ASH

MARK RUNTE

Printed by Kindle Direct Publishing, an Amazon company.

Requests for permission to make copies of any part of the work should be emailed directly to m.runte25@hotmail.com

Cover design by Jon Stubbington: www.jonstubbington.com Email: Jon@jonstubbington.com

Formatting by: Nicole Scarano Formatting & Design

Ash / Mark Jonathan Runte
Paperback ISBN: 978-1-990759-03-1
Hardcover ISBN: 978-1-990759-02-4

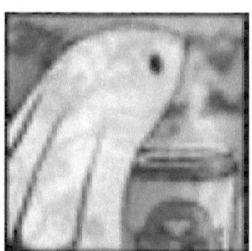

Contents

To everyone who helped make this book possible, thank you.

PROLOGUE

The hospital smelled too much like bleach and cleaner to him. Something sour and unpleasant in his nose, mixed with a smaller, bitter scent half buried beneath it. Death, if one knew how to look for it. The light overhead cast their shadows into hard edges, stark against the gray tile of the hallway. Jocelynn was sniffling, wiping her nose on her hoodie sleeve. Alain and Athenais were remote, expressionless from where they stood at the foot of the hospital bed.

Corinne LaLaurie stirred briefly from her sleep, gaze drifting around the circle of faces. Her own husband and children, and then her brother-in-law and his family standing a step or two away from the immediate family, nearer to the hospital room door. "Daniel…"

She looked like a corpse already, her reddish-brown hair long since shaved short. Just thirty-six and she was skin and bone beneath the light cotton pajamas she wore.

Daniel took her hand, careful of the little tube placed at the base of her nose and the little device meant to measure her heartbeat placed on one finger. "Mom, I…"

Her laugh was weak, tired from the effort. "Just promise me that you'll look after your sisters, please."

It wasn't a question, or a request and she spoke in the language of home. French was for family; English was for public use outside the house. Daniel sighed, edging out of the way to let Jocelynn crawl up onto the foot of the bed. Athenais sat down next to their younger sister, one arm wrapped around the eight-year old's shoulders. "Alright, I promise."

Because he was sixteen and the oldest here, he was expected to be the responsible one in the family now. As much as he wished otherwise, their mother was well past medicine and medical solutions to save her life. The cancer had spread too quickly, had become too deeply wrapped within her body for any doctor to fix. Corinne was dying and he could sense it in her with a simple brush of his hand against the back of hers. It was little bits of darkness taking her by inches as her cells failed on her. It wouldn't be much longer now as the darkness spread, overwhelming internal organs. Liver, kidneys… her lungs.

Alain's hand rested on his shoulder and he looked away, trying not to flinch at the touch. It was unspoken but hard not to read what the gesture meant. Daniel chewed on his lower lip, tasting a little trace of blood from the cut. This was permission and acknowledgement, encouragement even but he couldn't bring himself to make the attempt. "Dad, no."

The grip tightened on his arm before relaxing and her closed his eyes, fighting back the prickly feeling in them as he reached out with his gift. Corinne's heart stuttered, slowed and stopped, matching the shrill sound of the monitor next to the bed.

Jocelynn whimpered, tears streaking her cheeks and she

curled up in a tight ball next to their mother. The tip of her nose was pink from crying. "Maman..."

She hadn't called their mother "Maman" since she was six, not since she had started elementary school, but no one seemed inclined to correct her right now. Daniel turned away, letting go of Corinne's hand and walked out of the room. There would be time for grief later, in private. Right now, he just wanted to be left alone.

The little garden was unoccupied as he pushed the glass door open and stepped out into it. Out of doors, quiet and in full bloom. It didn't stay that way for long. Not with the fresh shallow cut trailing blood over his right wrist. A thin, bright red line trailing over his hand and spotting the paving stone underneath it.

Little orange sparks lit the nearby leaves and grass, growing into small flames as the greenery charred, curled in on itself and turned to gray ash. Only the small patch where he stood remained untouched by the fire though the heat of it was still warm around him. Anyone else would have been burned by the red gold creature, he had enough control not to let it near him. The heat was a penance or a punishment for not doing more for his mother. For taking her life when he shouldn't have. His vision wavered, sparks dancing in front of his eyes that had nothing to do with the fire he'd started in the garden.

He never felt it as he hit the ground and woke to see his uncle and father nearby. One clearly concerned, the other restrained and unreadable, Alain's hand covering the fresh but no longer bleeding cut on his wrist, holding his forearm to the sunlight overhead.

He was only sixteen and their mother was only hours gone. It was up to him now to take care of his younger sisters.

Jocelynn was only eight, Athenais, only thirteen and three years younger than he was. There was no one else able to.

CHAPTER ONE

TEN YEARS LATER...

"C'mon," Daniel gently shook his brother awake, keeping a wary eye out for any unwelcomed passerby as well as Jocelyn's own peculiar talents. Jocelyn wasn't a light sleeper at the best of times, he was unlikely to be happy about being dragged from his bed in the middle of the night for a hushed and hasty explanation. The last time something like that had happened, the unlucky recipient had been rushed to the hospital for a massive heart attack. "We need to go."

Sooner rather than later, preferably as he looked over his shoulder. The bedroom door was closed, the light from the hallway unbroken by inconvenient shadows. That was good then, a blessing he hadn't counted on as he hauled a pair of backpacks onto the foot of the bed. "I've got your things. We just need to get my car."

The keys to the silver Audi were already in his hand, warm against his skin as he stood. "Jocelyn."

Jocelyn mumbled something unintelligible and rolled over beneath the coverlet, throwing a spare pillow at him. Daniel sighed, shaking his head at that. Things could have been worse, the pillow could have been a ball of fire cast by reflex, or a sleepy, half aware attempt at something more dangerous. A pillow was good, safer and better than any other method of assault, but they couldn't afford to waste any more time than they had already. "Now, Jocelyn. I mean it. I know when your asleep and when you're faking it. You woke up three minutes ago."

His brother glared at him through untidy shoulder length hair and fumbled for the thick, ugly glasses on the nightstand. "Asshole, I was happy, and you ruined it."

Daniel flushed, trying to overlook the expletive. His eighteen-year-old brother might not have a problem with foul language, he did. "Don't be crude. Dad would wash your mouth out with soap if he heard that from you."

Jocelyn snorted, throwing the coverlet aside to reveal the t-shirt and little else that he was wearing. As well as the delicacy of his build. Narrow shoulders, a shirt that barely concealed the curve of her- his hip and chest. "Dad isn't here, Dani. You got me up, now get me out before I throw more than a pillow at you. Unless you want a fucking empath leaving you in a coma somewhere."

The threat was only halfhearted despite the expletive laced language. They both knew better than that, Alain had ensured it. Daniel shook his head, only averting his gaze to give Jocelyn the privacy he needed to get dressed. And in truth, out of discomfort as well. It wasn't easy dealing with the parts where his brother had to deal with sports bras and women's underpants were expected, not the comfort. "Done yet?"

"Done," Jocelyn's voice still had a brief, acidic note in it.

6

"No thanks to you, Dani. I could feel your anxiety without having to look at your face. Now where the hell are we going?"

"Doesn't matter," Anywhere would be better than New Orleans, in truth. Daniel looked away as a shadow passed by the closed door and let out a breath when the doorknob didn't rattle under the shadow's owner's touch. It was likely just Carla going to bed at long last. The older woman had a disquieting tendency to make eleven her bedtime, not before. Still, she wouldn't tell anyone about their flight if she was asked. "Remember that old bible story about the mother looking to protect her son from the Egyptian soldiers? It's like that, we have to be fast and quiet like mice here."

"Quiet I can do," Jocelyn looked towards the rats in the cage on the dresser before he scooped the imaginatively named Biscuit and Mouse into the pull over hoodie pocket. "It's the why that I object to. I'm not thirteen anymore and this isn't a three-night stay in some shitty motel. You aren't giving me enough information here and I'd love that before we go anywhere, Dani."

"No time," He wasn't going to bother changing out of the dress shirt and slacks he wore, not when they were cutting it as close as they were. Not after what he'd seen at the gala. Alain wouldn't leave a charitable event or dinner party unless the building itself was on fire. Others might, not his father. "C'mon, just grab the cage and go."

Uncertainty flickered across Jocelyn's face, but he obeyed, glancing away as he shouldered the backpack. "Fine but just to let you know, I disagree with this crap."

Daniel ignored the use of the childhood pet name and moved to the door, listening for any further sounds or for coming footsteps. "Would you really stay here?"

Jocelyn swore low under his breath at the question. "No,

not with that tone in your voice. Just give me the keys. I know how your driving is, Dani. Mine's better. I didn't wrap the rental Honda around a lamp post when I was sixteen because I fainted mid exam. I'm pretty sure the Louisiana state driving school tried to ban you from ever getting behind the wheel after that."

That was a low blow even for Jocelyn. Daniel winced, gritting his teeth. "Things are better now; I haven't fainted behind the wheel for over four years. I know you're grumpy, Jocelyn but I'd prefer not to get into a fight right here."

Jocelyn sighed, looking away again. "Fine, I never did enjoy Dad calling me a girl anyway. You can tell me why your shirt sleeve has blood on it later anyway. Let's go."

Daniel covered the blood spotted cloth with his free hand out of reflex. The bandage he had improvised wasn't enough to hide things if Jocelyn had noticed the dark red and drying splatter there. "Thank you,"

"This doesn't mean I've forgiven you for waking me up in the middle of the night though," Jocelyn spoke over his shoulder as he closed the bedroom door behind them. "Thought you were at some gala or something of Dad's anyway."

"I... was," Daniel said. "It's complicated."

Comprehension crossed Jocelyn's face, followed shortly by distaste. "Dad arranged for someone's conveniently timed stroke, wasn't it? You're too nice, Dani. You know that. I mean, I don't like the idea either – it's murder disguised as bad luck but you have to consider our family as well. Uncle Christophe quoted it once, public virtue, private vice or something. How the hell do you survive the political games around here?"

"I play- played to protect you," The protest was weak at

best but the only answer he could give right now. "That helped."

"She's fine, better where she is," Daniel forced an attempt at shrug. "No-one's going to bother her at the institution."

The last word was sharper than intended and he made a face, shifting the weight of the pack on his shoulders. "Let's go, please."

Daniel backed the car out of the driveway as a light flashed across the dash and rearview mirror. Jocelyn's snide remarks about his driving aside, there was no time to care about running over the corner of the lawn in the process. Alain had always been ambitious, the power behind the throne as it were but to make a move so openly at the gala was either careless or overconfident. Even if the move in question bore a strong resemblance to a fatal stroke. "Remember what I taught you?"

Jocelyn rolled his eyes, pulling the glove compartment open and lifting the disposable plastic water bottle from the insurance and registration mess of papers. "You would be better off with a gun, Dani. I remember, you taught me a couple tricks Dad doesn't know or he didn't bother to learn himself. Cousin Jared on the other hand…"

He shrugged, trailing off. "Throw the bottle and call one of the numbers you insisted I memorize. Mississippi or Lyra Highsmith?"

Either of the two women would be a good call but Missy lived within the city itself. It would be too easy for his family to track him if he went to his old teacher. "Lyra."

With luck the reddish film on the inside of the water bottle would be enough to confuse the trail for a few hours. They were overdue some good fortune right now. Word would eventually get back to their father but for the time being he was going to take any scrap of fortune passed their way.

Jocelyn pushed the glasses back up to the bridge of his nose and dialed, using one of the cheap gas station cell phones purchased as an emergency. "Lyra? Dani's calling in whatever favor he owes you. We need a place to stay for a few hours."

A pause as he listened to her answer before his voice dropped, going tight. "I don't know all of my brother's plans, it's safer that way but if you want me to make a damned guess, I'd say either Chicago or Memphis. It's still a long car trip and we need a gas stop before then."

Daniel took a breath, trying to overlook Jocelyn's tendency to curse when stressed. It was unfortunate but understandable given the circumstances even as each expletive had him wincing inwardly. His brother's mouth was far from clean at the best of times. "Throw it,"

Jocelyn cast him a dirty look and rolled the window down, casting the used bottle into the grass by the outer edge of the highway. "That was Dani, Lyra. Interrupting our phone call. No, not the bleeding car chase you're picturing, just the kind of littering that might save our lives. Got a place in mind?"

He listened for another moment, a small frown evident in his expression before he hung up and switched to the factory reset portion of the settings, wiping all history and records from the phone before dissembling it into back plate, battery, and the phone itself. "Give me your pocketknife."

Daniel swerved, recovering in time to avoid drifting into the oncoming lane as he searched one handed through the center console. The small blade should have been there but all he found was an old chocolate bar wrapper or two, a box of tissues and a battered paperback from a used bookstore. "Oh…"

If he had been capable of swearing, the end of that sentence probably would have ended in a 'damn', as it was, he just let it trail off into silence.

Jocelyn made an exasperated sound and reluctantly encouraged Biscuit to climb out of his hoodie pocket. "Sorry, Biscuit but our… lives are more important than yours."

The rat looked up at him, looking oddly trusting- hopeful almost before she slumped to her side in Jocelyn's lap, a bead or two of blood at her mouth and small ears. Another victim to an aneurysm. Jocelyn sighed, shoulders dropping as the phone he held, burst into flames in his hands. It smelled too much like burning plastic and charring metal and he wrinkled his nose, dropping the half-melted phone out the window a mile or two after the water bottle. "I hate this, even if I can't kill anything bigger than a rat. She died so I could set a phone on fire."

"I'm sorry," Daniel turned the wheel, pressing down on the gas pedal.

"She was only a rat," Jocelyn's voice was tired. "I can always get another one from a pet store if I want it. Lyra said to meet her in Baton Rouge, it's not exactly out of the state yet but it'll take time for Dad to trace us, longer now that you don't have the water bottle to connect us to the rest of the family. Let's… just keep going. The sooner we get there, the better. It's a little motel outside the city. Sunshine Acres."

He rested his head against the back of the seat, twisting so that he could stare out the window rather than at the road in front of them, Biscuit's cooling little body still in his lap. There was no more conversation between them until they reached one of the last few twenty-four-hour gas stations left in the Baton Rouge area. "Pull over, we need a refill and I need some, err, things that could get a guy in trouble for buying. Fifteen minutes tops, yeah?"

"Fifteen minutes, yeah."

It wasn't quite agreement, but it was all he could offer under the circumstances. Dani could handle refilling the gas tank, he had to deal with the unpleasant sensation of wet stickiness between his legs. The time of the month that he always hated and couldn't do anything about. "Even though this little drive of yours dragged me away from school before I could finish my last semester and graduate."

And freedom at last from being under Alain's roof. Freedom to be who he was and not who he was perceived to be.

She looked back at him in the mirror as he pushed the door open. Too thick glasses perched on her nose, shoulder length hair that hadn't seen a brush since the hasty escape from New Orleans a few hours ago. He bit down on his lower lip, trying to ignore the uncomfortable knot in the pit of his stomach as he reached for the pink and violet box and a milk chocolate bar for later. "You don't happen to have a key for the bathroom around here? I need to clean up a mess."

The woman behind the counter barely looked up from her book as she shoved a block with the key attached by a little leather cord. "Here you are, miss. Ladies is on the right by the freezer."

Miss. He had to fight the dry taste in his mouth at her choice of word and took the key, darting a look over his shoulder at the cashier. There was no need to worry, it seemed like – she was more concerned with lighting her cigarette than caring about a stray late-night traveler.

That was just as well then. He put his hand on the door handle, glancing away. Some tricks not even Daniel knew.

Fire was one thing, incinerating a phone without a lighter or easily apparent fuel source. Breaking a lock was another and one he'd worked on for six weeks a few years ago. All it took was a little twist to the latch mechanism from the inside and it opened under his touch, the key left behind on a nearby shelf.

Though it was regretted a few minutes later as he turned the lights on. The men's bathroom hadn't seen the better side of a mop or cleaning for what looked like over a month. And the toilet paper was an empty cardboard tube in the dispenser. "Men…"

Would it kill them to treat washrooms as well as any woman did for one?

Daniel passed him in the doorway, a faint look of concern on his face and the cash needed for the gas already in hand. Jocelyn shook his head, glancing away. "Avoid the bathroom, it's filthy and I think I saw black mold in the corner. Goddamn attendant."

At least he was cleaner now, the soft cotton of the pad between his legs. It would do for four or six hours now. Or until they caught up with Daniel's Baton Rouge friend.

Baton Rouge had plenty of places to hide in, but it also had the misfortune of being visited often by their family on business. On the other hand, Sunshine Acres was the last place anyone with common sense would have visited. The small parking lot was cracked concrete, the paint marking stalls faded from age and the potted plants guarding the entrance to the motel were as dead as it came. Jocelyn hung back, watching as Daniel paid for the room and turned away, key in hand. "Not even a card lock?"

"No," Dani tucked it into his jeans pocket. "And we aren't staying more than a few hours."

That was a relief, a couple hours would be more than

enough time to unpack his shopping and get a shower before they were on the road again.

And pray for the best while doing that. Daniel glanced at the sloppily printed number taped to the key's base, sighing before crossing the parking lot again. Their room was on the second story of the motel, behind a revoltingly orange door. "Here. I'm going to get my backpack from the car and see about… things. Do whatever you need to."

Jocelyn nodded, wrinkling his nose at the graying tartan bedspread and pulled a pair of sandals from his knapsack. There was no way he was going to go barefoot into that shower after the filth of the gas station bathroom or the dubious… quality of the shower connecting onto the bedroom. "It's yours afterwards if you want it. Change the plates or borrow another car?"

Though the silver Audi was like Biscuit, well loved and cared for. It would break Daniel's heart if they had to torch it.

"Change the plates, if I'm lucky," Daniel paused, bracing himself on the doorway for a moment, looking like he needed a moment to catch his breath.

Jocelyn ignored the hesitation, shutting the bathroom door behind him. There were more important things on his mind. Things like the much-needed shower.

He was bent over the trunk, digging through the boxes and the spare sleeping bag before the hair on the back of his neck prickled. Daniel went still, one hand dropping to the knife sheathed on his hip. "Show yourself."

A woman's laugh sounded; her voice marked by a Brooklyn accent. "I could think of less cliché things to say, Daniel."

Daniel lowered his hand from the combat knife and turned to see her, folding his arms over his chest. "Lyra,"

She smirked, brushing a hand through long pale blonde

hair. At some point she had shaved the sides so the top and what remained, resembled a horse's mane. "Yeah, that's me."

"At some point, someone's going to call you out on that name and call you a liar," Daniel said dryly.

Her smirk widened, almost becoming a smile at the remark. "Who's to say I'm not already that, LaLaurie? So, what brings you to Baton Rouge so badly that you need my help?"

Daniel tugged the sleeping bag out from under the nearest box, folding it over his arm. "I- we need helping in getting out of state. If you have a Ford or a Mazda or something available. Or a stolen set of license plates, I'd owe you for that."

A shadow crossed Lyra's face and she glanced away, the amusement fading towards concern as she took in the silver Audi. "It's a nice car, I'd hate to see something like it torched in a ditch somewhere. Alright, I can help, and I won't ask for much in return."

The smirk returned, brief but genuine on her face. "Keep your money, Daniel. There's nothing you have at the moment that I can accept or need unless it happens to be that you're willing to put up with a large black panther in the backseat. You owe me, sure, but I'll call that favor in later if I need it."

Her expression was sly as she put a hand on the hood of the Audi and closed her eyes for a moment. Daniel watched, wary and sensing the barest flicker of power in the back of his mind. The car didn't change, didn't look any different to him but for that ripple of whatever power Lyra had been able to draw upon. "You're a witch?"

She laughed, dropping her hand back to her side. "Nah, I can't do any of that blood magic psychic shit you do. I'm just very talented with illusions. You won't lose your car in the parking lot but to anyone else, they'll just see a fifteen-year-old little Ford Escape. There wasn't as much I could do about the license plate without copying someone else's down to the dirt but this should slow your hunters down for a while."

"Now," She looked past him, appraising the motel's poorly chosen paint scheme with an expression of distaste. "I brought supplies if your sister didn't. Hair dye and scissors."

"That won't be necessary but thank you anyway," Daniel said. "The room's this way. How did you get here so quickly?"

Lyra sniffed; the distaste being replaced by dismissal. "I had business in the area. I thought a New Orleans psychic or witch would be able to help me but it turns out that was a dead end. Baton Rouge is just one stop on the way back to New York."

The young woman shrugged, avoiding his gaze. "The usual shit when it comes to family and shadow work. Truth is that my brother almost died protecting me last year. Gave up a lot to do it and now he's... in a place I can't reach. I think you'd already know something about that without having to ask me."

"Prison? A hospital?" Daniel frowned as he slipped a pair of fifties over to the graying haired, older man behind the small desk for a room. "Just for three hours, thanks. You should still be able to visit him."

Lyra grimaced, good humor fading from her eyes. "It's more like shell shock or trauma than anything physical. Alex's there but he isn't, you know."

Daniel accepted the key from the man behind the desk and pushed the stairwell door open, holding it for Lyra. "Yeah, I know. My sister's the same way."

The less said about Athenais the better in his opinion. Their escape wouldn't have been half as successful if they had attempted to take her from the hospital. He paused, bracing himself on the stair railing for a second to catch his breath, pressing a hand to his side in an attempt to ease the stitch there.

"Dani?" Jocelyn's hair was damp, loose over his shoulders and he wore a graying towel around his body as concern crossed his face. "What's wrong?"

"Nothing," He straightened, pulling Jocelyn into the motel room. "And you really shouldn't stand outside in nothing but a towel. I'm better now, Jocelyn."

"Okay," Jocelyn still looked unconvinced, but he didn't press the issue further until they had the door shut behind them. "What's our next step?"

"We'll discuss that after I have a shower," Daniel said dryly.

His brother tangled his fingers through the damp strands of hair. "Better you wait, I saw a cockroach behind the toilet. This isn't... worse than the gas station but it isn't much better either."

"I see," Daniel grimaced, gesturing for Lyra to take the lead into the cramped bathroom. "If you don't mind."

Lyra arched an eyebrow at that and kicked the thin door shut with the toe of one combat boot, twisting the sink tap so that rust colored water flowed into the bowl. "To cover our conversation, not that Jocelyn will pay any attention to it. I wanted to ask, that stitch thing on the way up was more than that, wasn't it?"

Daniel hesitated, looking into the cloudy mirror over the vanity. "If you're asking whether or not I'm out of shape, I'm not. A three or four mile run every day, or as often as I can manage it."

"So, a flight of stairs shouldn't have been a problem, usually." Lyra's expression matched the mirror for a moment. "Could you roll your sleeves up?"

Daniel sighed, pulling the shirt sleeve up to reveal the white cloth bandaging wrapped around his forearm. "Happy?"

Lyra gave him a brief look and unwrapped the cloth, laying it aside to show the old silver lines of scarring that crisscrossed over his skin. She traced one of the thin marks with a fingertip before she looked away. "Car accident?"

"Only if that's what you want to believe," Daniel took one end of the bandage in his teeth and used his free hand to wrap his arm. "I use my own blood for my magic. I won't kill or sacrifice a life for power. Not like my dad."

She was quiet for a long moment. "Necessity makes us regret things after the fact."

Daniel pulled his shirt sleeve down, covering the white inch wide cloth with cotton. "Yeah? Who told you that one?"

Lyra shrugged, avoiding his eyes. "Experience mostly, but my aunt taught me a lot about how far people will go and the regret afterwards. She was caught in a fire years ago and how her hunt for the soldiers responsible for it ended. It didn't solve all of her problems in the end and she still regrets leaving the Italian family without a father even though he helped start the fire in the first place."

That sounded like there was more to the story than Lyra was willing to say but he wasn't going to ask for more details unless given permission to. "I'm sorry,"

"Don't be," Her mouth quirked in a bitter smirk. "I'm not a witch but my aunt Helen is close to that. Some Christian fundamentalist tied her to an old telephone pole and accused her of witchcraft. Bastard even went as far as to set the blasted thing on fire."

She snorted. "And that is as much of that story as I'm going to trust you with while in a shitty bathroom. Watch the roach under the toilet."

Daniel winced as he saw the aforementioned bug crawling away to safety behind the toilet. "I'll skip the shower."

Better yet, they needed to be on their way. "Thanks, Lyra."

"Don't thank me yet," Lyra's expression was pensive as she pulled her necklace from around her throat and pressed it into his hand. "Freya's kitten. It should hold the illusion I put on your car, for when I can't be around to fix it myself."

Daniel dangled the pendent before him, frowning a little. "Christopher would have been preferred but I guess a Norse myth is as good as any."

Lyra snorted, looking away. "Let's see, the patron saint of travelers and runaways versus Freya. Forgive me if I put more of my trust in a goddess than anything of Christian make. Plus, I know a Christopher back in New York. I didn't want to be confused between the two."

"Fair point," He had to give her that, however dryly it was spoken. "Expect I'll see you again?"

Personally, he doubted it but it couldn't hurt to ask regardless.

"Maybe, maybe not." She shrugged, one hand on the doorknob. "We'll see if I can shake my grandfather's ravens off my trail first. Those two get everywhere."

It was his turn to give her a briefly askance look. "If you're hinting at something with your talk of your grandfather's birds and Freya, I hope you're just kidding because I really don't need to know about that."

Lyra grinned and went into the small living room space. "Am I? Or am I not? You decide. See you around, Daniel."

Lyra. He had to shake his head at her retreating back down the hallway and gathered up his backpack. Jocelyn's hand clasped lightly in his free one. It wasn't so easy to tell whether Lyra meant half of what she said, or if she got a great deal of fun out of her mythological references at his expense. "You're a liar, you know that."

If she heard him, she chose not to answer. Daniel shrugged and looked at his brother. "Shall we?"

.

CHAPTER TWO

They were on the road an hour and a half afterwards, Jocelyn curled up in a sleeping bag in the backseat despite an offer to take over driving for a couple hours. Daniel looked at his brother in the rear-view mirror before focusing on the road ahead. They had a long day of driving in front of them, coupled with the early hour and departure from New Orleans. A plane ticket would have been the more sensible option but that would have implied advanced planning he hadn't been able to afford. And flights were closely monitored. So, it was travel by car with occasional stops for fuel and meals.

Daniel rubbed a hand across gritty feeling eyes. Even with coffee and just the slightest use of his magic, at some point he was going to have to sleep or risk a car accident. It wasn't healthy to get three or four hours sleep in a gas station or truck stop parking lot before driving again. Mundane people couldn't do it for very long and while he could manage it briefly, there was still danger in using his magic that way.

What would have been a full day and night driving if the

passengers swapped out in the driver's seat was longer and it felt like only luck that no one had been seen tailing behind him.

A car horn blared, and he jerked at the wheel, swerving briefly onto the shoulder of the road before recovering. And cursing the unfamiliar landscape around him. Snow and ice were uncommon in Louisiana, so it was taking all of his remaining focus to not to roll the car into the ditch.

Maine might have been a mistake, but it was one of the few places his father didn't do business in some form or fashion. Much less so in a town as small as Calais.

There was still danger, admittedly but he was going to take this place for what it was worth even if he hated the cold Maine winter in front of them. "Jocelyn?"

Jocelyn mumbled something and sneezed, wiping his nose on his shirt sleeve. "Why's it so cold?"

"It's Maine," Daniel slowed the car down, cautiously navigating the turn into Calais. "Not much farther north of here unless you count Canada. Or Toronto, I think."

"Oh," Jocelyn bit down on his lower lip. "Where's that?"

Daniel grimaced as the first buildings appeared to either side of them. "Remind me to complain about the state of our education system to the Louisiana governor or senator if we ever go back to New Orleans. You'd think Americans would have at least a basic idea of geography."

"You sound like Dad," Jocelyn said.

Did he? Daniel blushed, shoulder checking behind him for a moment. "Maybe just a bit, he was no happier about the poor public-school system here than I am."

"So, where the hell is Toronto?" His brother wasn't looking at him as the question was asked.

Daniel took a hand off the wheel to pinch the bridge of his nose in exhaustion. "I'll show you on a map later, Jocelyn.

But this is something you should be able to look up on your laptop."

"You left my laptop in my bedroom when we ran away," The younger boy's voice held an acidic note in it. "Timing couldn't have been worse, halfway through my senior year."

"This wasn't exactly expected," Daniel said. He was tired and trying not to show it in front of the irritable eighteen-year-old. "I'll see what I can do once we find a hotel room for the night."

"Fine," Jocelyn folded his arms over his chest, eyes narrowing behind the thick framed glasses. "But nothing less than three grand and I expect the best graphics possible for it."

"Two and a half," Daniel slowed the car down at the traffic stop, wishing they weren't faced with a wall of white fluffy snow coming down in front of them. "That's my final offer."

"Two and a half," Jocelyn's agreement was only grudging but at least he hadn't fought for more than already budgeted for the new laptop. "And you toss in a couple hundred for a scanner, printer set."

"No promises," Daniel glanced away, rubbing a hand across his eyes in an attempt to erase the beginnings of the ache behind them. "We're trying to hide here, that means limited credit card transactions and smaller purchases if we can. Let's just try to find a place to sleep and consider our next steps in the morning."

He remembered little after that beyond a brief argument with the hotel receptionist and stumbling up to the fifth-floor hotel room before collapsing fully dressed onto one of the two beds in the room. Jocelyn's tentative hand on his shoulder was an uncommon reversal of things but one he was grateful for once. The headache had eased somewhat, and he was feeling better after too long on the road. "Thanks, Jocelyn."

Jocelyn blushed, one hand going up to pet Mouse perched on his shoulder. "Uh huh, so what're we going to do now? I'm hungry and you slept forever."

"Food first, I guess." Never underestimate the appetite of a hungry eighteen-year-old boy after all. "And then we get a better sense of where we are."

The mental list of errands could be done as they drove around the small town. There was breakfast or lunch to deal with, getting gas for the car, groceries. A whole host of things that needed to be taken care of if this was to be home for the next little while. "We've got a busy couple days ahead of us."

Maybe more than a couple but for now he was just focusing on their immediate needs. Food, gasoline and groceries. "C'mon, Scooter."

"Scooter?" Jocelyn made a face at the pet name but didn't argue with that. "Just 'cause I wanted to be a puppy with a butt problem, you still use that one on me?"

"I was fourteen and an idiot," Daniel said dryly. "I won't if bothers you, but it stuck better than what our sister called you."

Jocelyn flushed pink, gently placing his rat back into the carrier. "Cauliflower rabbit thing, I guess. Wish she could be here with us."

"That... wouldn't be advised," Daniel glanced away. "She's better off where she is, Jocelyn. It's safer for everyone."

He idly glanced at the bank account displayed on his phone before turning the device off and disassembling it before pocketing the pieces. There would be time to destroy it later, in the meantime he was badly in need of a job. And Jocelyn... "What say we fit in a visit to the local high school and register you? It's a bit late but I do have a copy of your transcripts."

"Thought of almost everything, have you?" Jocelyn's voice was bland. "Too bad you missed the important stuff."

"Planning, yes. Thinking that I'd actually have to run away with you, no," Daniel said. "The night of the gala was... complicated. C'mon, let's go before the cleaning service gets here."

Getting gas came before breakfast and he sighed, crumpling up the receipt before tossing the little ball into the back of the car. All that slip of paper was a reminder of how little remained in his bank account after the past few days. "Looks like we'll be sleeping in the car tonight if we don't find a cheaper place or two to stay."

Jocelyn was silent for a moment, staring at the two-story brick building that was the high school. "What if I don't want to go? I'm old enough that I could get a part time job somewhere and no one would care about me working."

Daniel folded his hand over his brother's. "No one's going to hire a guy who doesn't even have his diploma, Jocelyn. You need this. For me if nothing else? You'll be able to go as the boy you are rather than the girl you were for the last three and a half years. Think of it as a fresh start."

"I guess," There was a noticeable lack of enthusiasm in Jocelyn's voice. He pulled away, reaching for his backpack. "Okay, let's go."

It felt strange without the weight of the hunting knife on his hip and he had to resist the urge to drop a hand there to check for it even if the reasons for leaving the weapon behind were valid. He was in enough trouble as it was, there was no need to add a police charge to an already dubious record.

Jocelyn led the way to the principal's office through some unerring sense of things or was just better at following the signs. Daniel hung back, wary until his brother tugged on one hand.

The principal was a thin woman, brown hair streaked with gray and seated behind a wooden desk. The ten-year-old desktop computer was the most modern thing in the office as near as he could tell. Daniel sat in one of the two chairs, pulling the file from his backpack. "Mrs. Chandler?"

She gave him a lingering look. "It would have been more appropriate if you called beforehand, Mr...?"

"LaLaurie," Daniel said.

She arched one eyebrow at that, and he flushed, looking away. His surname wasn't common this far north or well known but to have a principal of a small Maine high school know it. "I..."

Mrs. Chandler shrugged offering a box of tissues to him before setting it aside at his refusal. "I was more inclined to comment on your accent, Lauren."

One of those people then, that was almost worse than an askance look or two over his long dead ancestor. Daniel felt his mouth tighten in irritation at the deliberate mistake. "My dad was born and raised in Paris. No doubt any trace of foreignness you hear in my voice came from him. It was always French at home, not English."

"I see," She turned her gaze towards the transcripts on the desk between them. "So what brings you to Calais in the middle of the school year? I see your sister was going to an all-girls academy before this. Why make the switch now, midway through the year?"

"I hated the skirts and uniforms," Jocelyn interrupted before Daniel could speak. "And I was one guy in a not particularly tolerant school."

Daniel flushed, quieting the half-formed protest before he could speak it. This was Jocelyn's story, not his to tell. If

Jocelyn wanted to do it in an abrasive way, so be it. "That, and that we had some family stuff we didn't want to get caught up in. I've had custody over him since he was eight. Mom made Dad promise to give that to me when I was eighteen myself."

The principal's eyes narrowed in something like displeasure. "Very well. Though I must question why you refer to Jocelyn as male when her transcripts clearly say female."

Jocelyn opened his mouth, shut it again and stood roughly shoving the chair out of his path. "Take it or leave it if you want to but I'm transmasculine. My preferred pronouns are he and him."

He walked out of the office without a backwards glance. Daniel slumped, feeling the headache as it flared behind his eyes again. "I'll go talk with him later."

"Of course," Mrs. Chandler's gaze drifted from the transcripts to the computer screen again, no longer interested in the conversation. "Thank you, Lauren."

"Excuse me, Mrs. Chandler?"

Daniel started, turning to see the young woman hovering by the door with a file in hand. She gave him a quiet, short lived smile and set the manila folder on top of the transcripts before retreating through the doorway.

The principal flipped through the new file, pointedly ignoring him. Daniel sighed, giving it up as a lost cause for now. "Excuse me, Principal Chandler."

He sagged against the corridor wall, fumbling for the small pill bottle in his jacket pocket and swallowing the tiny oval dry. "Which way out of the school?"

"I'll show you the way to the parking lot," The young teacher or receptionist's voice intruded on the beginnings of his headache.

Daniel graced her with a short-lived look, relieved. She was pretty in a way that appealed to him. Light brown hair styled in a pixie cut and a blue streak dyed into her hair. "Thanks, Miss..."

She smiled shyly, toying with a stray strand. "Haydee Ashworth. Since I doubt that we'll have much contact with each other, let's just use first names."

"Daniel LaLaurie," He glanced away, holding the door for her. "What do you do here?"

Haydee laughed, leaning against the corridor wall next to him. "I'm a part time receptionist and a substitute teacher at the junior high. The pay's not great but it's better than nothing. Just got out of college and the principal has me delivering her mail or coffee. You?"

Daniel hesitated, weighing his answer carefully. One way would gain Haydee's trust despite how little they knew of each other. The other might lose that fragile beginning. "Oddly, I wanted to be the same back in New Orleans but custody over my brother complicates things. Some severe food allergies and a... conflict between his physical gender and how he feels on the inside."

She winced, a light blush staining her cheeks. "Ouch, about the allergies, not that you had plans to be a teacher yourself. She- he seems like a nice kid."

"I'm right here," Jocelyn's voice was brittle. "Is true what the principal said?"

"No," Daniel pulled his brother close to his side, wrapping an arm around the younger boy's shoulders. "And if it does, I'll talk to her and the school board if I have to."

Haydee seemed more pensive than concerned now. "It's none of my business but if you're new here and need a job, I think the sporting goods store is hiring. It's midseason now but their stocker broke his arm, and they haven't found a replacement yet."

"I'll look into it," It was the best he could promise for the time being. "I don't suppose you know a cheaper place to stay, I'm tired of the hotel room."

A shadow crossed her face, mixed with unhappiness. "I know, yeah. My parents run a bed and breakfast in town. If that's cheaper then I hope you don't mind that they're the vegan, hippy-dippy sort of witches."

"Vegan's fine," Daniel glanced away, concealing his disquiet at the witch remark. "Jocelyn's allergic to shellfish, eggs and peanuts."

She made a face at that. "I'll call ahead and tell them about the diet restrictions. These wouldn't be the lethal kind of allergies?"

Daniel sighed. "Yeah, peanuts are the bad one, but he can manage shellfish and eggs in small amounts."

"Oh," Haydee's expression cleared, sympathetic. "I'll call and tell them. You?"

"What?" He frowned, distracted from his own thoughts. Haydee was being so helpful that there had to be a catch somewhere along the line or later. Something she wanted as a favor when the time came for it.

She snorted, running a hand through her pixie styled hair. "Any allergies of your own? I saw the bracelet on your wrist. Peanuts? Soy?"

"Oh," He flushed, looking away. "Penicillin, severely. There was an infection and I nearly ended up in anaphylactic shock because of it."

There was little point in talking about the source of the infection or that the cut had been self-inflicted with a dirty pocketknife. Emergency aside, it had been his own fault in the end. "I've got a car."

Haydee laughed, looking at him. "Is that an invitation to

drive me back home or do you just want a navigator to the bed and breakfast?"

Daniel went a deeper shade of pink at her teasing. "Both, but I could use the navigator more. Also, where's the nearest Catholic church around here?"

Haydee smiled shyly. "Tell you what, I'll give you the tour on the way back to my parents' place. C'mon."

CHAPTER THREE

"And there's the church you were asking about," Haydee gestured out towards the left side of the vehicle. "Though I don't know why it's so interesting."

Daniel noted the modest structure and shrugged. "Better a Catholic than Protestant, right? Faith is... kind of important to me even if I disagree with their black and white ideas on marriage."

She arched an eyebrow at that, leaning back in the driver's seat. "Sex before the wedding?"

Daniel flushed, picking a stray thread from his jacket sleeve. "I'd prefer not, to be honest. It was more people like my brother than anything else. I'm alright with women dating their own, or men."

Haydee grinned, pulling the car to a stop outside the bed and breakfast. "You're cute. A virgin at what was it? Twenty-three?"

"Twenty-six," He corrected her dryly. "Clearly you aren't,"

Haydee winced but the laughter was still in her voice. "I

was eighteen, so yeah. Gave that up nearly ten years ago. You know how it is, prom night."

"Are you flirting?" Jocelyn leaned between the driver's and front passenger seats, curiosity on his face. "Because Dani needs a girlfriend. And a life."

Daniel snorted, ruffling his brother's hair. "Leave my sex life out of it, kit."

"The lack of it," Jocelyn said brightly.

Daniel cuffed him alongside the shoulder. "It's none of your business, Jocelyn. What I want to do or not, okay?"

"Okay," Jocelyn subsided, retreating into the backseat long enough to struggle with rat cage and backpack before climbing out of the car.

Haydee gave him a bemused look. "Your brother's cute, Daniel."

He rolled his eyes, retrieving his own backpack from the backseat. "He's innocent, I'd like to keep him that way. My… family wasn't always so…"

"Kind?" A brief shadow crossed her face at that. It vanished as quickly as it had appeared. Just as she cut the engine of the pale gray little Ford outside a nearby house.

"Unambitious," Daniel shouldered the bag, making his way inside the bed and breakfast.

Jocelyn lingered behind them, gaze taking in the New England style house. "It's bigger than I thought it would be."

Haydee forced a laugh, stepping onto the porch. "The money isn't what it used to be; apparently, hence the bed and breakfast deal we have running but we make do. All I know is that the only reason I'm still living at home is because I can't balance student debt with rent and car insurance. What were you expecting?"

Jocelyn shrugged, shifting the weight of his backpack so

that it was seated more comfortably on his shoulders. "It's a nice place, for Maine. That's all."

Haydee graced Daniel with an uncertain smile. "Is that an insult or a compliment?"

He made a face, running a hand through his hair. "Knowing Jocelyn, probably both. Baton Rouge isn't New Orleans, but we grew up fairly well privileged."

"I see," Haydee glanced away and fumbled for the house-key, twisting it in the lock before gesturing them inside.

The small lobby space smelled of incense and cat. Daniel wrinkled his nose and accepted the leger book Haydee handed to him, paying with his card as a tabby wound its way around his legs. "Your pet?"

She gave the cat a dark look. "My mom's familiar, actually. She doesn't believe in 'pets' and subscribes to a PETA rag of a magazine. It's both my parents but more my mom who believes in the Wicca shit."

"You don't?" Not that he expected otherwise. Haydee seemed too grounded and rational to give any credit to the Wicca form of magic some people practiced. "I've known one or two in Baton Rouge."

Haydee shook her head, pressing the small antique key into his hand. "Do you?"

There was subtext in her question, and he grimaced, looping the flower-patterned tail onto a delicate chain. "Let's say, hypothetically, my dad knows what real power is and how to use it. Stuff like that isn't kind or pretty. It's a... weapon more than anything else. There's nothing about the threefold law or a god or goddess as far as he cares. And I think he would have suffered a massive heart attack or stroke by now if that law wasn't more than made up."

Haydee laughed. "That's a refreshing view of things if a bit dark to consider. I take it you avoid Harry Potter then."

Daniel smiled thinly. "Oh, no. I read them. Gave up halfway through the series when Harry lost what was left of a small personality."

She smirked and gestured to the door leading into the house. "Second floor on your right. I'll go tell my parents that you're my guest for dinner. It's spaghetti if my dad hasn't managed to burn it or turn the pasta into a gluey mess at the bottom of the pot. If not, I'll place an order for vegan pizza or something."

"Isn't that just a cheese pizza?" Daniel asked.

"You'd think," Haydee said. "But apparently vegans have a problem with cheese. C'mon."

It was pasta after all, and Daniel breathed a sigh of relief as Haydee's mother dished the spaghetti out. His fear about the food was unfounded and it smelled delicious. "This is good."

Haydee's mother smiled. "Thank you, Daniel."

She sat after a moment, dishing her own portion out. "So, tell me, where are you from? Your accent doesn't sound local."

"It isn't," He was careful in his answer. "Somewhere in Louisiana, actually. Baton Rouge. Haydee said you were a witch?"

A brief smile and a laugh. "Yes, Haydee doesn't think much of it but I am. You're welcome to join the circle when we meet next week."

Daniel hesitated, seeing the discrete twitch of Haydee's mouth. "I think I'm going to have to pass, Mrs. Ashworth. My family's always been conservative. I don't think he'll find out if I did decide to go but I'd rather not take chances. Plus... it's witchcraft, he wouldn't approve."

Not of the Wicca variety anyway.

"Oh," Haydee's mother looked down, seemingly disappointed. "Well, I could always give you a little sage or lavender incense to cleanse with. Good for the soul, it's said."

What did she know of his soul? Daniel felt his mouth tighten at that. She had unknowingly touched a nerve there with her words. So far as he was concerned, no sage or lavender would ever burn away the years he'd played games to keep his brother safe or the blood magic his family used. "Thank you but I'll pass for now."

He looked down at his empty plate and stacked Jocelyn's on top of it. "Dinner was perfect, either way."

Haydee's mother gave a brief smile, no sign of hurt at his refusal apparent in her expression. "You could learn a thing or two from your boyfriend, Haydee. He's a good one."

She went scarlet and shook her head, muttering something under her breath. "Thanks for that. You know, there's a couple places I forgot to show Daniel around here on the tour. Why don't I take him there while Jocelyn entertains himself with the cat?"

Her grip on his wrist was more insistent than expected but he followed her regardless, catching the door before it swung shut on them. "Haydee?"

She lifted her gaze to his, heavy winter jacket half on one shoulder and half off. "It's nothing, Daniel. Really…"

"Something," He said.

Haydee sighed. "Mom likes to play matchmaker, I guess. Wouldn't be the first time she assumed a good-looking mid-twenties guy was my boyfriend."

Daniel blushed despite himself. "Good looking? Who were the others?"

Haydee grimaced, tugging on the zipper and pulling the fur lined hood up over her head. "One Malachi Blackburn. Thankfully, the guy is gay or that relationship would have imploded within the first week. He doesn't mind my mom's crap."

"You do," Daniel noted dryly.

"Yeah," She looked away. "Not that I haven't pretended otherwise, exactly. C'mon, the Cat and Crown's a local dive bar but I could use a drink and if you're quiet enough, no one will notice a foreigner there."

Her nose wrinkled slightly. "Someone took their love of British pubs a tad too far when naming the place but it's decent. Ish. Rumor says that the owner or maybe manager is some sort of Greek Scottish or Irish or something."

Haydee went a shade deeper pink. "And I'm chatty, that doesn't usually happen."

Daniel shrugged. "Maybe you're just starved for someone to talk to. Doesn't sound like Malachi really listens if you ask me."

"Maybe," She was quiet for a long moment. "I don't know, I'm just not a big fan of secrets and he's full of them. We better go before we freeze here anyway. Kate MacKinnon makes a mean Bailey's style hot chocolate. Never drink more than one but shit if it isn't to die for on nights like this."

He accepted the offered hot chocolate more out of politeness than any desire for a drink. Haydee might have used the time to unwind after long day. He was here to people watch, nothing more than that. And what he was seeing was a rather ordinary scene for the night. A handful of middle-aged men arguing over a football game, another man staring bleakly into a half full beer glass and a college age student holding a pool cue in one hand. The bartender was a woman with a look of boredom so well placed it had to be an act. "What's Calais like?"

She gave him a lingering look and a half-hearted shrug.

"You know, small town, not a lot to do in the off season when the tourists aren't here. I-"

"Beth! I'm not paying you to stand around and chat when you have glasses piling up in need of washing."

Beth's expression darkened and she scowled. "Fine, I'll get around to it, Kate. Damned bitch."

Daniel sighed, setting the dregs of his drink aside as the newcomer approached. "Kate MacKinnon, I'm guessing. Haydee mentioned you. A little."

Kate laughed, looking away. "Ashworth's girl. Good old family here, that lot, *cherie*."

She snorted, noting the askance look he gave her for the accent. "And yes, I've spent my share of time in Louisiana. Always had a love of the cypress and the city. It being the crossroads for people."

He grimaced. "It... just seems unlikely finding another Louisianan this far north. I came here to escape family, not find them."

Kate rolled her eyes, wiping down a sticky patch of scarred wooden counter between them. "Adopted home, not born I'm afraid but I always did like the place. It suited, even for a mongrel pup like me. Where else would you find a Scots Greek woman after all?"

"Fair," Though he was grudging in his assent, gaze and senses following a dark-haired man with a bird feather stuck through the shoulder length ponytail. "Who's that?"

The unknown guy's presence was stronger in the back of his mind than Kate's more muted bearing. She was something but it was just as likely someone- something had just brushed against her arm earlier in the night.

Kate's mouth and expression were neutral. "Since I doubt it would be any sort of woods creature, my guess would be the son of a... man best not spoken of lightly."

"I see," Daniel pushed away from the counter, leaving his drink behind. Kate had given him something, but he wasn't sure of its worth yet since she hadn't given him a name or identity to place the stranger with. All she appeared to be warning him about was that the guy's father was a risk to learn about. "Thanks for the tip."

He didn't need to search for the newcomer when his path was plain, seeking out Haydee. As was her irked expression when he found the pair. "He's not bothering you?"

She dropped a hand back to her side, flushing in embarrassment. "Not more than usual, Much, anyway. Daniel LaLaurie, meet Malachi Blackburn."

Daniel regarded Malachi warily, taking note of the shoulder length hair tied out of his eyes and the blue jay feather stuck through the leather cord holding it. "You were Haydee's mother's attempt at matchmaking?"

Malachi's expression flickered, a shadow crossing it so quickly it might not have been there. "It never would have worked out. My mother would have preferred the notion, herself but I have no intention of playing pretend where my homosexuality is concerned."

The other man inclined his head in Haydee's direction. "Mistress, Daniel."

Daniel waited until Malachi was out of sight and earshot before frowning for a second. "Mistress…"

If it was possible, Haydee's flush went a shade darker at that. "It's just something he uses from time to time. It doesn't mean anything."

Maybe not to her off the bat but it was likely she hadn't had the historical education to put the pieces together. Daniel shook his head, looking away. "Maybe, maybe not but mistress is just another way of saying miss or Mrs. Malachi…

maybe he just likes playing pretend but his phrasing, his words- that was an eighteenth-century pattern of speech."

Haydee arched an eyebrow at that, looking skeptical. "More likely he's done his share of historical re-enactments, Daniel. I don't see how else you could possibly guess at what an eighteenth-century man spoke like."

He managed a wry smile, one tinged with a bit of bitterness. "Just wait until your dad makes you read a pre-revolutionary era journal in French as a lesson. You... learn what the English sounds like eventually. Trust me, revolutionary war actor or interpreter or not, his phrasing wasn't anything from this century or after the first world war."

His phone vibrated against his leg and he sighed. "I guess it's time to go back now. Jocelyn has school in the morning and he's really bad at getting up in the morning."

"Oh," Haydee looked disappointed. "Go on then, I'll pay my bill and see you back at the car."

Not before he paid his share of the bill. Daniel pulled a twenty from his pocket, pressing it into her hand. "My dad might not be the nicest of men out there, but he made sure I knew my manners where it came to women. I owe you for the drink."

Haydee looked down but didn't reject the twenty. "See you in ten?"

"See you in ten," It was a promise he intended to keep, so far as he was able. "I'll meet you at the car."

The parking lot was small, filled with drifting snow and he had to keep his gaze downward while taking careful steps to keep himself from falling on the slick ice. The hand that steadied him a moment later had him biting back on an invented expletive and the reflexive use of his magic. "I could have killed you."

Anything else he wanted or could have said in protest died as he pulled away from Malachi. "What do you want?"

Malachi shrugged, looking at ease in just a denim jacket despite the chill in the night air. "I doubt you could have succeeded, Daniel. You're stronger than you look and well taught, but we're all taught to counter another witch's power. You couldn't kill me unless I was caught off guard."

"Did my dad send you?" Daniel asked.

Malachi glanced away with an unreadable expression. "No, I've never had the pleasure of meeting the man."

That was only marginally a relief so far as he was concerned. "Why are you so open about being a witch then? Why me?"

"Because you would have found out eventually and I wanted to avoid any...unpleasant conflict between us." Malachi said. "Besides, we have a friend in common."

"Kate, I'm assuming," Daniel said.

"Haydee," Malachi's tone was as unreadable as his expression. "Truth be told, I prefer warlock to witch but that's of little relevance tonight. Hurt her and you'll find me an enemy."

His hand tightened on Daniel's wrist, twisting firmly but not enough to hurt as he pulled his shirt sleeve up to reveal the cloth bandaging his forearms. "Ah,"

Daniel pulled away and pulled his sleeve down to cover the bandage wrapping his arm. His cheeks were burning with humiliation at being so easily tricked into revealing his secret. "I won't hurt her. All I want is safety and peace from my dad's games."

"Protecting someone?" Malachi said.

"My brother," Daniel turned away. "He shouldn't have to be a part of my world."

"And what world is that?" Malachi's voice was dry. "You

won't be able to protect him forever, however much you want to."

Maybe, maybe not but he wasn't going to stop trying. "I should find Haydee again. I promised her ten minutes."

"So be it," Malachi shrugged, taking a step away from him before searching out the little Ford car in the parking lot. The engine started a moment later and then the taillights faded into the darkness.

Daniel sighed, relieved. Whatever else Malachi was, he was disconcerting, and it was nice not to be in the other guy's presence. "Haydee? Sorry about that."

She tried for a smile and nodded. "Nothing to forgive, I know Malachi can be... weird sometimes. Ready to go back to the bed and breakfast?"

"Yeah," He was ready for that and the prospect of a nice comfortable bed. "Guess I'll be getting Jocelyn up early for school and looking for work then."

Whatever else happened, this would be a new start for both of them.

CHAPTER FOUR

F irst days were always the worst. Starting over in a new high school in the middle of the year was even less lucky. Jocelyn glanced through his glasses at Daniel and shouldered his backpack. "I think I hate you. I'd rather be working than this shit."

His brother had called this a new start for the two of them, he was less convinced by the optimism in the words. "Where are you going to be?"

"Looking for work, I think." Daniel put a hand on his shoulder. "Someone has to feed your rat and provide toys for her. That costs money."

"Okay," Jocelyn brushed Daniel's hand from his arm, looking away. "Hope you get a job soon."

He didn't want to see the flicker of hurt that crossed his brother's face at the way he pulled away. "I'll see you after school."

The little car charm hanging from the rear-view mirror was new. It wasn't something that had come with the Audi and must have been a gift from Lyra a day or two earlier. Freya's kitten as a pendant looped around the mirror. Whatever charm or magic it held, didn't work for him despite the explanation Daniel had given him. The car looked like an Audi, not the ten-year-old vehicle it was masquerading as.

He slipped out of the car, closing the door with a dull thunk just as the bell rang. "Thanks so fucking much, Dani."

Whatever else happened today, at least his first class was going to be an easy one. Biology was something he- his family had excelled at.

A low snicker sounded as he walked inside the classroom and made his way to the back. Children were cruel with their teasing, teenagers more so – he'd learned to brush the whispers off or fight out of necessity. And no one had accused him of hitting like a girl either. "Where's the teacher?"

His seatmate gave him a long look, flipping blonde hair out of her eyes. "Mr. Jacobs? Late as usual, why?"

"Just curious," Jocelyn glanced down at his textbook and opened it to the last quarter of the book. "Who wrote this shit? The human heart is myogenic, not ampullary. And the nucleus absent blood cells are platelets, not lymphocytes."

She gave him a look somewhere between affronted and uneasy. "We aren't even halfway through the textbook and you're checking the answers in the back. I'm, well, I'm Brittney."

"Jocelyn," He barely glanced up from reading. "I had a couple very good tutors through high school and less interest in the cheer squad or the silly rumors my old classmates liked so much. My brother has the equivalent of two years medical school, by correspondence and my dad expected a ninety average from the both of us."

Brittney looked like she had been about to offer him her hand and was regretting it. "Guess you don't need much catching up to do then. We're supposed to be dissecting rats today. Optional, I guess but…"

She shook her head, glancing towards the whiteboard at the front of the classroom. "Never mind, you don't sound like you're from around here."

"Baton Rouge," Jocelyn leaned back in his seat, putting a black runner up on top of the desk. "Nowhere as interesting as New Orleans but the this is almost the first time; I've seen real snow in the US."

"Almost the first time?" Brittney arched an eyebrow at that, pulling her own textbook from her messenger bag. "When was the first?"

"Paris, France," His voice was dry. "Summers and winter break there for every year I can remember, visiting my grandparents. Skipped out one year when I was fifteen and took off to New York instead. Hopped on the bus and rode it all the way north, ala that Christmas movie with the kid in it."

Brittney stifled a snort, going pink. "Weren't your parents freaking out?"

He was saved from having to answer that question by the teacher's belated arrival, a coffee cup in one pudgy hand and the pointed glare directed at him. *"Je m'en fiche…"*

The teacher was followed a moment later by another student pushing the cart with the chilled bodies of rats wrapped in plastic. Jocelyn looked, a dry taste filling his mouth at the sight. "Partners or independent studies?"

Brittney shrugged, turning a hand over to inspect her nails. "Thirty of us, fifteen desks. We're comparing notes together even if we have to cut the rats open ourselves."

Her expression fell. "I heard about this from my ex-asshole boyfriend- he was a year older than me before graduating. I hate this part of the biology class, but I need it if I want to stay on the basketball team. It's not only the stupid football players who need good grades to keep their places, but also the women's basketball lot as well."

"Squeamish?" Jocelyn moved his foot as the package hit his foot rather than the little metal tray it was supposed to rest in.

"A little, yeah. You?" Britney gingerly opened her rat's bag and swallowed.

"I had a pet rat, had two of them but one died of a hemorrhage," Jocelyn glanced away. "So, kind of but not enough to avoid the project. It's more... a pet related thing than cutting them open."

"Miss. Jocelyn Lauren. If you could refrain from talking while I'm trying to explain the purpose of this assignment,"

Mr. Jacobs' voice was as unpleasantly nasal as he was pudgy, Jocelyn bristled at the snide tone. "If you're going to address me, at least try to get my gender right, Mr. Jacobs. It sure as hell isn't she or her."

Brittney went a deeper shade of pink and tugged on his arm. "Don't, just let it go, Jocelyn. Whatever Miss means to you, it isn't worth getting into an argument with the teacher over it. You can tell me about this at lunchtime, seniors are allowed off school property."

He bit down on his lower lip, forcing his temper back into the little box where it belonged. "Fine. For now."

She let out a breath that sounded relieved. "Thanks."

The teacher's opening lecture wasn't anything he hadn't heard before. Jocelyn tuned it out in favor of absently filling in the worksheet that had come with the project. Paper assignments were one thing, cutting the little labels out for the organs was another. "They banned this project at my old school, you know."

Brittney looked a little green as she set her scalpel down, shoving the rat away from her. "They did? Why?"

Jocelyn forced a smile at that. "All girls' Catholic academy, what do you expect? They didn't like teaching evolutionary theories and we got religion instead. Thankfully, my dad disagreed enough with that to find me a biology teacher in need of a fast buck or two."

Heart, lungs, and liver were already neatly placed in the metal tray and labeled with toothpicks. The intestine and stomach came next before he put the scalpel down by the hollowed-out corpse. "Faith and science don't have to be mutually exclusive. My brother is devoted but it doesn't stop him from believing in evolution or that the world is older than six thousand years."

The bell saved him from answering to Mr. Jacobs' scowl as he packed his bag up and returned the completed assignment to the teacher. "Go out for lunch like you said or the cafeteria?"

"Stay here," Brittney shouldered her backpack with a wince. "Normally I'd take my chances, but the roads are too icy."

She blushed a little, looking away. "And you aren't likely going to get many friends here if you keep irritating the teachers. C'mon. You can tell me about Baton Rouge until gym starts after lunch."

Gym... was going to be a problem. Jocelyn rummaged half-heartedly through his knapsack for the apple and whole wheat sandwich in it as they sat down at an unoccupied table. "Yay..."

Brittney peered at him curiously. "I thought you would be happy about that; you seem like the kind of girl who enjoys running and sports."

Jocelyn twisted his medical alert bracelet around his wrist, cursing the next period's class. "It's... complicated. That was the one class I hated more than the gossip trade back home. There was no guy's bathroom at my old school."

He flushed, picking apart the ham and mustard sandwich

47

rather than eating it. "Try sharing space with other girls when you realize you identify as male."

Brittney grimaced, pulling out her own lunch. "I screwed up, didn't I? Calling you a girl? Share a sandwich or cookie as an apology?"

"Can't," Jocelyn looked away. "I've got allergies. Peanuts are the big one, but I can't have shellfish or eggs either. Took a bite of a cookie once and found out one of the unlisted ingredients was a soy paste or something. I'd still take a severe peanut butter allergy over what Daniel has. He cut his hand open on a rusty knife or can lid once when he was my age and it got infected. The penicillin they gave to treat it nearly killed him. Dad was pissed."

The remainder of the day was only bearable by Brittney's presence. By the time three-thirty came around he was almost sorry that the day was over. She was one of the few who didn't judge him on his allergies or the gender he preferred.

Daniel almost seemed to notice his relief as he climbed into the passenger side seat. "Good day at school?"

"Good," Jocelyn wrapped his arms around his backpack, resisting the urge to reach out with his power and get a read on the reason behind his brother's exhaustion. That would be an invasion of privacy at best and at worst, an assault Dani wouldn't take kindly to. "I made a friend and pissed off a teacher in the same eighty-minute block. Biology is fun, the textbook sucks. You were a better teacher than Mr. Jacobs."

"That's good," Daniel coughed, wiping a hand across his mouth before focusing on navigating out of the small visitors' parking lot. "I thought you might."

"Yeah, thanks," The least he could do was be grudgingly grateful for Daniel's faith in the faculty and students at the high school. Not all of them were as transphobic as he had feared that morning. "What are we doing for supper?"

"I think Haydee's mother was planning some sort of vegetarian casserole, maybe." Daniel aid.

"Soy free? Yum," Jocelyn watched the snow fall outside the window until they pulled up outside the bed and breakfast. "Maybe this... will be home after all, for as long as we can manage it."

It was optimism unwarranted of him, but he couldn't help it either. The first day, as rough as it had been, had been better than anticipated. "Is it alright if I invite Brittney over at some point? For a study period somewhere. My math sucks as much as her biology does."

"It isn't our home, we're only renting a room until I find us an apartment somewhere but if she asks you over to her place, sure." Daniel cut the engine off, pulling the keys from the ignition.

The remainder of the evening surrounding the dinner was filled by homework, helping their hosts with the dishes, clean up and later, a long shower and bed. For once, he felt warm and safer than he had since their flight from New Orleans. Sooner or later, he'd have to admit the truth to Brittney but right now, that was his to keep.

Sleep was welcomed for the hour or two he claimed it, until the sound of coughing woke him. Jocelyn opened his eyes a crack, silently cursing the darkness of the night as well as his need for glasses; he couldn't see much but he knew Daniel's blurry shape even here. "Dani?"

Daniel shifted position, turning to look at him with a small white ball clutched in his left hand. "It's nothing, go back to bed."

If that was nothing, then he was well below idiot on the intelligence scale but there was little point in confronting his brother right now. Attempting would only make Daniel close off even more than he typically did. He'd tell in his own time and when he wanted to, not before. "Okay,"

Truth be told he was worn out and oddly, looking forward to the next day of school. It meant seeing Brittney again after all. As worried as he was by the way he had been brushed off, it was probably nothing. Daniel had always been prone to colds or sniffles for as long as he could remember. Among… other things but neither were worth dwelling on right now. Not when there was school in the morning.

He drifted off into a dreamless sleep.

CHAPTER FIVE

He hated lying to Jocelyn but until he got more information or an inconveniently necessary doctor's test, he wasn't going to do anything about it. Those files were with the man in New Orleans and any attempt at transferring them to a new doctor would only betray their hiding place. Daniel glanced away, briefly noting Jocelyn curled up in the other bed before crumpling the tissue paper up in one hand and tossing it into the waste bin where it turned itself into a small, smokeless fire before going out.

No-one needed to know that the coughing fit had brought up small spots of blood yet. The spasm had subsided as quickly as it had come and he could breathe again. Daniel pulled the coverlet over Jocelyn's shoulder, tucking a strand of hair out of the younger boy's eyes before closing the door behind him.

Haydee greeted him on the landing, a folded set of bedsheets in her arms. "What next? We didn't have much time to talk earlier."

Daniel shrugged half-heartedly. "What do you want to do?"

She smiled, looking ruefully down at the sheets she was carrying. "I was going to put these on the bed and then maybe... do you want to go on a date? A real one? I know it's late but..."

"I'd like that," He cut her off midsentence. "If it isn't being too forward."

"Too forward?" Haydee laughed. "Wow... you really are the Catholic school guy. I don't suppose one of your child-hood ideas was seminary school at one point?"

Daniel colored, looking down at the carpet under his socks. "No, at least nothing I seriously considered after Jocelyn told me who he was. Too many kids get hurt by priests. I value faith but not to the point where I'd consider taking any vow. In any case, my dad has a complicated rela-tionship with the church back home. So..."

He regained his train of thought. "I'd like that date, actually."

"Cool," Haydee edged past him, placed the folded sheets on the bare mattress before locking the door behind her. "I know a half decent Italian place we can go to."

Italian sounded just fine to him and it would be nice to explore more of the town than he had already seen so far. "Sure,"

The restaurant was small, something that would have been called a hole in the wall back home but here, it was nicely intimate with soft music playing from the speakers. The kind of place that someone proposed to their girlfriend in after the dessert was served. Daniel arched an eyebrow at that, glancing at Haydee. "Not that I know you very well but aren't we getting ahead of ourselves here?"

She rolled her eyes, seeming not to take offense to the question. "Welcome to Calais' only decent Italian restaurant, Daniel. The only other options were takeout or Chinese-

Italian fusion and the second one is under a health and safety warning. And no, if you're thinking what I am, I don't plan on proposing to you on the first date. My mom would be overjoyed if I did."

"Ah," Daniel took the door for her and let her go first into the restaurant before following a step or two behind her.

The waitress took their jackets with a brief nod and returned a moment later with the menus. Haydee flipped hers open, scanning the listed items idly. "Tagliatelle, please."

"And you?" The waitress looked to Daniel curiously.

He shrugged, closing it. "Penne arriabata, *grazie*."

She beamed, responding in the same language. "I'll be right back with your meals."

Haydee watched the exchange with a little envy apparent on her face. "You speak Italian?"

Daniel glanced away, self conscious despite himself. One language shouldn't have been that unusual and it wasn't in any place outside of the US, but he couldn't help a slight flicker of discomfort at Haydee commenting on it. "My dad was born and raised in France, he insisted that I get a better education, language wise, than my classmates. So, I'm fluent in French and Italian. Among other things."

"Among other things?" Haydee looked at him bemused. "What are the others?"

"Medieval French, Ancient and modern Greek and Latin," Daniel shifted in his seat in discomfort. "Alain was big on the classical languages."

Haydee gave a low whistle. "I'm actually impressed but I wonder what good learning all that is."

"It isn't, not really but Dad has a few antique books at home written in those languages that he wanted me to read," Daniel said.

He was careful to omit the titles of said books in the

unlikely case Haydee had heard of them. The others had no titles on their covers though they had been written in the languages he had listed. Those books had been the works of long dead witches and Alain had spent years collecting them. "There was no English translation available, and I doubt any historian would have enjoyed reading the contents of the books in my dad's library."

The dishes placed before them neatly cut short what was, for him, not an enjoyable subject. Daniel dug into the penne, savoring the spice in the sauce. "It's perfect,"

Haydee looked pleased, taking a bite or two of her own meal. "I thought you might like it here."

That was enough about him for the time being, now it was Haydee's turn. "What about you?"

She had the grace to blush and look down, stirring a fork through her pasta. "Probably boring compared to you, to be honest. The only language I know is English and I grew up here in Calais. Haven't even had a chance to see the original city, I'm afraid. I'm actually kind of jealous, you lived in Louisiana. To us northerners, that's as exotic as it gets and still be in the United States. All that history…"

Her voice was dreamy. "I'd love a chance to visit New Orleans some day."

"It's not all its cracked up to be," Daniel said. "Bourbon street is a tourist trap and, in some places, you have to watch out for pickpockets."

"Oh," Haydee looked disappointed for a moment. "Okay,"

Her hand slipped and she cursed softly, bending down to retrieve the fork she'd dropped. Daniel got to it first, shirt sleeve riding up to show the white of the cloth bandage on his wrist underneath it. Haydee blinked, gratitude for the return of the fork mixing with confusion as she caught sight of the wrapping on his forearm. "What happened to you?"

Daniel felt his face burn as he tugged his sleeve over the bandaging. A lie was necessary, however much he disliked telling a story. "Car accident. I didn't get the thing wrapped around a lamp post like most guys, but I did skid out enough and slam on the brakes hard enough to send me through the windshield."

Haydee looked skeptical but she didn't press further for now, much to his relief. There hadn't been a car accident and all the scarring on his arms, he'd done to himself in practicing the witchcraft. His family's and most of the other New Orleans families blessed or cursed with it, relied on blood to power their magic. "Out of curiosity, how well do you know Malachi?"

A slight frown crossed her face at the question. "He's been a friend for the past couple years. Said he came from North Carolina and one of those obscure little towns that even the locals forget exists from time to time. Before that, Boston, I think. I do know that he's on cautious terms with his father or stepfather and that the guy is Native American. Runs something out of Seattle maybe. Why?"

There was no way to tell her that Malachi was as much a witch as he was. Daniel pushed his cleaned plate out of the way, making room for the small brownie and ice cream dessert the waitress put in front of him. "Blackburn's an old name, English. Not something a Native American man would use very often."

"Mixed blood, maybe," Haydee shrugged, taking a bite of her coffee cake. "He said he was half Native, half white once. The rest you already know, I'm sure."

Her gaze dropped lower once they paid the bill and stood before looking back up at his face with a quizzical expression. "Not to comment on your personal habits but most people don't take a combat knife into a restaurant and not tell their dates. Is that a big city thing or just you, personally?"

Daniel flushed, pulling his jacket on in an attempt to hide the mentioned blade. "Better say paranoid but its nothing on you or this town. I just… got out of something back home and I don't want my brother to end up in it. He's too gentle for that life."

"Huh," She was looking pensive, biting down on one fingernail as she regarded him. "Good Catholic school guy, shy and reluctant to have sex before the wedding night. Carries a knife on his waist out of some paranoid need to protect his brother. What did you say you did before coming here?"

"I didn't," He quieted, uncomfortable. "And that's personal stuff I can't mention right now."

Haydee sighed, shoulders slumping. "Alright but from where I'm standing, switch the combat knife for a gun and you have a pretty credible picture of a runaway mafia body-guard to me."

For a moment he was tempted to tell her everything, about his family, about what Alain LaLaurie was capable of and the influence his father had in politics. The moment passed and he sighed, running a hand through his hair. "I guess ex mafia bodyguard works as good as anything else. It isn't the whole story but its close enough to it in the end. You can't tell anyone about this, Haydee. I… don't want you hurt and if my cousin tracks me down, he will."

Jared picked up the plastic water bottle from the side of the road, noted the reddish film coating the inside of it and swore in French as his grip tightened on the disposable material with a crackling sound. His prey had been smart enough to hide his trail or at least delay him but there were other ways to find the one he was looking for.

This had only bought a little time, not stopped him for good. Blood was power after all and he had saved an old tissue from his cousin's last nosebleed. "Better that you have left your sister behind, Daniel. Clever thinking of the bottle trick but you forgot Jocelynn's blood."

He drew back, throwing the plastic bottle into the air and watched as it fell back to the earth along the highway. The man behind him choked, put his hands to his throat and dropped to the ground, gaze unseeing. Blood smeared across his throat and mouth, spots on his shirt collar from the broken eardrums. "Well, we know that they aren't within the state anymore."

In this, their families were briefly united though Claudia Deveraux would stay behind in Baton Rouge. This was his hunt after all. She looked down, nudging the dead man's side with the toe of her sandal. "Where? You say you know but that's still miles of territory to look through."

She was no witch, but he liked her all the same and he smiled briefly, the expression cool. Whatever power her family had, had passed by her but she was aware of enough to still be useful. And she was good in bed as well, once he'd dealt with any future prospect of children. Early menopause or sterilization was a wonder sometimes. "Just get me a map, I'll do the rest."

It still wouldn't be a precise art, but he could narrow down Jocelynn's location to a state or two from here. Once within a closer distance then he could rely on a stronger blood tie to find the girl and her brother. The two weren't likely to very far apart after all. Jocelynn was thirteen and legally blind, Daniel was her guardian.

He spread the map out, closing his eyes for a second as he searched inwardly and then moved further out, penciling a line from Baton Rouge northwards. And cursed again at the end of the trail. "New York, New Hampshire or Vermont, *merde*."

There was worse he wanted to use in regard to the possible states and their climates, but a simple shit would have to do for now. "What in His name possessed you to go that far north, Daniel?"

"Because we can't drive very well up there?" Claudia asked.

He gritted his teeth and forced a smile at that. His girl-friend was a ditz and a dyed blonde one at that but occasion-ally she had a logical thought. "Maybe, c'mon. We're going back to New Orleans and getting on the next flight to Vermont. Leave the body for the animals. I've got what I needed from him for now."

And he didn't even have to mark his arms up to do it. Daniel might have preferred to use his own blood, but it limited his cousin's power in a way that a life sacrificed didn't for him. "Let's go,"

They were one step closer on their hunt now.

CHAPTER SIX

Bartending at the Crown and Cat was less than ideal but they were the only place that had called back with an answer after he'd dropped off a resume. And working at the bar was the kind of job he was looking for, for the time being. Temporary until he found something more permanent or risked his chances and requested his transcripts from university.

And it was a good place to catch what passed as local gossip in Calais. If anyone new came by or asked questions, chances were that someone would bring the news to the bar. Kate MacKinnon appeared to collect that information and share it for a price in addition to managing the bar.

Daniel wiped the sticky counter down with a sigh, watching Kate out of the corner of his eye for a moment. She might have appeared ordinary to most of the handful of patrons frequenting the place, but they lacked his... sense for the odd. Whoever she was, she didn't lack for power.

Neither did Malachi but the other guy wasn't around, easily memorable for the shoulder length dark hair, his way of speaking or the gray feather stuck through the elastic tie he wore. Malachi, at least, had readily confessed to being a witch. Kate hadn't said one way or the other.

"Break," She mouthed the word at him, gesturing to the staff room down the short hallway.

He nodded, dropping the cloth into the sink and turned away. A half an hour away from serving drinks or cleaning up the mess left behind by said drinks was something to be grateful for and he sat heavily in the ancient gray cloth armchair in the staff room. "Thanks,"

Kate lingered for a second, briefly touching the pendant she wore at her throat before dropping into a crouch in front of him and taking his hands in hers. Daniel nearly drew back, pulling away from her until he felt the slight, oddly comforting sensation of power giving him strength. "How...? Why?"

And because the situation warranted it. "Is everyone in this town a witch or did I have the bad luck to stumble into Roanoke's new home?"

Kate laughed, tucking a strand of hair behind one ear. "*Cherie*, Malachi's the only one who might be considered a 'local' here. You and I are wanderers, seeking a hiding place or answers to mysteries. As for why I lent my power to you, I daresay you needed it."

Her smile turned sly, almost fox like in its expression. "Believe the old tale if you want to or not but you may call me the first real witch around. My mother calls me a fool for ever teaching mortals the shadowed arts, but she has been long dead and had no skill with the craft."

Daniel pulled free of her touch, disquieted. "Kate, Hecate then?"

She smiled again, inclining her head for a moment. "The lady of the crossroads, some say. I wouldn't be so open with just anyone, but I feel you need a little bit of truth tonight."

He swallowed, looking away. "Shouldn't you be dead? No one believes in the Greek gods anymore."

Kate laughed and sobered. "Perhaps, perhaps not. I'm not what you would call human, though mortal, yes. I gave up the goddess given power for a more... mortal perspective. I still answer to my father though. And his three headed beast of a dog. My mother passed on long ago, surrendering her people and her name to become Erinyes."

Her gaze moved past him to focus on a space by the old outdoor patio table in one corner. "And she lacks the sense sometimes to keep out of my business."

Daniel followed her look, seeing nothing out of the ordinary. "Er,"

She pinched the bridge of her nose and looked down, rueful. "I see the dead as much as I'm a witch, yes. My mother isn't best pleased that I confessed to you, Daniel. Now I should ask you to get back to work before Beth comes back here."

He nodded, putting one hand on the doorknob. "Thanks for the help."

She shrugged carelessly. "So be it. A warning though if you find yourself in the woods outside town at night. It isn't only the cold you need to fear, be careful around the spirit kind. They aren't human and can't think like you or I."

"I'll keep that in mind," Though the chances of him ever being caught out at night in the middle of winter were almost zero. "Are there... any wardings I need to do to keep Jocelyn safe?"

"Are you asking for lessons?" Her question was wry. "Come by tomorrow then. I'll keep the bar closed for our privacy. By the way, how was your date with Haydee?"

"It was... good," Daniel lifted his gaze to meet hers. "How did you know about that?"

She laughed, shaking her head. "Nothing as trite as shapeshifting and pretending to be a waitress, Daniel. I wouldn't invade your personal life like that. The dead like their gossip as much as the next living person. You're fortunate you can't see them."

Maybe he was, but it would have been nice to see the apparent observers. Daniel sighed again and returned to his place behind the counter. At least now there were only three or so hours left of his shift before he was free to go home.

Haydee greeted him at the front door, taking his hand shyly for a moment before dropping it. "How was work?"

He pulled the winter jacket off, hanging it from the coat hook. "Mostly sticky and it smelled too much like beer but at least I didn't have to handle breaking up a fight tonight. Kate has a guy for that. Jocelyn?"

"Making friends or at least one friend," Haydee said. "Brittney seems to like him. I saw them in the lunchroom together again. I think she finally asked him over to her house for a study session since I saw them in the cafeteria working on another biology assignment. I think she- he was tutoring her in it."

"That's good," Daniel pinched the bridge of his nose, in an attempt to ease the beginnings of another migraine behind his eyes. "At least it's the weekend. I can sleep in and get an afternoon instead of an evening shift tomorrow."

The evening work and closed period Kate had promised him were for the lessons she had offered during his break. "And then church on Sunday."

At least for him if Jocelyn wasn't interested in going to the service. Talking with the priest would help if nothing else.

Haydee hesitated, chewing on her lower lip. "I can't say I'll understand half of it or be able to sit through all of this thing, but do you think I... could go with you? Faith isn't really my strong point, I'm too cynical for that but I'm willing to listen."

Who was he to say no to her request? Daniel gave her an attempt at a reserved smile. "Sure,"

Her company would be welcomed, at least until after the service ended and he needed to talk with the priest. But between that time and the remainder of the night, all he wanted was his bed and Kate's lesson.

Haydee seemed to note that because she let him pass and climb the stairs to the bedroom. He gave her a grateful look in passing and closed the door behind him. His sleep shirt and sweatpants were where he'd left them last, folded on the top of the rest of his clothes before he pulled them on and drifted off into a dreamless sleep.

Morning brought too harsh sunlight with it and he winced as the frost caked outside the windowsill threw icy sparkles into his vision. Even with medicine taken just before going to bed, the migraine lingered and forced him to fumble for a pair of sunglasses on the nightstand.

Jocelyn, inexplicably, was up well before him and sitting at one of the tables in the dining room, chatting with Haydee over a bowl of cereal. Both looked up when he walked inside and slumped at the table. She was quizzical, his brother merely curious. Haydee spoke first, a dry note in her voice. "How much did you have to drink last night?"

"Water," He wasn't in the mood for sarcasm at the moment. "I was working, remember? The migraine came after I got here."

"I'll need your car for the morning," Jocelyn dropped his dishes into the sink, turning his back to it. "Brittney gave me directions to her house but I'm not going to hike it in this cold."

"As long as you bring it back before five, alright," Daniel

took the leftover toast from Haydee's plate and buttered it, cautiously testing it against the nausea induced by the headache. "I've got work this afternoon."

"Fair," Jocelyn gave him a cursory nod and took the keys from a small bowl placed at the center of the round table. "Shouldn't be later than two, maybe. Brittney hates studying."

"Alright," Daniel said. "I'll see you tonight."

His brother was as good as his word, bringing the car back half an hour earlier than promised though he was evasive on what the study period had been related to. At any other time he would have pressed for an answer but Jocelyn was allowed to have his own secrets. He was eighteen, that was worth giving him a little bit of trust or freedom in exchange for privacy.

Still, he felt a pang at leaving his brother behind, but tonight was about more than the errands he had said needed to be done today. It was winter and they were in the wrong state for it, but sage could be useful if he was able to find a place that sold the dried plant. A can of spray paint- the color didn't matter to him- and thread. Even the smallest, mundane object had a little power in it, for warding or traps. It was just a matter of knowing how to use it.

If anyone thought the collected items on the table were odd, they weren't around to comment aloud about the nature of the collection. Not all of the craft was standing around a pot of water and boiling a frog to death in it. It was biology, chemistry and a little bit of physics gathered under one umbrella.

The can of spray paint lay on its side next to the spool of thread, a handful of sticks were wrapped in a ragged bit of cloth next to it. A gas station lighter lay on its side a little way apart from the rest.

Kate was expected, Malachi was… not. Daniel glanced warily at the male witch before looking back at her. "I thought it was going to just be the two of us tonight."

She shrugged, studying her nails before dropping her hand back to her side. "He's here for moral support."

The question remained for whose moral support, but he bit back on the words, looking towards the collected items again. "Alright,"

He drew back, wary as the two exchanged a look with each other before Malachi grabbed his wrist, holding tight and pushed him against the staff room wall. One hand placed between his shoulder blades. "Counter it,"

Daniel sucked in a quick breath, fumbling one handed for the combat knife at his waist. The shove hadn't been expected but maybe that was part of the lesson, he could sense Malachi's power teasing, searching for an opening in his defenses. Any small hole and the entire wall would crumble around him, leaving him vulnerable to whatever the other witch wanted to do. "Get… off."

He sank to his knees as Malachi let go, breathing hard as his heartbeat slowed to a normal, healthy rate. "Were you trying to send me into cardiac arrest?"

Malachi's expression was neutral, unreadable. "You could have fought me off if you wanted to. You treated this as a normal assault instead. Against another witch, you would have been dead, Daniel."

He lifted his gaze, using the table to brace himself in a standing position. "I won't kill. I made a promise to myself about that."

And it was one he wasn't sure he would be able to break if worst came to worst. "You didn't get in, did you."

Malachi offered him a thin, short lived smile at that. "I'll give whoever taught you first, some credit. You know how to protect against a brute force attack. You did well, considering I was trying to stop your heart but there's no subtlety in your use either. Given a few minutes or a distraction, I would have found a way through your guard. But then I've had nearly four hundred years practice, some of it against opponents with several times the power we do."

"We'll live that long?" Daniel closed his eyes, trying to suppress the dizziness that washed over him.

"Some, a few." Malachi glanced away. "Not all like us. Most don't, truthfully. Those that do, either made a bargain with a god or cheated their way to a longer life. Or they were born to it like I was. You're just mortal though."

That was more of a relief than he was willing to admit to. He couldn't imagine a lifetime of potential centuries rather than a decent seventy or eighty years. "You bargained with a... err..."

Malachi's brief smile tightened slightly. "I didn't, my mother did for the sake of my father's life. Dysentery nearly took him before the hangman's noose did."

"Coyote?" That didn't add up with the story Haydee had told him at the restaurant the other night.

"Tobias Blackburn," Malachi's expression was once more unreadable. "He may have sired me, yes but Coyote's... influence was greater in the end. And shapeshifter might be a more apt description of him if near god is uncomfortable to dwell upon."

Kate had been quiet, seeming content to observe for now. Now she spoke up, pulling the chair out and sitting down in it. "Willing to come back again tomorrow?"

She'd addressed the question to him. Daniel hesitated, unsure of his answer. On one hand, he was wary of anything Malachi might say. On the other, he needed to protect his brother and if that meant learning whatever the bar's manager was willing to teach him. "Do I have a choice?"

"Likely not, if you want to keep Jocelyn safe," Kate said. "The kid loves you."

"Yeah, I know," Daniel looked away. 'Guess I'll bring my journal tomorrow night. Reading that might help you figure out a way of showing me differently from what my dad did."

"If you think it'll help, I'll read it," Kate looked towards the table but didn't clear it off. "We'll try again tomorrow."

Her gaze drifted toward Malachi. "A word in private, please."

He nodded, letting her lead the way back to the small office in the hallway. Daniel lingered for a moment before leaving. There was nothing more to do and he needed to return to the bed and breakfast if he was going to get Jocelyn up in time for the church service.

CHAPTER SEVEN

Haydee was the first one up and at the table in the kitchen, dressed in a fleece sweater and jeans. A half-finished plate of pancakes by her elbow as she scrolled through something on her phone. "There's hazelnut coffee if you want it."

Daniel took the offered mug, taking a seat at the table opposite her as he sipped at the barely warm liquid contained within. "It's lukewarm at best."

She flushed, putting her phone down. "Sorry, I hope you don't mind but I was trying to put a list of potential services down for Jocelyn, just in case but there isn't much in the city that I've been able to find."

That was both unnecessary and unwanted. Daniel looked away, covering his mouth as he tried to suppress the slight cough that emerged. "It's... appreciated but I'm pretty sure Jocelyn can figure this out for himself. He doesn't need us hovering him over like he's a little kid."

She sighed and smiled shyly a moment later. "You know, I love how you say Calais. You don't give it that hard, ugly sound most people around here do."

He managed a weak laugh despite himself. "My summers and sometimes winter vacations were spent with my grandparents in Paris. I guess more of the Parisian accent stuck than I thought. You said there was nothing here that could help my brother?"

Her good mood seemed to fade a little. "Not much, I'm afraid. And nothing involving a gender therapist. You've me the high school principal. She's not the most transphobic person around, just one of the more... obvious ones."

"So, it's Augusta or Portland then?" He would have been grateful if there had been someone who suited Jocelyn's needs here, but it seemed that luck was against him for now. And if the principal was an example of the less transphobic people in the town, it didn't seem wise to ask who was more against it.

"Yeah," Haydee tore the sheet with the numbers and addresses from her notebook. "Take a weekend or two and see what fits."

He sighed, resting his forehead on his clasped hands before lifting his gaze to look at her. "I'll do my research later. Right now..."

"Church?" Haydee asked.

"Yeah," He nodded tiredly. "Shall we?"

The winter sun was weak but through the stained glass of the windows, still beautiful. Daniel paused for a moment, listening to the beginning notes of the hymn. The words were in English rather than French he was used to in Parisian services but there was still some comfort in hearing it.

"You like this?" Haydee glanced at him intrigued. "I mean the church is pretty and I'd love to take a few pictures of the stained glass but it's just a song to me."

He shook his head, unable to explain his faith to her. "It's more than a song to me. It's… complicated but this feels right somehow."

She subsided, taking her seat in one of the pews as the hymn ended and the priest stepped up to the front.

Daniel glanced away, willing to let his guard down for now. The peace brought by the man's sermon was worth it. And then it was over before he wanted it to be. Haydee's hand slipped over his before she blinked and pulled away, a blush staining her cheeks. "I'll be outside for you. This was nice but it was just a service to me."

He nodded, not hurt by her words. Faith was difficult to put into words at the best of times, telling someone how he felt when they didn't share that same faith was nearly impossible. "Alright,"

She gave a shy smile and nodded, pulling her mittens on before she made her way to the heavy oak doors at the front of the church.

The priest greeted him with a brief duck of the head. "Yes, child?"

Daniel hesitated, searching for the right words to use. "Can we talk? I could use your advice."

He didn't mind the man's use of child this time since the man appeared to be in his late sixties with more silver in his hair than mouse brown. "There's nowhere else I can go to and well..."

He trailed off with a sigh. "I always found faith before."

"I see," The priest looked pensive. "Try to describe your difficulty and I'll do what I can to help."

"It's more than one thing but I'll start with the more normal thing first," Unless pressed, he wasn't going to mention the witchcraft or what he was capable of just yet. "My brother was born female, but he never liked the dresses and skirts my dad insisted he wear on Sundays. I'm trying to

71

protect him, but I can't be there at school for him. From what Haydee said, the principal is transphobic."

"Ah," The man frowned, taking a seat on a nearby chair. "Wouldn't this be an affair better taken up with the school board and not a pastor?"

Daniel sighed, folding his hands in his lap. "Maybe but I was wondering how you felt on the matter first."

The priest glanced away, contemplating the nearest stained-glass window with a depiction of Mary and child in the frame. "The bible says that there are only two sexes, male and female and that such roles are set in His eyes, but I find the interpretation decidedly narrow. Jacob made his home in the house while his brother hunted."

"Genesis," Daniel noted the priest's expression of surprise. "My father made sure I knew the bible as a kid. It... mattered to him."

"Hm," The priest lifted a shoulder in a shrug. "I think some of the congregation would disagree, but I believe that He wasn't mistaken where it concerns your brother. In his sex, perhaps but not his gender or how he decides to express it. This may be a strength of his, not a flaw or weakness to be erased."

A thoughtful look crossed his face. "I wonder, if you don't mind, telling me what your name is."

"Daniel," He was quietly spoken despite giving it over. Trust was a hard thing to come by after all.

The pastor gave a brief, kind laugh. "God is my judge. I suppose the name suits you. I must admit I was expecting an Alexander or David."

Daniel snorted, making the sound wry. "It almost came close to that, Alexander. The protector. David was near the end of my mom's list of names. Why ask?"

"Curiosity, largely," The priest said. "You're a far better person than you give yourself credit for."

"I don't know about that," Daniel passed a hand over his eyes and dropped it back to his side. "I'm trying to be good, but I don't know how well it works with- with witchcraft."

"With witchcraft?" The skeptical note in the older man's expression was genuine, not something feigned or a mask concealing something else. "Surely you know there's no such thing."

"If only," Daniel sighed. He glanced towards one of the heavy votive candles left behind by one of the parishioners in front of a portrait of Edward the Confessor. There was an oddity in finding the painting in an American church, but someone clearly had liked it regardless. "I'm one of them."

It was less a prayer than simply drawing on his power, but the words seemed to help focus, direct the little internal spark enough to light the wick with almost a thought. Much more than that and he couldn't have done anything else, LaLaurie magic was unpredictable at best and little more than worth-less when it came to consecrated ground. Some blessing or faith itself made the magic beyond the reach of its user in the face of the sacred.

The priest's eyes widened in disbelief, and he crossed himself hastily though he didn't move from his seat. "I... see,"

Much more faintly this time, certainly without the surety he had had when discussing Jocelyn. Daniel looked away, tasting something bitter and acrid in his mouth. "Well?"

"Truthfully, I have no answer to how you accomplished lighting the candle without a match," The priest looked almost guilty at that. "I think this is one question you may have to answer for yourself."

He had expected as much even if the lack of an answer was disappointing. "Thank you,"

Haydee was waiting for him outside the front doors, fiddling with her phone as she finished up a text. "Anything?"

"Sort of," Daniel said. "He helped with Jocelyn, other things- I think I'm... looking in the wrong place. Or to the wrong person."

She pocketed her phone with a slight shrug. "Some help is better than none, right?"

"I guess," He would have liked an answer to the theological questions, but she did have a point about the help. "Who were you texting?"

A shadow briefly crossed her face at that. "Jocelyn. Don't ask me how he got my personal number when he shouldn't have it. Mom or Dad must have given it to him."

"And?" There seemed to be more to the story than the little she'd given him.

Haydee sighed, pinching her nose with a gloved hand. "How should I know? I don't hang out in the same places your brother does. All I know from the text relay is that he's asking to go to a study session with a couple of his friends and that he's bringing the snacks. Or so he says anyway. Brendan's family has an indoor pool in the basement."

Daniel bit down on his lower lip, looking away in discomfort. On one hand, Jocelyn deserved a chance to be just another guy and spend time with his friends. On the other, there was the obvious... euphemism within those handful of text messages. This was less about studying and more about a party. "If he thinks he can be safe, sure. He can go, just tell him I don't appreciate the lying to me about it."

Haydee frowned and typed out the message, waiting a minute for the answering beep before she relaxed. "He says he's alright so far. And that the chemistry is going swimmingly."

Her mouth quirked in something that was almost a smile. "Got to respect a kid who knows how to imply either getting off with someone or actually going swimming and still make it sound like the chemistry homework is easy."

That was something of a relief, however small it was. Daniel sighed, relaxing marginally. "Alright, shall we?"

If there was nothing else left for them to do it would be nice to curl up on the couch with a good book. It was deserved in his mind after the morning they'd had and the lack of answers the priest had been able to give him.

CHAPTER EIGHT

Brendan was more Brittney's friend than his but that hadn't stopped the other guy from inviting him over to his place for a party. One disguised as a study session from various parents or relatives but it didn't stop the tiny seed of discomfort coiling in his chest as he looked up at the house. Daniel had always been around to offer help or support. Or protection when he'd needed it. Now, this was the first time he was going to a "study" session on his own. At least before, Daniel had been there to drive him even if the reasons for said prior sessions were a lie.

Daniel had never been good at spotting or making up stories under pressure. He was too honest a person to be skilled at it.

Brittney had been his first friend at the new high school, Brendan was his second after her. That was all the circle of friends he needed until summer break started. Neither of the two seemed to mind how he identified and just treated him like a person instead of a freak or confused about which bathroom was better suited. Brendan had even offered to be a guard and lookout just in case any teachers came by and accused a girl of using the wrong toilet.

Jocelyn bit down on his lower lip, holding the hard-earned case of beer in one hand. It hadn't been easy to come by, even with a fake ID making him twenty-one and the briefest touch of skin on skin contact to make the cashier's mind. The guy would probably wake up in the morning with one hell of a headache for his reward. "Hi?"

Brittney answered the door, one step ahead of Brendan as music played from the living room. "Brought the stuff? Thought your brother would have objected to you drinking."

"He doesn't know, or he fell for the text message I sent to Haydee," Jocelyn's mouth thinned, wry. "And even if he didn't, our dad would have overruled him. It's illegal here, in France – kids are allowed to have a sip or two of alcohol. So, someone got the rules right."

"Really?" Brittney looked past him to see the taillights of Daniel's car vanishing into the darkness. "No offense to Daniel but he seems…"

Odd? Conservative? Uptight? There were lots of words he could have guessed at but none of them really fit his brother. "Cautious? Yeah, he kind of has to be around alcohol and driving. It's complicated."

He passed the beer case off to Brendan, seeing the graphic arts student beam at the sight, black streaked blond hair falling into his eyes. Brendan's style was difficult to determine, he seemed to rotate between punk, a basic t-shirt and jeans combination and a basketball uniform from his previous year on the team. "You're welcome."

The reason for Daniel's caution also wasn't his secret to tell – Dani would be furious if he found out, but it was too big for one person to hold onto. Jocelyn let his shoulders sag, giving in. "He- he was epileptic for as long as I could remember. My family doesn't like talking about it much but it's there. Dad just called it a faint and be done with it rather than face it right on. Things… have been better for a while but I remember the arguments over the phone. I think one of the treatment options suggested was surgery, but Dad refused to go through with it. Something about the horror stories my grandfather used to scare us about the asylums."

He rested his head against the doorframe, offering the box to Brittney. "He didn't want to go through with something he called mutilation so Daniel's taking pills- has been for a few years now. Still means no drinking and very careful behind the wheel."

Jocelyn forced a smile he couldn't feel. "He's eight years older than me and he never learned how to swim. Water and seizures don't mix."

Epilepsy and whatever psychic thing they shared a talent with didn't mix. It didn't take an expert to picture the damage that combination could do if it went wrong.

"I was going to say gentle," Brittney's expression was tired. "But I'm sorry about Dani for you."

"Yeah," That was one way of describing his brother. "He's gentle,"

He edged past her, trying not to get snow on the expensive hardwood floor. "Brendan's got a nice place. I like it. Nothing like home."

Brittney laughed, setting the case down into the cooler plugged into the kitchen wall. "What's home like, or was, I guess?"

Invent something or stick to the story of a boring middle-class family that had been his and Dani's agreed upon narrative. "Just me, Dad and my brother, I guess. You know, normal. Mom passed away a few years ago and my sister's doing a… residency in a New Orleans hospital."

It wasn't quite a lie where Athenais was concerned, right? The only thing he'd fudged was her position as a patient rather than a nurse or doctor. "Haven't really seen her for a few years. She's not on speaking terms with our dad."

The beat of the song changed, quieting for the first few opening notes. Jocelyn dropped his jacket on the back of a kitchen chair, going into the living room where the party was in full swing. A couple of his classmates were laughing, flirting with each other on the couch. Three more were goading another into a drink.

Brittney's hand slipped over his shoulder for a second. "Fun, yeah?"

"Maybe, honestly- this is my first real party," Jocelyn said.

"No kidding," She smirked, giving him a slight shove into the living room. "At least Brendan's parents aren't here, they'd freak out. Go on, enjoy yourself."

He popped one of the beer cans open, wincing at the taste of the amber liquid. "Maybe not for long. Dani's on shift, bartending but I wouldn't be surprised if he took his break to take me home a couple hours on."

"Then we'll make the best of that time," Brittney said.

She pushed the other couple from the couch and tugged him into sitting next to her. Brittney's mouth met his before he could pull away. Her scent was light vanilla and cinnamon, clinging to her skin. "Oh…"

Her kiss was nice. He hesitated, placing his hand at the nape of her neck once they broke contact with each other. "You… don't mind that I look like a girl?"

Brittney laughed shyly, running a hand through her hair. "Honestly, Jocelyn. I prefer it. You're pretty for a guy and you don't have inconvenience of something between your legs. Be a shame to lose that, though… I admit your explanation wasn't easy to deal with at first. I cried when I thought I was losing a chance at getting a girlfriend."

"Girlfriend?" It always paid to ask for clarification about certain words, just to be on the safe side.

"I… uhm, like girls, yeah." Brittney's cheeks were pinker than they had been a moment earlier. She looked away, swallowed and leaned forward, pressing her mouth to his. Her words were muffled, barely a breath over his skin as she kissed his cheek. "You're the first guy I've ever actually kissed. Wonder if that makes me still a lesbian or more on the bisexual kind of scale."

Jocelyn shrugged, glancing away. "We'll figure that mystery out later, maybe. Probably best if you don't meet my dad though. I can't call him a bigot but he's conservative and doesn't like much about the gay community. We're all sinners and this is something we chose, not what we were born with." Whatever else he wanted to say died unspoken as the half-finished plastic cup chilled under his touch, feeling less like plastic now and more like refrigerated glass as the living room wavered around him. The music faded to an indistinct background hum, to be replaced by something scratchier and more bad eighties themed than contemporary. One sniff told him enough about the cigarette smoke and spilled alcohol than he wanted to know. Someone's dimly lit bar rather than Brendan's party.

Daniel was behind the counter, in the midst of pouring and serving a drink before he went still, a flicker of emotion no stranger would have noticed as it crossed his face. He steadied himself on the scarred counter, brushing a hand across the back of his neck.

Jocelyn watched, helpless to do anything as the glass his brother had been filling from the tap, shattered on the floor.

Scattered pieces of glass and amber liquid skittering across the grubby tile. Dropped from a suddenly nerveless hand.

Just for a moment, it felt like Daniel's gaze was on his before his brother crumpled behind the long counter. The plea for help unspoken but still there.

"Jocelyn?" Brittney's question echoed Daniel's own use of his name, intruding on his thoughts. "What's wrong? You kind of spaced on me."

Jocelyn looked down, seeing the spilled red cup at his feet and ignored it as he grabbed for his jacket on the way out of the front door. The lingering taste of Daniel's fear still in the back of his mouth. "I don't know, but this is important…"

A lie but a necessary one for the time being. Just give me your keys or let me take the nearest damned car I can find. I didn't space out on you, my brother did. For the first time in a few years."

She caught his hand in hers, restraining him. "How could you possibly know that? Jocelyn, talk to me? The only decent bar around here is clear across town and I wouldn't call it high class. This isn't…"

"Let's just call it a psychic thing and be done with it," Jocelyn swiped the keys she held out for him. "I know I'm not giving you any information at all but it's safer that way and I… well, I just know my brother's in trouble. He's not the kind of guy who throws a beer glass across the open bar space. His temper is better than that."

Brittney's mouth tightened in unhappiness. "So, I'll ditch the party and go with you anyway. It's not like I was enjoying this shit much otherwise. Talk to me, please."

Jocelyn sighed, pulling the jacket on over his shoulders. "Fine, so long as you don't tell anyone else or freak out on me. I'm not going to do this justice, but I just saw a… daydream thing where Dani seized. His epilepsy was supposed to be in control. The pills helped him for as long as I could remember reading the label. Now… I just need to deal with this. He's in no condition to drive back on his own."

"I'm going with you," Brittney said. "He isn't, neither are you in this state. Not on icy roads."

What choice did he have? Brittney was right. Several years of driving on mercifully dry roads in Louisiana were in no way preparation for the snow-covered streets of Maine. Jocelyn sighed, relenting. "Fine, hope your fake ID's as good as you think it is. We're both eighteen."

"It's worked before in Augusta," Brittney flipped the plastic rectangle over in her hands. "Are you gong to explain the psychic thing to me later on? 'Cause I'd kind of like more information than you zoning out on me and leaving in a rush."

Tell her or not? Jocelyn glanced away from studying the space beneath the steering column of the Ford. "It's complicated, psychic makes more sense than an accidental bit of tracking magic when I was sixteen. I'm still not sure what went wrong or if I was always a little sensitive to Dani, now it's kind of… hyper focused. I'll always know when he's in trouble. Empathic talent gone somewhat sideways, and I can't always ignore it. Distance helps, a little but that's not always an option."

He was working as he spoke, stripping the wires underneath the steering wheel and touching them together. The car started without complaint as Brittney watched him, disbelief crossing her face. "You know how to hotwire a car?"

Jocelyn shrugged briefly, looking away. "Lyra Highsmith taught me much to Dani's embarrassment. I have a… complicated family back in Baton Rouge but she isn't related, thankfully. I'd be worried if she was since I'm pretty sure Lyra isn't her real name. From what little I know about her; she loves her wordplay. Lyra sounds like liar and Highsmith- well, it isn't much a stretch to make her surname sound like that label of everyone's favorite Norse trickster."

He sat back in the driver's seat. "I'd almost believe it, except that she's blonde and female, not the dark-haired guy from the movies."

Brittney looked at him, chewed on her lower lip and climbed into the passenger seat. "I'll add that to my mental checklist about you. Damned good with biology, hotwires cars for fun and a psychic."

"Yeah," Jocelyn skidded on a patch of ice in the driveway, recovered and put a foot on the gas pedal. "Not as fun as you think it is. Or as useful. I can only track him; this doesn't tell me street addresses or locations in advance. I could still get lost on us."

Brittney was still biting down on her lower lip. "Where – what did the bar look like to you?"

"Small, seedy," Jocelyn stepped on the brake a little harder than intended and earned a frightened squeak from her. "The kind of place tourists avoid."

"The Crown and Cat," Brittney's answer was automatic. "Everyone calls the owner weird. She's Greek, or maybe Irish but she doesn't give a damn about who comes in there, so long as they're well behaved."

The Crown and Cat was as seedy as Brittney had described it being. Jocelyn ignored the man loitering at the doorway in favor or going directly to the back of the bar and the cramped staff room. Dani was sitting on an ancient tartan patterned couch, head in his hands. A red-haired woman in a black tank top was sitting next to him, concern apparent on her face.

Like the man up front, the bartender was ignored as he dropped to the balls of his feet in front of Daniel. There were more important things to worry about right now than acknowledging the bartender. "What happened earlier? I felt it when you fainted."

"I'm fine now," Daniel lifted his gaze. "Whatever it was, it passed."

Deny it all he wanted to; he had never been much of a liar. Jocelyn brushed a hand roughly through dark brown hair. "Lie to Brittney or your employer all you want to, don't try to lie to me, Dani. I'll always know when you're not feeling well. You seized again, didn't you?"

"I fainted, that's all." Daniel's tone went flat, warning. "Leave it alone, Jocelyn."

That might have been his brother's wish, it wasn't his. Jocelyn stood, folding his arms across the loose-fitting navy t-shirt he wore. "Keep your secrets if you want to but Brittney already knows about your epilepsy, Dani. I told her."

"It wasn't your secret to tell," Daniel felt his mouth tighten at the admission. "It was private-"

"And that's shit," Jocelyn dropped his hands back to his sides. "Deny it if you want to, it doesn't change what happened and that I felt it. Or did you miss the part where I'm able to track you clear across town thanks to what I did a couple years ago. I'll always know how you're feeling."

He took a breath, trying to calm the rising tide of fear in the back of his mind. "I won't insist on seeing a doctor this time but if you... faint again, I'll call the emergency whether or not you want me to. Just don't give me the crap about not eating or missing a meal or something. You're- you were always careful about diet and exercise. This isn't like before, you know that. I don't know what's going on but it's beginning to scare me."

Shame flickered across his brother's face. "It was just a faint, Jocelyn but if it happens again, I'll ask a doctor about it, promise. I've always been better at keeping my word than lying."

"Alright," Jocelyn looked away. "I'm still not happy about this but it's better than nothing. Though... at some point you're going to have to tell Haydee about everything. She likes you; you know. Grandma always said that omitting things was as bad as a real lie. You were better at editing than making a story up."

"That falls under the if statement, but I'll keep it in mind." Daniel said.

It was as good as he was ever going to get out of his brother. Jocelyn stood, putting his hand on the staff room doorframe. "Fine, fair enough. But I should tell you that I borrowed someone's car and hotwired it to get here. Also, I have a fake ID that makes me twenty-two, not eighteen. Just thought you should know."

"Jocelynn Isabeau LaLaurie,"

It was hard to tell whether Daniel was more outraged or disappointed by the mention of the illicit activities and he was in no mood for any lecture of his brother's. He was already out the door, rubbing his hands against the cold of the winter night. Brittney could return the car to its rightful owner after she drove him back to the Ashworth's bed and breakfast. Daniel could beg a ride or do it himself later if he was of a mind to. The silver Audi was still parked in the far end of the small lot.

CHAPTER NINE

I t seemed like longer, but it couldn't have been much more than an hour or two before his shift ended. Kate drove, he sat in the front passenger seat next to her, staring quietly out the window until she slowed, stopped the car outside the bed and breakfast place. "Thanks,"

"Anytime," She wasn't looking at him. "Just try and eat something before your next shift, Daniel. I can't have you fainting on me again."

"I'll try," He pulled the keys from the ignition and pocketed them. "How will you get home without a car?"

Her smile was forced but still held a little fondness in the expression. "I have my ways, don't worry about me, Daniel."

If she said she was going to be alright, who was he to stop her, but he couldn't help the slightest bit of concern about his employer. "If you're sure,"

"I'll be fine, your brother's waiting for you," Kate said.

Jocelyn was sprawled on one of the two beds in the room, one arm under his chin, the other holding a book down at the page where he had fallen asleep on top of the open book. It couldn't have been a comfortable position or pillow. Daniel lifted the glasses from his brother's nose, smoothing a bit of hair out of his eyes. "Everything will be alright, I promise. I didn't mean to scare you like this."

When he made a promise, he tried to keep it no matter the circumstances. Daniel pulled the blanket up over Jocelyn's shoulders and turned away from the bed. Sunday nights meant school in the morning; it was on him to drag his brother out of bed when the alarm clock went off. "See you in the morning."

Morning brought a pounding headache and the shrill shriek of the alarm clock through his hearing. Daniel groaned, covering his eyes before fumbling one handed for the dark glasses on the nightstand. "Ow...."

The sunglasses only did a little to ease the pain as he walked into the dining room. Jocelyn unusually was already up before him, texting someone on his phone and paying little attention to the toast and pancakes Haydee's mother placed in front of him. "I thought bartenders weren't supposed to drink on the job. What's with the sunglasses, Dani?"

Tell or withhold mentioning anything about the migraine? Dani looked away, choking down a bite or two of Jocelyn's cooling breakfast. "They don't, this is just a... headache."

He hoped anyway. Jocelyn snorted and tossed a blue and orange labeled bottle at him. "Midol, it works better than Tylenol for headaches."

If it was alright with his brother, he was going to stick with Advil or aspirin instead of Jocelyn's remedy for menstrual cramps. "I'll pass, thanks. You're up early."

"It's a school day," Jocelyn dropped his textbooks into his knapsack. "And biology is boring. I was planning on cutting the class for tutoring Brittney before the next test. She asked for it."

He frowned, tilting his head towards Daniel. "And you have a date for tonight with Haydee. I already booked the reservation since you're so quiet around her. And by quiet, I mean passive. She likes you but you haven't done anything nice for her yet."

"I never- I mean..." Daniel looked away, a bitter taste in his mouth. "I'm nice to her,"

"Girls don't want that," Jocelyn's smile was short lived, closer to a smirk. "Tell that excuse to someone who hasn't spent the last sixteen years living as a girl. She's been dropping hints from the first time you walked into the principal's office and you haven't noticed. Take her out for supper, charm her with the Italian I know you have and make it a date. Some of Dad's language lessons should pay off for once."

"Fine," He relented at that, leaving most of the waffle untouched in front of him. "But I'm not going to make any promises about this turning into anything. You know how our family is."

"I know, that shouldn't hold you back, Dani." Jocelyn said. "Are you going to finish that, or can I?"

He was looking at the waffle on Daniel's plate. Daniel made a face and pushed the maple syrup-soaked treat towards him. "It's yours. I'm going to see if a nap and Advil gets rid of the migraine before your date."

Time and the nap, thankfully, did seem to clear up the worst of the headache and he was almost in a place where he could choke down a light meal of cheese and crackers without feeling like he was about to throw up again. The little blood spots on his tissue on the other hand... they weren't worth worrying Jocelyn about right now. No one needed to know that his brief coughing fit had brought up bits of scarlet on the paper. It flamed up in his hand, turning to black and then ash gray as the former evidence drifted into the wastepaper bin.

CHAPTER TEN

"Can I ask about the psychic thing you mentioned earlier?" Brittney kept her voice to a low murmur despite the secret little corner of the library they were in. "How does that work exactly? You weren't what I'd call detailed when we rescued your brother."

Jocelyn hesitated and let his textbook fall on the table with a dull thud. "Sure, I guess. I'm not like Dani, shy like, but I normally would have asked him about telling anyone outside my family first. Why?"

She shrugged, staring down at the diagram printed on one page of her textbook. "Just curious. Can you find anyone else or is it just Daniel? How does the talent work?"

"Daniel's easier, always has been but that's because we're related," Jocelyn finished labeling his worksheet. "Making it... permanent was an accident of mine. But the rest of it, tracking anyone else needs, well, their blood on a bit of t-shirt or fabric."

"Ew," Brittney's nose wrinkled in disgust. "Can you do anything else that isn't gross?"

Jocelyn flushed, trying to figure out her tone and whether

it meant she was about to leave him sitting alone at the table. "If it, uhm, helps a bit, the owner of the blood doesn't have to be human. This is a bit less psychic than witchcraft, but I was trying to be easy on you earlier. I don't need Dani's blood to find him anymore."

He let out a sigh, trying to rephrase his explanation into something that an outsider would understand. "Let's try it this way. All those stupid sci-fi movies think telepathy is the bad thing. They got it wrong, the empath is the dangerous one. They- we, just need a touch and a few minutes to play with a person's head and we can... suggest them to do anything we want them to."

He swallowed, fighting back the burning sensation in his eyes. "There's limits, we can't make them shoot themselves or jump off a rooftop somewhere unless they're already halfway to that state but it's a bit more than your average hypnosis expert but- I thought you should be aware at least."

Brittney looked like she was about to falter or run, textbooks scattered around the table be damned before she spoke again. "Just as long as you promise never to use that thing on me, we're good."

"I won't," Jocelyn looked away. "Not even to save your life, Brit. I... I'm better than that."

She quieted for a long moment, the unease taking a little longer to fade. "So, if you're a witch, does that make your brother one as well?"

"Yeah," Jocelyn pulled the biology book towards him, highlighting a paragraph or two in the glossy pages. "My whole family was- is. Dani isn't half as good at tracking as I am but he's the stronger of the two of us. He can do more than me, er, magic wise."

He made a face at that, wrinkling his nose. "I hate that word, people hear it and think Harry Potter, but it isn't, not really. Dani got the blood magic crap, but he can't track, I got the empath talent or whatever you want to call it. My sister…"

It was lucky that their table was hidden behind the one shelf devoted to folklore in Calais. It was easy to retrieve the book he wanted and flip it open to the right page. "Athenais ended up like my grandma Delphine. Somewhere between a witch and psychic vampire."

That was one theory anyway and a lighter way of confessing to his grandmother's crimes. It was debatable whether the old woman had been born a striga or earned the curse. "She… isn't very nice. From the family stories, the first time Daniel saw her, the attempt at driving her off, blew out both windows in his bedroom when he was younger than I am."

Daniel had been thirteen then and virtually untrained then, now his control was better, or his temper was. It was probably a mix of both.

"Could I… see?" Brittney sounded tentative, looking down at the woodcut printed photograph on the book of eastern European folklore. "If you don't mind showing me, I mean?"

Jocelyn shut the textbook and shoved it out of the way. "I guess if you're sure you want to see this. The empath thing is kind of my talent, I could get away with credit card fraud if I wanted to or make a couple pissed off drunk guys get into a fight as a distraction, but I have to say again, I'm not like my brother. The stuff I can do is a lot more subtle, not as… uhm, physically destructive but that didn't stop me from trying to learn some of Daniel's tricks."

He swallowed, glancing downwards. "If I'm angry or scared enough, I could stop someone's heart or tear it to pieces with just a touch on their arm. My… first real experiment with the gift ended up with a classmate dead of an aneurysm. No one blamed me for the accident it looked like but it's something I'll have to live with even though he was a bully with height and weight on me at the time. Darren was only thirteen when he died. His kind never change, and he would have been a bully into high school, but he didn't deserve death either."

Brittney swallowed, looking like she was dearly tempted to run and never look back at him again, but she forced herself to remain seated at the table despite the lack of color in her face at his story. "I had to... ask, didn't I?"

"I'm sorry," Jocelyn looked down, interest in their tutoring session evaporating just like that. "I did say what my family was capable of, is dangerous. Not like the pretty stuff in most fantasy books. If you want to leave, I won't stop you or- or change your mind."

The look of relief on her face almost made up for the earlier fear though the sour taste lingered in his mouth. "Keep on with this or call it a day?"

Brittney's hand covered his, a slight chill lingering in her touch. "Honestly, I'm still terrified of this, anyone would be but maybe if you showed me, I'd get over being afraid?"

If that was how she wanted to recover from hearing a horrifying story, who was he to stop her? Jocelyn sighed, gently pulling away. "Sure, if that's what you want. Just... save the questions for afterwards, okay?"

Their books and the backpacks would be safe enough for the few minutes it would take to demonstrate his talents to Brittney in the safety of the alley despite the cold. Fire was easy, one of the first things Daniel had taught him after the unintentional murder of a classmate and he drew on that, trying to call a baseball sized ball of flame to hand but only sparks showed, quickly fading away in the cold. "Sorry. It's just not coming today."

The relief on Brittney's face almost made up for the disappointing show. "Honestly, I'm glad whatever you were trying, didn't work. What you told me already is freaky enough."

"I guess," Jocelyn managed a weak smile. "At least you didn't run away or call a hunter on me. I was afraid you might."

Brittney laughed, running a lock of hair through her fingers. "There's still time, Jocelyn. But I like to think I'm tougher than that. Or is it less superstitious?"

"Both?" Jocelyn asked.

She snickered, rolling her eyes. "Has to be, can't think of anything else."

Her giggle still sounded halfway hysterical. "I'm not really in the mood for more studying, to be honest. I just need a little time to process this. Think, maybe and I can't do it here."

"I get it," Jocelyn looked away. "At least I think I do. This stuff is almost normal for me, I can't picture not knowing *something* about it."

"Thanks," Brittney said. She stood, trailing a hand over his shoulder. "So, uhm, talk to you tomorrow at lunch or in biology?"

"Yeah," If only the promise didn't feel like it hurt so much to make. "Lunchtime, at school."

CHAPTER ELEVEN

It was during biology, not lunchtime when Brittney greeted him with less of her usual sparkle. Jocelyn tossed his backpack into the locker and shut it before any of the debris could send papers and a pair of t-shirts that hadn't yet seen a washing machine onto the brown and pale tan tiles of the floor under his boots. "Brittney? How... are you feeling after yesterday."

She looked as tired as he felt, hair mussed and absent her usual light touches of makeup.

She gave him a weak smile. "Honestly, still terrified as fuck about what you can do but I'm trying to pretend it's all just psychic crap and deal with it."

He sighed, leaning against his locker. "Sorry, again. I never knew what it was like being an outsider and learning about this stuff. Even Carla knows, back home, but she took it in stride. It's Louisiana – people just tend to kind of accept the weird stuff and call it a movie effect or something the vodoun priests do. Real magic, as much as my family does it, barely gets noticed unless someone really screws up or decides to go Carrie White on the town. They tend not to live very long or wind-up dead at the hands of some hunter group after a few weeks."

Brittney bit down on her lower lip, keeping her eyes on the floor between them. "Okay, I guess."

She lifted her gaze to look at him. "Carla?"

If it was okay things shouldn't have felt still so strained between them. Jocelyn looked away, tasting something bitter in the back of his throat. "My dad's housekeeper. Tell you what, skip class? Maybe I can still fix things after last night?"

He was hoping anyway. "Please?"

Brittney hesitated, clutching her biology textbook as if it were a shield between them. "I- alright, sure. Got a place in mind?"

"The local library but I don't know how to get there, and Daniel needs the car more than I do," Jocelyn closed the latch on his locker and turned away.

"Sounds good," Brittney pulled her keys from her jeans pocket, leading him out to the student parking lot and a beaten-up Toyota car. "Here,"

The drive to the library wasn't very long, relatively speaking but the silence between them was awkward, uninterrupted by the radio or the news playing from the speakers. Brittney pulled into a stall, cutting the engine as she leaned back in the driver's seat. "Do you want to talk here or in the library?"

Which was safer? Which would be more comfortable for Brittney? Jocelyn looked into the rearview mirror, saw the girl there and pushed it back up to its folded position. "Where do you want to go?"

Her shoulders slumped beneath her parka and she swallowed, watching the snow fall onto the hood of her car. "Inside, it's warmer than the car. And they might have books on this, right?"

Jocelyn made a face at that, shoving his glasses back up to the bridge of his nose. "It's usually a point not to be noticed by anyone normal but I guess there are a few around. I just wouldn't trust them as far as I could throw them though."

Brittney's smile was wobbly and short lived but genuine. "I guess. I'm just trying to understand what happened last night."

"Fair," Jocelyn slipped out of the car, watching the patch of ice under his boots and hoping he wouldn't slip on it. "C'mon,"

They set up in a quiet corner of the library, taping a study session in progress sign to the glass front of the door for a little privacy. Brittney pulled a stack of books towards her and folded her arms on them. "So, uhm, what's the truth? Why don't more people know about, well, witches?"

Jocelyn forced a smile, resting a black socked foot on the tabletop. "No one wants a repeat of the witch trials, Brittney. Innocent or not, a lot of people died at the stake or being hanged for a non-existent crime. Believe it or not, yours was one of the more... positive reactions I expected last night. It could have been worse."

"Really?" She gave him a tired look.

"Yeah," Jocelyn skimmed the battered hardcover book he held, checking the printed date in the inside cover. "1950's, never a good decade unless the person in question is white and male."

He was deflecting in an attempt to gather his own thoughts. "Let's just look at it this way. Most people would either see a witch hanged or use her for their own purposes. It was a few decades before my dad but say, assuming the government found out about real 'psychics', what would they do with them? Putting it into a Cold War perspective."

Brittney looked down, tracing the hammer and sickle cover printed on her own book. Shame briefly crossing her face. "Depends on which government agency was interested, I guess. The empath thing you told me about, the guy or girl with it would make- make one hell of an interrogation expert, no water or sleep deprivation stuff needed. The tracking, no one would be able to hide from that if someone had a sample of the runaway's blood. Everything else,"

She shivered, pulling her sweater closer around her body. "You would put most of the CIA out of work if what you told me about blood magic is real. Killing with just a touch or something. That's a step past magic and crossing over into assassination."

"No one would be able to tell if it was a natural death or murder," Jocelyn looked away. "Yeah. War crimes would be harder to prove if everyone knew about psychics. That's mostly why we try to stay discrete. We're either victims of a hunt or the military government forces see us as assets, not people."

He slumped, moving his foot from the table to the floor. "I'd be able to handle it for a while, I'm used to having to tolerate crowds around me. Daniel never would. He calls me the gentle, innocent one but if it came to that scenario and his own power – he is. He's not a killer, even if his skills were meant to fall along that path. He chose running rather than hurting another person and he has the scarring to prove it on his arms. Anyone military would call that cowardice; I'd call it the bravest thing he's done since we ended up here."

"Alright," Brittney was chewing on her lower lip again, pulling the little stick of lip gloss from her jacket pocket. "I can't say I like all of this but at least I... understand more than I did yesterday. If I can help, I will."

"Thanks," Jocelyn said.

CHAPTER TWELVE

Bartending at the Crown and Cat was less than ideal but it was a better alternative to being unemployed. It provided a screen of activity and on busy nights, no-one had the opportunity to ask him about a background he couldn't give ready answers to. Jocelyn was right, as usual, he wasn't much of a liar. Occupying his time elsewhere was distraction enough after the earlier episode of fainting on the job. So far, nothing like that had happened yet and he was willing to count his blessings in that regard.

At least until the heated argument in one corner of the bar turned into the sound of breaking glass and expletives thrown both ways by the unhappy customers. Daniel held back until he caught the glimpse of metal glittering under the dim light. Like everything else, Kate seemed to regard Maine law as a guideline more than a hard and fast rule. As long as no one drew attention to themselves or they ended fights quickly, anything seemed to be permitted.

This didn't seem to be one of those nights though. He saw Kate out of the corner of his eye as she muttered something low under her breath in Greek before she stepped between the two men, eyes narrowing in dislike. "Wolf, Sieh, enough. One of you is a friend, the other was known as a racist bastard even before he came to America. Finish your territorial fight elsewhere or I'll finish it for you. And neither of you have any desire to meet my father, I daresay."

Sieh was lean, blond hair falling into his eyes where it wasn't halfway down his back and more deserving of the 'wolf' label than the man he had been about to punch. His eye color was an odd, pale amber that belonged more to the canine than a human. "For the sake of your... guests, so be it. I'll take my fight to the woods away from the den."

Kate's smile was thin, bitter. "I'd prefer out of my state, *Ly'ashain*, but sure. The woods outside of Calais are good enough."

Sieh's expression darkened but he left without another word or farewell. Daniel let out a breath he had been holding, relieved when the tension broke. "Who was that and what was the- I think it was a word- you used but it's nothing I know."

Kate relaxed, sagging against the counter as she poured herself a half cup of beer from the tap. "You're too observant for your own good, Daniel. That- he's a friend for all I can't trust him."

Her smile was less bitter now than touched with resignation and weariness. "As for what I called him. It's... unclear. I either gave him his birthname or called Sieh the equivalent of a motherless pup. I'm lucky he took it so well; he's not known for putting up with insults."

She looked down at the remnants of her drink and set it down on the scarred wood. "Or he wasn't that interested in a fight tonight, who can tell. How was your date earlier?"

"It was... good," Daniel lifted his gaze to meet hers. "How did you know about that?"

She laughed, though a thread of tension still ran through it. "I hear things, I owed the owner of the restaurant a favor, in exchange, he tells me what people get up to. That said, I didn't ask for details, I'm not that kind of woman."

Her tone went dry. "Or that kind of female but that's besides the point. I won't invade your personal life because I'm desperate for gossip."

Haydee greeted him at the front door, taking his hand shyly for a moment before dropping it. "How was work?"

He pulled the winter jacket off, hanging it from the coat hook. "Mostly sticky and it smelled too much like beer but at least I didn't have to handle breaking up a fight tonight. Kate has a guy for that. Jocelyn?"

"Doing whatever it is, he does," Haydee said.

"That's good," Daniel pinched the bridge of his nose in an attempt to ward off the beginnings of another headache beginning to make itself known. "At least it's the weekend, I can sleep in and get an afternoon shift instead tomorrow."

Haydee's expression clouded over with concern. "You don't think you're having too many headaches lately, Daniel? Isn't it time to see a doctor about them?"

"I- maybe," He felt his shoulders slump. "Doctors aren't my favorite kind of people to talk to but I'll think about it if Jocelyn doesn't drag us into another date before then. It isn't like I keep tabs on him, but he wanted something Japanese lite and said there was a place in Augusta that looked good. It's his turn for a first date and he's bringing Brittney with him. May as well make it a double, right?"

Jocelyn's idea of a good day in Augusta was spending an hour or two in a small, dusty bookshop and then onto an equally small but more dubious looking place for a fitted tank top. Daniel hesitated outside, unsure of propriety or manners until the younger pair emerged, laughing and holding their purchases in brown bags. "Ready?"

"I think so, yeah," Jocelyn absently touched his medical alert bracelet. "It's only Japanese, I'll be fine, Dani. You're really worrying about food right now. If I get a chicken dish and nothing involving peanuts, I'll be alright. I'm starving, c'mon."

The chopsticks were a little hard going but nothing compared to the embarrassment of using a fork when his brother and the girls managed the utensils so well. Jocelyn scooped up a little ball of rice, holding the bowl in his other hand before going for the grilled chicken next to it. "Glad this place checks out; I wasn't sure it would."

Daniel's expression was abstract, barely paying attention to him as the newly purchased phone by his hand rang. Jocelyn frowned, noting the buzzing of the vibrate mode. "That phone's new, who has the number?"

No one he was aware of right now. "Daniel?"

His brother shook his head, swiping to answer whoever was on the other end. "Not that new and this isn't a burner phone. I just never used it before now."

"So…" Jocelyn started.

"Hush," Daniel turned away, tone going neutral. "I don't know anything about what you're looking for, Lyra. I'm sorry I can't be of more help but I'm not the researcher you need. Not when you're chasing down mythological jewelry."

Jocelyn tuned the conversation out, occupied with stealing the last cucumber roll from Brittney's plate. If it was all about ancient stories and jewelry, there was little point in paying attention. Daniel had things well in hand. And even if didn't, there was a great deal of subtext behind his words.

At least until Daniel put a hand down on the table to steady himself, the phone slipping from his grip to land on the tile floor with a black screen, a crack running down the center of the face. The fall took only moments, but it felt like longer than that as his stomach turned into a little ball of fear. "Dani?"

Somehow, he was already out of the booth and kneeling by Daniel's side, anxiety tasting like ash in his mouth rather than the good flavor of soy sauce and chili pepper, before he was aware of moving. "Wake up, damn it."

Haydee was already moving with some sort of calm he couldn't manage as she pulled a small flashlight from her pocket and then pulled the winter jacket from his shoulders. She was already dialing a three-digit number one hand as she hastily relayed the address and everything else, she could to whoever was on the other end. He ignored her desperate words, closing his eyes as he found the combat knife at Daniel's waist and drew the edge across his palm. Gritting his teeth at the slight pain that flared as well as the thin line of blood visible from the shallow wound. "Shit, damn it, wake up!"

The empath thing might have been his speciality, but he had learned what he could from Daniel's teaching just in case things had called for it. Now, it seemed they had. Haydee looked horrified at the blood. "Jocelyn, I don't think-"

"You trust Daniel, right? Trust me," He closed his eyes,

searching, seeking deeper than he had managed before. "Figured he would have told you long before this but Jesus, guy's more stubborn than I am. Your boyfriend's a witch, same as me."

Haydee opened her mouth and shut it again, sitting heavily on the nearest chair. "Judging from your reaction, this isn't the wicca kind of witchcraft my parents like."

"It isn't, now shut up and let me focus. This isn't as easy for me as it is Dani." Jocelyn pressed his uninjured hand against the inside of Daniel's wrist. This wasn't like the time he had abandoned a party to race off to Daniel's side or even like the once or twice before when he'd caught Daniel in the middle of a seizure before they'd come under control. "Shit…"

This was worse, somehow and the best he could describe it to himself was as a slow, creeping creature sneaking up on Dani. Only its preferred prey wasn't a living person but the blood cells within them. "God damn it all to hell!"

And there was nothing he could do to slow or banish the thing. Daniel stirred under his touch and he edged back a step or two, tasting a bitter kind of relief in his mouth as his brother touched the lump forming on the back of his head. "You told me this was under control, that you weren't going to faint on me again. And now, fuck it, there was so little time that I couldn't sense what was wrong."

"I- I didn't want you to worry too much. This is my problem, Jocelyn." Daniel said.

Jocelyn rounded on him, not caring about the scene they were causing or who might overhear. "We're family, Daniel. Don't tell me that this has been going on longer than you let me know. I thought we were supposed to look after each other. That was the one good lesson Dad taught us, family always cared about each other. That they talked. It's one thing to keep a secret from your girlfriend, it's another to hide this from me."

The stricken expression in Daniel's eyes was more than enough for him. He stood, pushing past the EMT's walking inside the restaurant and finally slumped on a snow covered bench a block or two away. "Damn it all to hell…"

What else could he say?

CHAPTER THIRTEEN

The hospital stink brought back unpleasant memories of the last time he'd set foot within one. The last time he saw his mother alive, thirteen years ago. It didn't matter where the hospital was, whether it was New Orleans or a small city so far north that the residents were almost Canadian.

Haydee was watching him through worried eyes, arms folded over her chest. Irritation mixed with fear and dismay. "What just happened? What was Jocelyn talking about? Jocelyn mentioned a few things, but I need you to make sense of what he said."

He tried to sit up on the hospital bed, fending off the EMT who tried to push him back down upon it. The man meant well but he was feeling better than he had in the restaurant. He didn't need any help at the moment. "It's a… long story."

"Try me," Her voice was steadier than it had been an hour or two earlier.

Daniel slumped, hating the bright florescent lights overhead. "Fine…"

The story was as long and as ugly as he feared to say but

she had asked, and she hadn't left yet so maybe there was still some hope for salvaging the situation. There was truth now, everything he'd omitted or ducked away from answering before. Haydee's expression fell, looked sickened at the confession but she swallowed, putting her hand over his arm. "I... don't like any of this and it scares me, but I've heard too much to turn back now. Don't get me wrong, I'm pissed that you didn't think you could trust me before but if I was in your place, I wouldn't have said anything either."

Her voice dropped. "You've always been the kind of fair skinned that I like in a guy but the past couple weeks, well... you've lost color a little- if that's any way to describe it and you've complained about being tired."

She sighed, running both hands through her hair. "How long has this been going on?"

Daniel glanced away, trying to pull a crease from the beige coverlet over his legs. "Longer, I guess. There were... signs of something back in Baton Rouge. A stitch, winded when I climbed stairs. I thought it was just nothing."

Though given his family history, maybe he shouldn't have discounted things so soon. "But I'm fine now, Haydee. There's no concussion or headache and apart from the exhaustion, I'm feeling alright."

Haydee only bit down on her lower lip and turned his arm towards the harsh light overhead to show the ugly blackened mark on his arm. "You got that when you fell, Daniel. I don't think instantly bruising is a sign of alright. So... please for me, don't try and get those discharge papers done. Just stay for a couple tests?"

"Jocelyn? Brittney?" Though he cared more for his brother than his brother's girlfriend who had come with them to Augusta.

"I'll look after them, promise." Haydee said.

"Thanks, I guess." Daniel slumped in the bed, cursing his luck once more.

Haydee watched him for a moment, uncertainty crossing her face. "You don't think this could be, you know, your mom's cancer? If it runs in your family…"

He shook his head, denying it. "No, I don't. I hope it isn't, to be honest. By the time she passed away, all that was left was skin and bones. And later when the chemo took her hair."

Corinne hadn't let her husband cut and shave it off for her and had asked him to do it instead. He could still remember the thin silk of it as he cut it short around her head and ears. The small buzzing noise of the razor as he shaved the little that remained off. It had piled around her on the towel and coverlet. "There was raspberry soap scent around her for three days after I cut her hair."

His mother had cried as he had done it, he'd thrown a punch or two at the mirror mounted to the inside of his bedroom closet that night, hating the memory of the act. Glass lying in silver shards on the floor. "This isn't cancer, Haydee. I'd… know."

At least she had the grace to look around her and lower her voice to barely above a whisper. "Your magic or the anatomy lessons?"

"Experience," His voice was tired. "I saw my mom die from cancer when I was sixteen." It wasn't the EMT this time but a doctor standing inf the doorway as she cleared her throat with a slight cough. Haydee blanched, gathering up her travel sized backpack and vacated the chair. "I'll be downstairs in the cafeteria with Jocelyn."

Daniel sighed, taking note of the woman's delicately framed glasses and the way her honey brown hair was loose around her shoulders. She was appealing in her own way but he preferred Haydee's pixie cut style over this. "Doctor…?"

She gave an airy shrug, idly flipping through the pages on her plastic clipboard. "Persephone Sotaira."

Persephone... Sotaira. Daniel gave her an askance look and a resigned smile. "I hope that isn't your real name, doctor. I already know a woman who shortened Hecate to Kate. Family of yours?"

"Only in mythology," Her answer was cool, nearly toneless. "But I have heard of Kate, yes. A child playing with things she should not."

Was she really? He hadn't seen any evidence Kate MacKinnon was inexperienced or a child dabbling with dangerous things. "She manages a bar in Calais, there isn't much danger there. I work for her."

"A child," Persephone glanced down at her clipboard again, expression and tone sliding towards something gentler though no less reserved. "I'd like to run a few more tests if I can. You described exhaustion and migraines recently. Miss Ashworth added bruising and several instances of coughing up blood."

He tried to arrange the pillow to a more comfortable position to no avail. It was as flat as cardboard no matter how he tried to fold it in half. "What kind of tests?"

She seemed resigned but not surprised by his wariness. "A few basic things but it may require staying overnight for a day or two, I'm afraid. I'll need a blood count among other things. And an account of your family's medical history as well."

In other words, everything that could trace him back to Augusta from New Orleans. Daniel pinched the bridge of his nose and dropped his hand back to his side. There was no way to escape that if he wanted a real answer to whatever was killing him. "What do you think it is?"

Persephone remained impassive, unreadable despite the

look he gave her. "I won't know until I run those tests, Daniel."

He pulled the pillow out from behind his back, resting his head on the headboard as he held it. "I already know I'm dying, doctor. Kate said that Jocelyn crossed into a place I nearly didn't leave from and that was how he sa- guessed I'd fainted one night while working."

The doctor's mouth thinned into a grudging smile as she sat. "You have no fear of my suspecting madness then and calling on a psychiatrist."

"Not with a name like Persephone," Daniel looked away, tasting the bitterness of wet ash in his mouth. "Could be coincidence or just a mom too in love with Greek mythology but after Kate, I'm guessing not. And that you already know I'm a witch."

She inclined her head slightly, touching the back his hand before pulling it away. "I'd still like to run those tests, just in case."

He had little choice in refusing and in truth, if there was a way to buy him some time- he'd take any test the doctors wanted to run. "Alright,"

It wasn't the freedom he had wanted but at least he was able to leave the room and venture to one of the common areas though he didn't find much on the ancient tv to interest him. Some crime drama aimed at sixty-year-old women rather than a guy in his mid twenties.

Jocelyn came by the next morning, clutching a small brown teddy bear in his hands and deposited it on the bed. "Do they know yet?"

Daniel forced a smile, shaking his head as he looked at Haydee hovering in the doorway. She looked anxious and her hair was unkempt like she hadn't slept well and didn't care how she looked to anyone else. "They've only just started the blood tests, Jocelyn. It's too soon to say if I have anything."

"Oh," Jocelyn's expression was hard. "When?"

"Soon, I hope." He sighed, twisting the paper bracelet around his wrist next to the one that marked his penicillin allergy. "Look, can I trust you to run to the cafeteria and get me a coffee? It sucks but I could really use one right now. Do you have a ten on you?"

Jocelyn bit down on his lower lip and nodded. "Okay. Milk, no sugar, right?"

"Yeah, I-" His brother was gone before he could finish the sentence. Daniel glanced away, pulling hoodie around his shoulders for the sake of warmth or at least attempting to stay warm. It felt like he was always cold despite the layers he tried to put on. "Stayed up to three AM worrying about me?"

Haydee flushed, looking away. "Research but most of what I found was garbage. Stupid internet. But I've got the same question Jocelyn does. Do you know what this is yet?"

"No, the doctors still want to run a few more tests." Daniel looked down, smoothing a hand over the borrowed hospital gown and the pale gray pajama bottoms underneath it. "But… if anything happens to me, can you promise to take care of Jocelyn?"

"If anything happens?" Something like misery crossed her expression. "Yeah, but I don't think it will. You'll get through this. You don't need me to look after your brother."

"Please, just in case?" Daniel asked.

She bit down on her lower lip, swallowed, and nodded. "All- alright. I promise."

Haydee might have said something else but the nurse that entered the room stopped that conversation and pulled the bedside tray over to him, laying out some unidentifiable kind of meat on a plate next to a small bowl of peas and carrot bits. Desert was a banana yogurt container. Daniel wrinkled his nose and poked at the meal tiredly, losing what little appetite he might have had. "I wouldn't mind a peanut butter and strawberry jam sandwich over this, whatever it is."

There was no telling where Jocelyn had got to with the asked for coffee, but it didn't seem forthcoming despite his request now.

The woman glared at him before turning her attention to Haydee, "Time for you to go, miss. Visiting hours are over."

Haydee cast him a helpless look and stood, gathering up her jacket and purse sized backpack. "Tomorrow, promise. You'll get out of here."

Doctor Sotaira arrived fifteen minutes after Haydee left and ten minutes after the unnamed African American nurse did, almost as if she had been waiting by the door for a moment of privacy. Daniel lifted his gaze from the picked at remains of his meal and pushed the tray to the foot of his bed. "Hospital food sucks."

She regarded the barely touched food with the slightest look of distaste. "You should eat something but otherwise I would agree with you on the quality offered the patients here, yes."

"Those blood tests?" Hope wasn't something he usually let himself feel very often but if there was any time where hope was needed it was now. "You said you had a few answers by now."

Persephone Sotaira sighed, pushing her glasses back up to the bridge of her nose. "It is... possible we may have a diagnosis, but I would like to run two more tests first. Do you know what a bone marrow biopsy and aspiration are?"

Daniel slumped, closing his eyes. "One of those takes a bone marrow sample from the solid part of the bone, the other takes a bit from the fluid portion. I've seen it done before. My mom passed away from cancer. Is this…?"

The doctor shook her head, impassive. "It isn't cancer, you can be assured of that much, but your blood cell counts are far lower than they should be. I'd like to confirm just to be sure."

"And you'd like to run the bone marrow tests," Daniel gave her a dull look. "When?"

"I've already scheduled the tests for this afternoon. Truthfully, the sooner the better." Persephone glanced away. "After that, you're free to go home. It'll take at least three days to study the results of your tests."

Three days. He wasn't sure if that was the reprieve it was intended as but either way. "Thank you."

Regardless of whatever time he had left, there was still one or two things he needed- wanted to do for Haydee. "You don't need to explain how the test is run; I know I'll be sedated for it."

Surprise didn't seem like it came often to Persephone but when it did, she couldn't conceal it. "You're familiar with these tests?"

He nodded, tasting something bitter, acrid in his mouth and tried to rinse it out with the plastic cup of water on the tray. "I was tested as a possible donor for my mom's bone marrow transplant. I wasn't a match, but I… know about the tests."

If things were at a point where he needed a bone marrow biopsy, then his condition was worse than he'd suspected at first. "Why don't we get the rest of this out of the way and start talking about options?"

A little furrow appeared between Persephone's eyebrows and she pulled the chair closer to the bed, glancing at him.

"You wouldn't happen to be a medical student, yes? You seem… unsurprised."

"Or comfortable," Daniel managed a laugh, but the sound was colored with bitterness. "My dad taught me enough to get through two years of medical school and him, not even a doctor but he knew his anatomy and biology well enough."

"Very well," Persephone touched her glasses briefly and stood. "Get some rest, I'll come for you when it's time."

He never would have admitted it to the doctor, but the idea of a couple hours nap sounded better than anything else he could think of right now. As short as the conversation had been, it had also left him exhausted. "Thank you,"

She put her hand on his shoulder for a second and he remembered little after that until a man's touch woke him from the restless sleep. It wasn't quite dark or even dusk out yet but the shadows wee longer than they had been earlier, the light bouncing off the snow coated window ledge was less harsh and glittering in front of his eyes.

Persephone graced him with a lingering look but said nothing as one of the nurses helped him into the wheelchair.

From that point until the cliché question about counting sheep or numbers until the anesthetic took hold, it was barely worth remembering the path to the room where the oncologist was waiting. He barely felt the sting of the needle as it entered his hip or its removal a few minutes later.

It was dusk when he woke again, once more in his room and very much alone. A note tucked under his phone and written in a careful Greek script. Daniel looked at it, let the folded paper fall onto the beige coverlet and tried to get comfortable in the bed, putting less pressure on the leg where the test had been done. Whatever happened next, could wait for morning.

Chapter Fourteen

I t was a very lonely hotel room that they returned to with their purchases in hand and after the trip to the hospital. Jocelyn sat down on the edge of the bed, not bothering with his usual habit of bouncing on the mattress to test it for comfort. "Is he going to get better?"

Haydee looked stricken at the question. "I don't know, Jocelyn. I really don't. I hope he does but…"

He hated buts. Both the word and the other one. Jocelyn bit down on his lower lip, wishing he had a cat or his surviving rat around. Petting its fur would have brought a little bit of comfort to him. "I tried to help him."

"I know," She was quiet for a moment, sitting on the bed next to him. "Daniel mentioned everything to me now. I can see why you wanted to help and why he didn't want you to. If LaLaurie magic comes with that steep a price."

"I would have willingly paid it, he's family," Jocelyn sagged back on the mattress, staring upwards at the ceiling overhead. There as a pale-yellow stain on it that might have been a rat curled up in on itself or a water mark from the room over theirs.

"Jocelyn…" She trailed off, running a hand through her hair. "Never mind, I think there's still a mall open somewhere, I just need an hour or two distraction. Come with me. It's Augusta, nothing will happen. All your family is back in New Orleans."

Go with her or stay in the hotel room alone? Jocelyn hesitated and then nodded. There was nothing else to do and he hadn't packed his favorite books in the backpack sitting in the closet. "Okay,"

Maybe he would have a chance to help Haydee with something if Daniel never got around to it. "Can we look at a jewelry store?"

The look she gave him was puzzled. "I didn't think you were interested in that even if you had your ears pierced."

Jocelyn blushed, touching the little earring there. "Not me. For Dani. He's so happy with church stuff that he won't think of it until he's out of the hospital."

"Oh," Haydee didn't look any less confused but at least she led him out into the hotel hallway.

That was fine with him, he could feel the small plastic shape of Daniel's credit card in his pocket and the piece of paper wrapped around it that held the password numbers. The plan had come to him in seeds, watching the way Haydee and Dani interacted with each other. Sick or not, Daniel needed to be with her and what better way than introducing a couple rings into the equation.

He gave Haydee the slip as soon as she entered the small changing space with a white lacy blouse over one arm. Girls would always take forever when trying on clothes, it was like them to care about fit and size on their bodies. There was at least half an hour before he would be missed, and the information booth started using the intercom to call for him.

The first jewelry store sold costume pieces, things that

were too big or gaudy looking for his tastes. Nothing that suited Haydee or his brother. Jocelyn wrinkled his nose and turned away, reading the next possible shop on the map. It sounded promising and he ventured inside, peeking into the display cases. What would suit more than anything else here? Haydee wasn't the kind of girl to like the color of gold or diamonds.

A silver ring caught his attention and he paused, biting down on his lower lip as he looked at it. A delicate weaving into a Celtic pattern and wrapped around a small amethyst stone. The one intended for his brother was slightly heavier and absent the little gem but no less a match for Haydee's. "Please, can I look at this one?"

The saleswoman glanced at him and frowned slightly. "Aren't you a bit young to be shopping on your own, miss?"

He tried not to flinch at the label and looked away. "My brother wants to propose to his girlfriend. He showed me the one he wanted to get for her. I'm just picking it up for him."

"I see," She seemed skeptical but willing to give him the benefit of the doubt for now. "Well, I hope you have the money for it then."

He held out the credit card for her to take. "I know the pin number. Daniel told me it." Her expression seemed more uncertain than unconvinced. "I-okay, I guess."

Maybe it was cruel of him to do this to the woman, she hadn't hurt him or done anything other than wonder about an eighteen-year-old kid trying to get an engagement ring on Daniel's behalf, but he really needed it for his brother's sake. He brushed a hand over hers, trying to gently change her mind. "Please?"

She blinked rapidly several times, rubbed a hand across her eyes and then swore softly as she pulled a tissue from the box underneath the counter. Her nose was bleeding slightly.

"Sure, alright. Just let me ring the purchase up for you. Anything else?"

Jocelyn hesitated, tying in the five-digit code and shook his head. "Just that."

He clutched the small bag in hand and hurried away before Haydee could notice his absence and ask about it. Part two of his plan could wait until they visited Daniel in the hospital again. Everything else was just minor business. He was a store or two away from the jewelry place before the saleswoman swayed and sat down heavily on a chair before slumping into a faint.

Haydee was just finishing up her purchases by the time he came back, slightly out of breath. "Find anything yourself?"

Jocelyn shook his head, stuffing the little velvet boxes into his hoodie pocket. "Just looking."

Haydee gave him a strange look but seemed to accept it. "Fine, alright. Shall we?"

If he was lucky, then there would be a few minutes time to return Daniel's credit card to the wallet before it was missed. "Wait, Haydee? There's actually... something Dani wanted me to tell you on his part. I'm just the birdie- a messenger but he wanted me to give you this."

He pulled the little box out, chewing on his lower lip. "For you,"

Haydee blinked but accepted the little box warily. "You- he wanted you to pass an engagement ring onto me? You know it's more traditional for the guy to propose personally rather than get his brother to offer on his behalf."

"Dani's in the hospital," Jocelyn said.

Haydee's cheeks blushed pink. "Fine, hope he's in on this little scheme, Jocelyn because if he isn't, you're one hell of a manipulative kid. LaLaurie thing?"

"Yeah, LaLaurie thing," Jocelyn shrugged. "Maybe? You're nice together and hee needs a girlfriend."

"I think the word you're looking for is fiancée," Haydee said.

He wasn't really sure what finances had to do with giving a ring over but if that was what she wanted to call it, who was he to argue? "Can we go back to the hospital now?"

He had to give his brother credit, Jocelyn was smarter than he looked and more devious at that. How else to explain the man's silver ring he held in one hand. Or the one Haydee was now wearing on one finger of her right hand. "Brat,"

Haydee's expression could have been best described as pink. "I swear I wasn't in on this."

Daniel sighed, slipping it onto his own hand. "Neither was I but I guess this means we're engaged now. I thought I'd misplaced the damned card or left it at the restaurant when I fainted. Never thought that Jocelyn was a decent pickpocket."

Haydee laughed, though the sound was strained. "You mean to say you didn't teach him that? You do everything else."

"Not everything," Daniel shifted position, wincing at the brief flare of pain through his hip. "I'm not much of a mechanic. I barely know the difference between the windshield wiper fluid place and the oil container."

"Are you alright?" Haydee asked.

Daniel glanced away; gaze focused on the water pitcher on the little nightstand by the bed. "Tired, mostly. Bored. My leg still hurts from where they took the bone marrow sample. I think they want to rule out leukemia after all."

"So, it… is cancer?" Haydee's shoulders drooped as she sat down next to him. "That bloody family history bit you in the… err, you know."

He tried for a smile, doing his best to reclaim optimism for her sake. The doctors hadn't come back with a diagnosis yet and Persephone was all but unreadable whenever he tried to ask. "They don't know for sure. I only had the test done last night after you left. There's still time."

"Yet," Haydee said.

That was the one thing he was trying not to dwell on right now and he sighed, turning over his arm to look at the scarring that marred the skin there. Old silver lines crisscrossing his forearms. One of the nurses had taken the bandaging off last afternoon and blanched at the damage. "I don't like that word much. I'm sick, maybe. I'm not dying."

The words tasted like ash in his mouth as he said them. It hadn't taken much effort for him to sense the shadow that was slowly claiming his life. The only question was how much time he had left to him, not if or when he would die.

"So…" Her eyes blurred and she wiped a hand roughly across her face, leaving a smear of makeup across the back of her hand.

Daniel looked down at the Celtic patterned ring on her finger and briefly touched it, hesitating over the words. He wanted this to mean something regardless of the location and time but every word he could come up with felt trite, small and not worth Haydee. "I never wanted to rush this. It…"

He trailed off despite himself. How could he square his faith with a hasty proposal? He was no soldier to propose to a friend, days before leaving for a desert or European conflict zone but it was just as unthinkable not to say anything and hurt her in the process. "Haydee,"

Her hand covered his for a moment as she glanced at him.

"It's alright, I understand. Daniel? Will- will you marry me? I mean I don't know what I could bring to the wedding in terms of money or whatever but…"

There were a lot of trailing off into silence moments here and he sat up gingerly, wishing the effort didn't leave him panting a little with the effort. "That's a little old fashioned even for me. My family's already well off enough. I don't need your payment on top of it."

The relief that crossed her face was easily apparent. "Well, good. Because I've got a pile of student debt I'm still trying to work off."

He laughed, feeling lighter than he had in a long time despite the circumstances they were currently in. For a moment he could ignore the fate hanging over his head and just focus on his girlfriend. And this time it came naturally to him without stumbling over the thought. "No, thank God. Mom would have killed me if a dowry got involved in any girlfriend's proposal. You don't owe me anything."

She didn't owe him anything, he did, and he was willing to pay if it meant Jocelyn had a legal guardian other than his father. "I'll help with the student debt if you'll let me."

Haydee blushed, looking down but not before he saw the gratitude there. "You can afford to throw away several thousand just to make sure I'm free of debt? Why are you paying thirty dollars a night at a bed and breakfast and not renting an apartment downtown instead?"

Daniel cupped the side of her face briefly before letting his hand fall back to the coverlet. "Because it isn't in the bank my family uses for business."

"Offshore bank account, huh." Haydee twisted her ring around her finger. "I forgot that your family is involved in stuff. How long were you planning on this little runaway excursion again?"

In truth, from the time he had been nineteen, but he hadn't needed to act on it until recently. Daniel glanced away, biting down on his lower lip. "A while. I know it sounds like I'm some mafia leader's child, but Dad was never interested in trafficking people or running drugs. His business was legitimate if a bit the power behind the throne."

"Not exactly comforting but at least your family aren't real, ah, criminals," Haydee said.

The faintly sour taste returned, and he glanced away, taking the glass from the small table and trying to use the tepid water to rinse the flavor from his mouth. No murder had been successfully proven again Alain LaLaurie but then it was all too coincidental to be murder in the first place. What was a brief touch or inadvertent brush up against another and then an inopportune heart attack or stroke when witchcraft was no longer a crime itself? And for a bit of power or a forgotten relic somewhere. "Yeah, I guess. To that and to your proposal."

Haydee grinned and threw her arms around him before he could protest the action. Even as the gesture left him winded. "Thank you,"

He pushed her off gently and she blushed pink, putting a foot of space between them. "Sorry, sorry."

"Don't be," Daniel said.

Haydee looked sheepish and retreated to the hospital room door just as the doctor walked inside, clutching a clipboard and half of what looked to be a mint dark chocolate bar in the other hand. "When do you think they'll let you go?"

The doctor frowned, looking from her to the clipboard and then to Daniel before looking back at her. "Today but there'll be a follow up appointment in a few days, just to see how things are going and then Doctor Sotaira may want to discuss a treatment plan with you."

A few days in a place he was starting to consider home and then back to the hospital again. Daniel sighed, taking the news with as much optimism as he could muster. "Thanks,"

His backpack was hanging on the little hook taped to the bathroom door and he closed it behind him, trying to fight the wave of dizziness that threatened before it passed. Even the brief walk from the bed to the bathroom had left him exhausted, Daniel closed his eyes, splashing water over his face in an attempt at refreshing himself before he pulled the t-shirt and jeans on. The short sleeves left his arms bare but that didn't seem like anything that could be helped in this moment.

All he wanted now, more than anything was to go back to Haydee's parents' place and as normal a life as he could. Even if the reflection in the mirror was something to be dismayed about. "No,"

Luck and genetics had given him the kind of looks one or two coffee shop girls would have happily shared phone numbers with him and had once or twice before. Now... seeing the exhaustion and the pallor in his skin, as well as the lingering bruising on his arms where the scarring wasn't. And judging from the way the bones of his wrists showed against the skin, he'd lost a little weight as well. Though that might have been more from the unappetizing hospital fare than any medicine or drug.

"Daniel?" Haydee's voice sounded from the other side of the door. "Ready yet?"

"Ready," For better or for worse anyway. Either way, he'd had enough of the hospital for a few days. "Coming,"

CHAPTER FIFTEEN

J ared pulled the computer closer to him, frowning a little at the screen before looking at the battered woman next to him at the coffee shop table. "Are you sure?"

The woman swallowed, tugging at the plastic ties binding her wrists behind her back and quickly gave up on the effort. "I- I'm sure. I don't have any reason not to be. If you'll look at the screen, you'll see the purchase in the last day or so for that jewelry store."

"Ah," He frowned again, opening up the internet browser and searching for the phone number and address of the store. "Should have taken more care, Daniel. Using a credit card at a jewelry shop."

Worse luck for his cousin, better luck for him. Jared smiled briefly, dialing the phone number on the website. "Hello? I was wondering if you could tell me anything about a purchase made in the last day or so? An engagement ring then? I see. Thank you."

He hung up, pocketing the phone as he looked towards the bank teller woman. "I appreciate your help, miss. I have a better idea of where my cousin and his sister are now. I never would have thought of Augusta, Maine without you."

She squirmed and a lock of red hair fell out of her eyes, showing the messy tear streaked makeup and the long cut across her temple. "Can I go?"

Jared shrugged, pulling a pocketknife from his jeans pocket and sliced through the plastic tie binding her hands together. "I suppose so, yes."

"Thank you," She stood, relief apparent on her face as he held the door open for her.

He nodded absently, catching her arm in his hand as a long cut opened up under his touch.

The woman gasped, covering the bleeding wound with her other hand. She fumbled, trying to wrap her sweater around it, one handed. "You…"

Jared regarded her impassively and brushed a hand over the side of her face, cupping a cheek before it dropped lower, closer to her chest. "I'm what?"

Her heart stuttered under his touch and she sank to her knees, gaze looking up at him. "Please…"

Jared smiled thinly, pulling his hand away just enough to put an inch or two between them. "Please what?"

She clutched at one leg of his jeans and he took a step back, away from her as he drew on his power again, forcing her heartrate upwards to a dangerous point. Either it would fail on her or she would suffer from a massive heart attack in the coffee shop's doorway.

Her breathing was ragged, desperate as she struggled to focus on him. "Help…"

What was she to him now that he'd gotten what he needed from her? Jared folded his arms and leaned against the door-frame, watching her curiously for a moment. "You're days away from a heart attack. What can I do about it?"

"Call," Desperation made wet tear tracks down her face as she slumped at his feet. "Hospital, please."

"Might, might not," Jared shrugged, dropping into a crouch next to her as he put a hand on her shoulder. LaLaurie magic could be used at a distance if the right tools were used or eye contact was made with the man or woman on the other end but touch, physical contact was always the easiest. "You'll have to make it worth my while."

Words aside, there was nothing she could have offered or that he wanted of her.

She choked, staring up at him with her hands at her throat before the light faded from her eyes. Her body staying upright for a few seconds before it slumped against the glass door. Jared glanced at her- it, now and bent down, pulling the medical alert bracelet from her wrist and studying it in the light cast by the lamppost. Who knew that the bank teller had had a severe allergy to tree nuts?

His car was the warmest place in the state, and he cursed the cold, warming his hands in front of the heater before he turned the key in the ignition. Augusta was his next stop in finding his wayward cousins. Luck willing, it would be worth it so he could get back to a warmer climate.

He'd never thought Calais would ever become a home, much less a home while living in a bed and breakfast but somehow it had despite the northern chill and heavy white blankets that covered the ground. Home was more than a few personal touches on the walls, it was more... subtle than that. More so since he hadn't let Jocelyn decorate the walls with drawings. That likely would have tested Haydee's parents' hospitality a degree or two. This wasn't meant as a permanent place to stay after all.

Even so, he couldn't help dropping his backpack on the bed with something like relief. It was nice to be in a place where the food was good and the bed, comfortable.

At least until his phone chirped with an incoming text message. He sighed, swiping the message away and reached for his jacket. Jocelyn would just have to take care of himself for the hour or two it took to take care of Kate MacKinnon's business.

She didn't look happy as she greeted him at the door to the bar, stepping aside to let him inside. "The back, now."

"What's wrong?" It was a cheap question so far as he was concerned but one that needed to be asked anyway.

Kate graced him with a black look but didn't say anything until she closed the cramped office door behind her. Daniel sighed, making note of Malachi for a second before fixing on the stranger seated casually in the room's only chair. "What now? And who's that?"

Judging from the same tanned skin and dark hair as well as the red gold feather stuck through a thin leather cord- Malachi had done that once before though not today- this had to be family. "Your father?"

Malachi swore under his breath in an unfamiliar language and shook his head, casting the newcomer a wary look. "No, thank God for that. Coyote's still in Seattle doing whatever it is he does. This is… someone else."

That didn't clarify much but it was likely better not to ask and wait for answers if any were forthcoming. "So, what's going on? Kate's text wasn't very clear."

She looked at him and tucked a strand of hair behind one ear wearily. "Have you read an Augusta newspaper lately?"

He had but it had been a small article buried at the very back of the paper. "Kind of, why?"

"Anaphylactic shocks in late night coffee shops don't just happen, do they?" Kate's voice was sour. "Peanut allergies don't usually make the newspaper, but this was a bank teller and the daughter of an Augusta city councillor. The funeral's set for Wednesday."

"Oh," Daniel looked away, slumping against the door. "Furballs. I've been in the hospital so if you think I did this, I didn't."

"Furballs?" This was from the stranger, casting him a bemused look. "Strangest way of cursing that I've ever heard."

Daniel flushed, making note of the oddly Russian accent from the Native American man. "I don't use the f-word. I can't swear at all, honestly. I'm Catholic."

"Ah," There was just the slightest hint of distaste in the stranger's expression before it vanished. "Fair enough."

Kate pinched the bridge of her nose before dropping the hand back to her side. "Fine then, I believe you but what mistake did you make that ended up with the poor girl dead?"

"I... didn't," Daniel looked away again, tasting uncertainty. "Jocelyn got hold of my credit card and used it in one of his little plans. Haydee kind of... proposed to me, I accepted. He bought the rings."

Kate swore in Greek, grip tightening on a letter opener before she forced herself to relax. "Jocelyn's sweet but he's innocent. This,"

She sighed. "Whatever you were running from, or whoever, I think Jocelyn just blew your hiding place wide open. Credit cards, bank transactions can be traced and if this person thinks you're in Augusta, it won't take much more effort to find the two of you here."

"So, what do I do?" Daniel asked.

"Nothing as trite as a screen of activity or running somewhere else," Kate said. "It's winter and as much as you've gotten used to Calais streets, the highways are worse for ice and snow. Stay here and let our... friend do the hunting."

"Our friend," He said it carefully, looking at the newcomer before turning his attention back to Kate. "Not that I mind, exactly but I'd like to know a little more about him before I trust any friend of yours."

She shrugged but the gesture was stiff, forced. "I can't tell you that, only that he agreed to help for a few days."

Agreed to help was not the same as giving someone trust. Daniel sat down on the desk tiredly, using the few minutes available to catch his breath. "Do you even know his name?"

For once, Kate looked shamed and uncomfortable, avoiding his gaze. "No, I don't. I'm not asking you to trust him but trust me, at least."

"Alright," Daniel said. There were no good other options in front of them, save for letting an unknown, nameless stranger help in whatever way he could. "Fine, help."

That seemed as good as permission because their "guest" inclined his head slightly and pushed the office door open, vanishing a moment later.

His departure left the three of them alone in the office, much to his relief. Daniel relaxed though he didn't take the vacant seat in the office. "What do I do? Jocelyn meant this honestly even if it was a mistake. I can't tell him it was wrong."

Kate sat down, putting black sneaker clad feet on the desk. "It seems like he was only trying to help you, so I'll forgive that despite the danger, whatever form it is. But I'd like to know more about your family, if you're willing to share, that is."

Daniel hesitated, tasting the bitterness of trepidation in his mouth. "Isn't the LaLaurie name enough? It isn't a common name up here and most people can run it through a search. Enough to find the Louisiana ghost story. Delphine wasn't... kind."

The bartender glanced at him; one eyebrow raised. "That much, I'm aware of. I was thinking more of your immediate family."

His immediate family, and presumedly the cousins as well. Daniel swallowed, bracing himself on the desk as a moment of dizziness threatened and subsided. "My mom passed away years ago, Dad- well, he can be cruel, but he isn't the bloodthirsty type. At least he never hit any of his children. His brother's more of the gambler and reckless one. I always remember him as calling Dad in the evenings asking for money or for the men, he owed debts to, to vanish and never come back. My uncle never had much of the LaLaurie talent. My cousin has more of it, I'm sorry to say."

He swallowed, grateful that the water she offered him was ice cold. This part of the story was much less pleasant. "Elizabeth turned out relatively nice. I mean she has all the power I do and she isn't afraid to use it to get what she wants but she won't always kill to play the game. Cousin Jared..."

Daniel set the glass down a little harder than intended, slopping water over the rim of the glass and onto the photograph of an ancient Greek vase. Hecate frowned a little and shook the water off, dropping the picture into her desk drawer. He ignored the reaction, needing to finish and get this out of the way so he wouldn't have to worry about it. "Jared is, well, he's never been diagnosed formally but he's pretty much a psychopath."

Kate's eyes narrowed slightly before she seemed to force herself to relax. "How do you figure that?"

Daniel hesitated. "Because I've got the equivalent of two years medical school and my minor was in psychology, both done by correspondence."

Hecate pinched the bridge of her nose. "Why are all the good ones related to the monsters? I bet you were the kind of guy who was top of his class in high school."

Daniel bit down on his lower lip, drawing a bead of blood from it. "I wasn't, actually. I preferred to stay in the middle of the pack but I think the teachers noticed I wasn't trying my hardest. Why? Other than the obvious danger Jared is, it shouldn't matter right? Unless...?"

The lightbulb flickered to life overhead and he colored, looking downwards at the brown carpet underneath his runners. "Your friend, the one you sent to look for that girl's murderer. You don't think he'll be in any trouble?"

She smiled wryly, shaking her head. "He can take care of himself. Has for as long as I've known him. I just pity the one who pisses him off. He's not one to mess around in a fight. Truth be told, he would be a match for any psychopath. He doesn't relate well to most people either though that's just age."

Somehow that wasn't particularly comforting. "Oh, so there are two of them now?"

Kate laughed standing to put a hand on his shoulder. "You're putting a human label on someone who isn't human, Daniel. Don't. He's his own... well, male would be the best way to describe it. Man isn't particularly accurate."

Then what *was* accurate? Daniel chanced a look at the bartender and decided it was better not to know. "Fair. I promised Jocelyn I wouldn't be long here though."

Truth be told, he was getting tired, and the winter chill was something he felt more now than he had before, even despite coming from a state much further south. Daniel put a hand on the door, looking back to see Hecate behind him. "Wait, something I almost forgot to mention. Do you know a Persephone Sotaira?"

Kate gave a long-suffering sigh. "My aunt, in a manner of speaking. The old tales mistook her and Demeter for mother and child when they're sisters, identical twins. Persephone claims the autumn and winter months, Demeter holds spring and summer. They only see each other a handful of times around the equinox. Why?"

"She... was my doctor in Augusta," Daniel said.

"Oh," Kate pinched the bridge of her nose again, looking weary. "She would take an interest, wouldn't she?"

She took a step closer, taking Daniel's hand in her own before releasing them. "I'm sorry,"

"It's nothing I don't already guess at," Daniel leaned heavily against the door of the bar. "They took a bone marrow sample. I'm getting a phone call back in the next few days, I hope."

Kate's mouth thinned at that, unhappy. "Phone calls, whoever created that, clearly didn't meet a ditzy woman and her empty little box."

Daniel sighed, shrugging. "I think out of the three of us, we're the only ones who actually get that reference. She let everything out but that. Still, I have to be hopeful for Jocelyn's sake."

She snorted, rolling her eyes. "Best call me cynical then. Alright, so long as you don't fall into false hope's little trap. She's a bitch."

Whether it was intended as a warning or just a little word of advice remained to be seen but Kate's words were well worth keeping in mind. Too much hope or a false hope of survival was just as bad as none at all or denial of the situation. "We'll see, I haven't had the phone call yet. Luck willing, we'll find a cure and I- I won't have to die over this."

If anyone else noticed the stumble in his words, they didn't comment on it as he turned and left the bar behind, driving the now familiar route back to Haydee's parents' place. She hadn't mentioned it to him yet but chances were they probably had noticed the Celtic patterned engagement band on her finger. The one that Jocelyn had pickpocketed and manipulated his way into purchasing.

Daniel slumped, resting his forehead on his hands and kept his hands on the steering wheel. "Fu- furballs."

What in God's name was he going to do next? Any sort of wedding he'd anticipated as a child, hadn't involved a small Maine town, an illness or a girl who wasn't interested in any kind of religion. Much less having to do without a church ceremony. Now… there was a distinct possibility, he would have to do without any of that. "I am not running off to Las Vegas for this."

Nevada was the last place anyone with reasonable morals or a budget would want to spend a week in, much less have a wedding. And yet the local registry office was out of the question as well. "What do I do now?"

Unsurprisingly, no one answered his question. Daniel lifted his head and finally cut the engine, fishing for the room key in his pocket as he entered the house. Jocelyn's running footsteps were the first thing he heard before the eighteen-year-old hugged him around the waist. "Took you long enough."

Daniel smiled briefly before pulling away. "Sorry, really I am but we're going to have to have a talk about the pickpocketing and using my credit card without permission."

Jocelyn blushed, scuffing a socked foot across the floor. "Never would have asked her without me, Dani."

"I would have, eventually but, Jocelyn- she's twenty-eight to my twenty-six," Daniel said.

"So?" Jocelyn glanced at him. "You love her, two years isn't that much of a difference Mom and Dad had four years between them. Grandma Delphine was fourteen when she married the first time."

The logic of an eighteen-year-old transgender boy. Daniel sighed, giving in for the time being. "We're still going to talk about the theft and fraud you committed later. I'm not going to forget about that just because you want me to marry Haydee."

"Okay," Jocelyn looked about ready to leave again before Daniel caught the younger boy's arm. Jocelyn paused, looking up at him. "What?"

Daniel pulled him close for a second. "Just promise me you didn't book a plane ticket somewhere... weird."

"Nah," Jocelyn hugged him briefly and took a step back. "Las Vegas's tacky. There's no plane ticket anywhere."

That was something of a relief even if he was dressing what might happen when or if Haydee's parents found out about the engagement. If they didn't already know about it. A new ring wasn't exactly subtle after all. "Thank you. Now, did you feed Mouse?"

Jocelyn's expression went tight. "Mouse's dead, I found her lying in her exercise wheel a few days ago. I know she was old and things but still, asking me if I fed her wasn't the best question you could think of."

"Oh," Daniel bit down on the inside of his cheek and winced at the pain. "We'll find a shoebox somewhere and bury her in it. I'm sorry about being tactless."

Jocelyn was quiet for a long moment before a quiet sigh escaped. "I think I did it, I was petting her and then she just fell over on her side, twitching. I felt it, Mouse's brain just turned funny on me and she collapsed."

"We'll give her a proper funeral first," Daniel said. "Deal with Biscuit and then... tell Haydee's parents about the engagement. Somehow."

Hesitation made him slow as he tried to come up with a reasonable excuse for the last few days. It was the least he could do while briefly omitting the hospital stay or whatever illness he might have had.

CHAPTER SIXTEEN

M orning greeted him with a shrill ringing sound that cut through the pounding headache and Jocelyn's ill-timed bouncing on the bed. Daniel groaned, trying to pull the pillow over his head in an attempt to block out the light. "Let me sleep."

"Can't," Jocelyn's muffled voice was more uncertain. "Your phone's ringing."

"Ignore it," Daniel forced himself to sit up though the movement made his vision swim in front of him. He buried his face in his hands, trying not to retch as his stomach knotted itself up inside. "Just find Tylenol or aspirin, please."

He doubted either would help with the migraine behind his eyes but it was better than going without.

Jocelyn hesitated by his side and clambered off the bed, rummaging through the backpack before he came back with a couple pills and the familiar blue and orange label. "Midol's like Tylenol, right?"

"Close enough," At this point he didn't care whether it was his brother's medicine for menstrual cramps or some-thing else. It just had to kill the pounding in his head. "You're going to have to get Haydee's parents to drive you to school today. I don't think I can."

Mercifully, the phone trailed off into silence and he managed to look up, fumbling one handed for the dark sunglasses on the bedside table and his medical alert bracelet.

"Okay," Jocelyn's worried glance lasted for as long as it took to get his backpack and slip out of the room. "You'll be better soon, right?"

That remained to be seen, depending on the headache and its resulting nausea. Daniel nodded tiredly. "Sure, go on before you're late."

Food was the last thing on his mind, and he only picked over the blueberry pancakes Haydee's mother put down in front of him. "Thanks, Mrs. Ashworth."

She blushed, shaking her head. "Anna, please. We're nearly family anyway. If you don't mind me asking, you look a little pale."

He'd always been pale. Daniel pushed the mostly untouched plate out of his way, not interested in eating just now. "Haydee just said that after the trip to Augusta. I'm more concerned about the migraine."

Anna smiled wistfully and put her hand on his before frowning a little in dismay. "You're burning up, Daniel. C'mon, I'm helping you back to bed. A little soup at lunchtime will be nice, yes? Chicken noodle?"

Though her nose wrinkled slightly at the non vegan nature of the soup. Daniel forced a smile and nodded. "Sure, alright. Could you call whoever tried to leave a message and tell them I'm sorry."

She dialed, listened for a moment and set the phone down in his hand. "It was an Augusta General doctor. Some woman who calls herself Persephone Sotaira? She wants to discuss the bone marrow biopsy with you?"

They were lucky it was still morning. Calais to Augusta was a three-hour drive on good roads, there was still time, but he'd have to give up on the dearly wanted nap and drag something other than his pajamas on. Daniel groaned and slumped in his seat. "Yay. Wait-"

Anna had already pulled the phone from his loose grip and was dialing another number. "Hello? Could I speak to my daughter when you have a moment, Mrs. Evans. And one of Jocelyn's teachers? Surely you can find a substitute receptionist for the rest of the day? There's something that needs them. Yes, it's important. I'll bring one of my vegetarian casseroles over Wednesday night. You always did like them."

Anna's casseroles weren't that good, but he was vaguely grateful for the effort she attempted to put into the conversation. "You don't need to pull Haydee and Jocelyn out of class for something like this trip."

She blushed pink. "Don't think I've forgotten how you just pick over that dish, Daniel. I know you aren't fond of it. Emily is, however so it's no trouble. No, no- it's alright. No need to bother them after all. I'm sure he'll talk tonight or tomorrow."

"Can I have my phone back now?" Daniel asked.

Haydee's mother ended the call, clearing the dishes and placing them into the sink. "Of course, shall we?"

They didn't have any other choice, did they? Daniel nodded, resigned. "Let's go,"

The trip was largely uneventful, but it didn't help the hard feeling in the pit of his stomach or the nausea at every gust of wind blowing snow across the highway despite his attempts to sleep. Or the bottle of ice-cold water Anna used to wet a cloth for him.

Persephone's office wasn't far from where he'd had his own room just a few days before. Daniel hesitated, knocking on the door before pushing it open. Her place was sparse, barely decorated beyond the desk, a couple leather bound books and the large woven tapestry decorating the wall to the right of the window overlooking an expanse of white blanketed park. "I like the scene, Artemis on one of her hunts and her dogs, right?'

She looked at him with just the faintest expression of approval. "You know your mythology then?"

"Some, Kate told me about you and your sister. The rest, I read when I was tired of my biology textbooks." Daniel said.

Persephone nodded, tucking a strand of hair behind one ear as she looked down at the reports in front of her. "We ran the bone marrow biopsy, and the results aren't... good, I'm afraid. You gave an account of your family and medical history and I can say, based on those tests, that we can rule out any viral infection or drug use but we were unable to determine the cause of your illness."

A shadow crossed her face as she turned another page in her report. "The biopsy confirmed it as aplastic anemia. Do you know what that is?"

Daniel looked away, swallowing back on the bile like taste in his mouth. "Not much, actually. I know what anemia is, my childhood doctor tried to get me to take an iron supplement for it but it made going to the bathroom tricky. I threw those out after the first couple weeks. Aplastic anemia, no... I don't know that one."

The doctor let out a breath, pinching the bridge of her

nose in a way eerily similar to how Kate did it. "Your body is failing to produce sufficient blood cells and aplastic anemia is causing a deficiency in all of your blood cells."

"I see," Daniel said.

Persephone regarded him for a long moment before turning another page in her report. "Please don't mistake my tone for any lack of sympathy but after seeing so many patients over the years, it is hard to… not be quite so matter of fact. I would like to discuss possible treatments with you, Daniel. Without a known cause, makes it a little more diffi-cult but not unmanageable."

"But there's no real cure, is there?" Daniel asked.

"There can be," Persephone looked at him over the rims of her glasses. "The bone marrow transplant is your best option but refusal or failure to find a match, there is an HSCT treatment. Are you familiar with that?"

"Yes," And the thought of that particular treatment scared him more than he cared to let show. "It could transplant my own stem cells or a matching donor's back in an attempt to cure this. Especially under thirty but you'd have to destroy my immune system to do it. And then pray infection or graft versus host disease doesn't show up. It's… too dangerous for me."

"I understand," She turned back to the first page of her report. "In that case, the bone marrow transplant remains your best option."

"If we find a donor," He pulled the report out from under her hand, skimming it wearily. "Is that the first or second line treatment?"

"First," Persephone inclined her head in acknowledge-ment. "And the best one for you, given your age. Refusal of any treatment at all, you may have a year at most. With the bone marrow transplant or drug intervention, you could have five years at a greater than forty-five percent chance."

He read the hesitation in her eyes even if it didn't show in her voice or tone. "Is it really forty-five percent for me?"

She looked down, a flicker of something replacing the shadow that crossed her face. "For your age, between twenty and forty years of age, it's closer to thirty-five percent. That depends on how well the donor matches you."

He nodded, brushing a hand roughly across his eyes. "Either way, I'm dead before five years are up. Stem cell or bone marrow it doesn't matter what the name is, I have a choice between crushing my immune system and risking infection there or the transplant failing on me. And that's only if I don't have a relapse at some point."

That was no choice at all, even if the alternative was only a year left. "I'm only twenty-six…"

Whether it was a plea or a prayer, he didn't know for sure. "So what do we do in the meantime?"

Persephone's hand covered his before pulling away. "Until we find a donor, the best course could be an immuno-suppressant and a corticosteroid."

"What's the catch with them?" His voice was dull despite the feeble attempt at optimism.

"The anemia may return, and you could relapse, Daniel." Her answer was soft, almost gentle. "This treatment will take several months, regardless. I don't think it likely given the season but do try to avoid indoor sports and germs."

"My girlfriend still needs to know, and her mother is still outside in the car waiting for me." Daniel looked away. "Could I have a copy of the medical report?"

"Of course," She nodded, separating the stack into two. "I made a copy just in case you though to ask."

"Thanks," There was little else to say to that as he slipped his copy of the report into his backpack and stood.

He paused at the door, turning to look back at her. "I'm going to have to find a place in Augusta, aren't I? I can't keep making a three hour drive every time for treatment."

The quiet knock on the door was somehow enough to cut the conversation short and he turned away, pushing the office door open to see the young woman huddled in a too big hoodie and an artificially colored wig. "Your turn,"

She nodded, tried for a smile and edged past him before the door closed behind her.

Anna was waiting for him in the car, nose wrinkled in concentration as she filled in a couple crossword puzzles squares. "How was the meeting with the doctor?"

"Alright, I guess," He dropped the paper bag onto the passenger seat, following it up with the box of medical masks.

She twisted around to look in the backseat and saw the masks there before her shoulders dropped. "Not as well as you'd hoped then?"

"No, it wasn't," Daniel pulled the seatbelt across his body. "I'd rather not talk about it until we get back to Calais. Let's just say that my life expectancy just got a best before date."

"Oh, come here," Anna wrapped an arm around his shoulders and pulled him close so he could rest his head on her arm. "It's okay to cry if you want to."

Maybe it was but he couldn't help a small feeling of shame at wetting Anna's winter jacket with his tears. It felt like weakness to him to show rather than bite down and conceal his feelings. He straightened, running a hand through his hair. "Let's- let's just go back. I'll need to talk to Haydee and my boss at the bar. She'll need to know I'm going to have to give my notice there."

Bars weren't always the cleanest of establishments after all, even when they were the high-class ones only available to the wealthy. Kate's place was nowhere near that standard. "Can't work there if I have to wear a mask or have the immune system to deal with the germs."

If Anna noticed the slightly pessimistic note in his voice, she didn't comment on it, only starting the car and pulling out of the snowy visitors parking lot. That was fine with him, he could have done with three hours or so of silence between them. It was better than talking, in his mind.

The lights were still on despite the late hour and a week-night by the time they arrived back at the house. Daniel glanced towards the report and the paper bag of medicine before resigning himself to juggling the box of masks in his other hand. Whether he wanted to or not, Haydee deserved to know about Persephone's test results and the report that accompanied it. It wasn't fair to hide something so important from her, not when they were engaged.

Anna gave him a wan smile, cutting the engine off. "I... would prefer something vegan for a late dinner but if you want something else, I think I can find my grandmother's recipe book in the bookshelf. A chicken burger or hamburger with cheese?"

As kind as her offer was, he wasn't hungry. "I'm fine but thank you. I think I'd just like to talk to Haydee and Jocelyn before getting an early night. I didn't sleep well last time."

"I see," Worry crossed her face but she didn't press the issue. "If you change your mind, I'll put sandwich meat in the refrigerator."

Haydee's knock came less than fifteen minutes after he dropped his backpack on the bedroom floor. Daniel unlocked the door to see her standing there, fidgeting with the hem of her t-shirt. "I don't know how much you know-"

"Nothing," She looked away. "Mom offered to tell me, but I said no, I'd rather hear it from you, honestly."

Daniel sighed, moving aside so she could sit on the edge of the bed. "The tests came back this morning. There was no way to drive the three hours and back again myself so your mom helped. I... have aplastic anemia."

Haydee winced but gently put an arm around his shoulders, tentative. "Is that as bad as it sounds? What did the doctor say?"

He swallowed, taking her hand in his as he smelled the raspberry soap she had used. So someone had told her something at least even if she had refused the details. Why else would she have made the effort to wash her hands before greeting him. "That if I don't get treatment, the most time I'll have is a year. With it, five, maybe. If I don't go into remission or have a relapse."

She bit down on her lower lip, gaze dropping to their clasped hands. "This sounds more like cancer than anemia."

Daniel offered a wan smile at that. "It can turn into leukemia sometimes, yeah. Most of the treatments are the same anyway. Chemo and a bone marrow transplant."

"I see," Her voice was soft. "So, what will you do next?"

He had been dreading the question, but it deserved an answer, regardless of his discomfort. "Try to use my magic as little as possible, I guess. It needs blood and since I use my own, now that any cut or infection could..."

Daniel shrugged helplessly. "Could potentially kill me, I can't risk it. There was no poison or source for it found so my best guess is that the same thing that I refuse to do to others, is taking its price out on me."

Haydee was quiet for a long moment. "Then... what do you say to a small wedding? Something in the living room with my parents, your brother and Malachi? I proposed sure but if you're worried about the time left then…?"

"I'd say yes," He hesitated and pressed his mouth gently against the back of her hand before lifting his gaze back to hers. "You're right, I don't know how much time I have left. Just…"

He flushed, trying not to think about it too much. "Just as long as you're gentle on the night afterwards. The anemia- I get tired more than I used to."

She gave him an arch look. "I'm not looking for a kid halfway through my first year of teaching, Daniel. We'll use protection."

Her wry tone faded into gentle now. "I'll be careful even if it means a little unflattering face mask in the process. You know me. I'd never do anything to hurt you, physically or otherwise. I… l love you. If sex is a problem, we can just spend the night cuddled in an empty room with a movie. That's good enough, err, consummating things, for me. My parents won't mind."

That was settled then. Daniel cupped the side her face in one hand before tucking a lock of her hair behind one ear. "A month or two onwards then?'

Haydee sniffed and the tip of her nose was pink. "A month or two on then. Don't you dare die on me before then, Daniel."

"I'll try," It wasn't a promise he could keep without knowing if there was a matched donor out there for him, but he would try for her sake.

Haydee sniffed again, wiping a hand roughly across her eyes. "Breakfast, bright and early. Mom's making waffles with strawberries tomorrow."

"Sounds good," Daniel said. He looked down at his phone, scrolling tiredly through the contacts, searching for

Kate's number. Whatever else happened tonight, he was going to have to give his notice for employment. Bars weren't known for their cleanliness at the best of time and Kate's was on the seedier side of that scale. "Do you mind if I make a call or two?"

She swallowed, lingering at the bedroom doorway long enough to give him a hopeful look before she vanished, shutting it behind her.

Daniel closed his eyes, murmured a soft prayer for luck and dialed Kate's number, hoping she would pick up tonight. All previous encounters with his employer had suggested she was prompt in returning calls or emails, regardless of whether she had something she was in the middle of or not. Sometimes when he was inconveniently occupied himself. "Kate? Listen, there's something I need to tell you and I think it would be best done in person instead of over the phone. I-"

His words were cut off by the irritating beep of her phone going to voicemail and he slumped hanging up on it before anything could be recorded. At the least she would see the missed call on her display. And if she didn't answer that, he could always try again in the morning after breakfast. "I'll try again later."

What choice did he have after all? Voicemail sucked.

CHAPTER SEVENTEEN

The underworld was a dangerous place but thankfully she wasn't being called 'home' for once. Only her father had that power, and he was rarely interested in such a mundane thing as working in a bar or the lives of mortals in general. That made some things easier, others much less so and she was already regretting the twenty minutes standing out in the chill of a New York city winter with her hand out for a taxi driver. One driver in particular.

Kate sighed, seeing the back of the man's head through the plastic partition. "Charlie. Last time I heard; you'd just started driving taxis around for stupid tourists. And charging them three times the standard fare at that."

He chuckled, rubbing his fingers together for the fifty in her hand. "A lead or silver coin isn't worth as much as it was once, girlie."

Girlie. She had to bite back on the low snarl that threatened at his mocking pet name for her. "Female, yes. A girl, no. You ought to remember that, Charon."

The driver scowled, dropping any pretense of affability

now though not the pronounced Greek accent. His appearance in the rear-view mirror shifted, aging fifteen years and the hair going to salt and pepper in the black coloring. He was as much a shapeshifter as she was though he had never given up the godlike power that came with it for some of the eldest. "Not wise to use my name, Hecate."

She smiled thinly. "And yet I can. You might be almost a god, but you answer to my father's will and he will not see me hurt or claimed by you."

Charon's scowl turned into a disparaging snort. "So be it, Hecate. What do you want?"

Hecate leaned back against the cloth seat, hesitating. "I need a favor. You know how to talk to your sisters, I can't."

"Ah," The black look he cast her turned into triumph. "You mean you don't want to."

She slumped, pinching the bridge of her nose. "No, I don't want to talk with the moirai. And yes, your sisters scare me, but I need that favor."

"Name it," Charon said.

"A life," She lifted her gaze to see his eyes in the small mirror. "Or at least an extension on it."

He twisted in his seat to look back at her, holding out a hand for her. "It'll cost you."

Hecate sighed, passing another hundred over. "I hope you're satisfied, Charlie O'Neil."

"Not quite, I could always use more money but for now, that I got Hades' daughter to beg me for a favor is enough," He smirked, starting the car before turning the lighted sign off.

She grimaced, regretting this already despite the necessity of it. "Fine,"

Charon lit a cigarette, blowing the smoke out of the

driver's side window before he dropped the butt into the street. "So, what is this one's name that you want to bargain with my sisters for?"

She wrinkled her nose at the cigarette smoke scent and shook her head. "No, that wasn't our bargain. You agreed to the favor. Not the identity of the one I'm trying to bargain for."

"Someone, I think," His voice was sardonic. "A lover, perhaps?"

Hecate flushed, speaking before her thoughts could catch up with her. "Gods, no. Daniel isn't my boyfriend or my lover. He's ill, dying but he's only twenty-six."

Charon chuckled again, turning the corner onto the next street. "Ah, so that was the name."

He'd tricked her into giving that up, Hecate cursed softly under her breath, giving in for the time being. "Wretch, have it your way. Yes, his name is Daniel LaLaurie and his own magic is killing him. I bribed my aunt with organic pomegranate juice and word of her sister for the medical records. I didn't know it then, now I regret learning what he has."

Charon swerved violently, nearly sideswiping a slower moving Ford truck carrying a couch in its back. "That Keltoi boy?"

Sometimes she forgot how old her father's ferryman was or how little information came to him that wasn't filtered by two thousand years or so understanding. Hecate winced, running a hand through her hair. "Creole, not Keltoi, Charon."

He shrugged carelessly. "Keltoi, it doesn't matter here he called home when his blood matters more. And the power he has came from those barbarian tribes."

His eyes narrowed in dislike. "I'll oblige your favor, but

I'm not required to be pleased about it, little one. You are a lady of Athens, of a civilized people and you would try to save the life of a Parisii whelp?"

She cupped her hand, calling a little fire to it before she extinguished the flame. "You forget that I'm the lady of the crossroads, friend. It was Athens first, and then Rome before it came to America. New York and New Orleans. So yes, that means I'll do what I can to save one Parisii whelp, a Creole one in particular."

"And if you can't save him?" Charon's voice was uncharacteristically kind now. "What then?"

"There's always a way," She said.

"Not always," He slowed the vehicle down, pulling to a stop and cutting the engine. "But I'll let you bargain with your father on that matter. You have my word that I'll speak with my sisters."

Hecate nodded, climbing out of the car. "Thank you,"

From now on, she was on her own to find a path onwards.

Charon cast her a dark look. "Don't thank me, girl. This might be more curse than gift in the end. Your mortal pet may not thank you either."

She'd chance that when it came to it. Right now, it was best to go on foot to where she wanted to. Modern machines and technology wouldn't work in the underworld. Hecate turned her back on the cab driver and ventured into the alley.

Shadow wrapped its comforting touch around her and a moment later she was in her father's domain, the pale marble of its pillars and the wall as familiar as her childhood home where Athens would one day and had been founded, nearly six thousand years ago.

"Hecate,"

She lifted her gaze to find her aunt and Persephone

Sotaira's twin standing there before the other woman wrapped her arms around her in a lingering embrace. "Aunt Demeter,"

Demeter was as warm as her twin sister was cool in her tone. "I missed you."

The woman laughed, running a hand through Hecate's hair. "What news then? There is so little to read of late."

Hecate smiled ruefully and pulled a week's worth of Times newspapers from her messenger bag. "I thought you might appreciate this then."

Her aunt accepted the bundle and gestured towards a nearby bench. "I'll read these later, perhaps. Your father is waiting. And your mother."

That was sure to be a warm welcome. Hecate glanced away, tasting something bitter in her mouth. "Mother..."

"Erinyes is... herself," Demeter's voice was cautious. "For one of her people anyway. I think it best if you take your natural shape rather than the mortal one you chose. She would appreciate it if her daughter had her wings."

"I see," Hecate said.

"Quite," Demeter looked down, smoothing a hand over the printed pages of the paper before leaving them on the bench. No wind blew in the underworld, so they stayed flat, unruffled by the breeze. "You are of her people as much as your father's- our kind."

Hecate nodded in resignation as she closed her eyes, leaving the human mask behind. Her natural form was nearly human in appearance save for the deeper tanned skin, golden eyes and the wings of her mother's race. She much preferred her human form.

Demeter's hand covered hers for a moment, warm, reassuring. "It will be fine, child."

So she hoped anyway as she stood, venturing into the gardens. These had been her aunt's attempt at introducing something green and living into the underworld. It seemed to have worked even despite the lack of a sun to warm the willow and aspen saplings. Peony and poppies grew at their feet. "Mother? Father?"

She found them at the end of the winding trail just as her father gave Erinyes a chaste kiss on the mouth. "Father?"

He started, seeing her there before greeting her with a reserved smile. "Daughter. It has been some time, yes."

"Only twenty years," Hecate tried for a shrug, self conscious about the massive wings folded against her back. She was uncomfortably aware of her mother's unreadable look. The avian woman had been dead for over five thousand years, her bones long since lost but it hadn't lessened her cool regard either. Only in the underworld did she have a shape beyond the shadow she was in the physical world. "Not that long."

The god glanced away; expression pensive. "A prayer could have been just as effective. I would have answered it,"

She managed a hollow laugh. "You well know the reputation your name carries, Father. I would sooner not draw your temper if I can help it."

He gave her a bemused look, running a hand through neatly brushed chestnut hair. "Far less of one than your mother, I think. If not to greet me, what brings you home?"

"A life," Hecate bit down on her lower lip, choosing her words carefully now. "A... friend. He is ill, dying and I'd like to spare him that fate. I already promised Charon a favor if he spoke with his sisters."

Her father snarled softly in warning, showing a hint of his cat like natural shape even in human form. His canines a touch longer and sharper than a human's. "Did I not warn you against any bargain with the ferryman? It may be a price you cannot pay."

His hands remained at his sides, but flickers of blue fire sparked around them.

"You did," She lowered her gaze, contrite under the brief display of his anger. "But the boy is a friend. I would rather not have you take him before his time."

"Ah, child," Hades cupped the side of her face in one hand, pulling her into a one-armed embrace with the other. "It may not be the answer you seek but who am I to deny nature or cheat it? If it is his time, there is little I'm willing to do to change that."

"But it need not be," Hecate said.

Her father sighed, exchanging a look with her mother before turning his attention once more to her. "Friend or not, if it is his time, so be it. Charon came before you and mentioned Daniel's... power as well as his ancestry. He was less than pleased about it but he can be ill-tempered as well you know. And though I suspect the tales about the Celtic priests to have been Roman rumor, it isn't something Charon is willing to put aside so easily."

"I know, Father," She quieted despite herself. "But..."

"You feel the Fates will be unfair?" Hades asked.

"He's young even for a human," Hecate said. "Not yet thirty."

Hades pulled her close, seeming heedless of the sober charcoal suit jacket and shirt he wore. "I've accepted the young before, little Kate. At his age, he would have been a man grown in another time."

"It's still too soon," Her protest sounded weak even to her ears and she let her shoulders slump, defeated. "If he lives or not, I can't just watch on the sidelines. That may be your duty and interest, it isn't mine."

Her father tucked a lock of hair behind her ear. "I cannot and I will not cheat the fates, Hecate. They need their due."

His expression darkened for a moment. "Bind his shadow if you are so determined to save his life but do not expect me to tolerate your attempts at imitating Asclepius. I will not permit your theft, Hecate. Christian or pagan, Creole or the distant son of a Celtic priest, he will be mine upon his death."

When her father made up his mind, it was made up and he rarely changed it. Hecate took a step back, looking away. "He's a good man, Father. Please…"

"So was Meleager and he passed away before a time you thought appropriate as well, child." Hades said.

This time, he made no attempt at affection or comfort, his expression going distant for a moment as though he was listening to something only he could hear. "They want to have a word with you, daughter."

One didn't refuse the fates, even when the sisters were ambiguously referred to as they. "Fine,"

She let her shoulders slump and stepped through the pale gray light of her gate, tasting something bitter in her mouth. Ash or something akin to acid, it was hard to say which was more unpleasant.

The sisters had… upgraded things since, by the looks of things. Rumor of their activities in the early days had painted a picture of a cave, a spindle and a loom and a pair of sewing shears. And to be sure, those things were apparent, but the loom was covered in decades worth of dust, the scissors tarnished and dull. Now a whiteboard – several of them were mounted against the walls of what could have been an ordinary apartment in New York. Computer equipment sat on desks, humming softly in the background. Hecate swallowed, nearly tripping over a stack of physics textbooks piled on a cream carpet. "Clotho?"

"In here," Clotho's voice sounded, muffled from under one of the desks as she cursed softly in ancient Greek. "Mind the quantum physics books, Hecate. Lachesis likes her order."

"Already tripped over them," She rubbed ruefully at her knee. "Invest in a bookshelf?"

"I know," Clotho sat up, tucking the pencil behind one ear. "She predicted that. And she doesn't feel the need for a bookshelf either."

Hecate dropped into a crouch, taking in the youngest of the fates warily. She wore the shape of a sixteen-year-old woman and untidy one at that. A gray streak of dust smeared unnoticed across one cheek and her blonde hair was pulled into a sloppy ponytail. "So, a computer lab?"

Clotho snorted. "If you expect astrology and flying cows, talk to the oracle of Delphi. She lost her job when the Christians came along. Now she works as the operating system for all this."

Her hand gestured at the computers around her. "Buggy and imprecise at the best of times. Hence the whiteboards."

"I... see," Hecate trailed off, unsure what she had expected of the fates but it hadn't been a sixteen-year-old computer expert either.

"Yeah," Clotho shrugged, glancing away. "Things improved. Slightly, when your father gave us Sisyphus as an admin. It seemed a better job than pushing the rock up the hill and watching it roll back down again. Delphi still crashes though."

She seemed to brighten despite the mention of the operating system. "You came here for a reason, yes?"

"I think you already know the answer to that," Hecate stood, taking a step back to give the young woman space.

"I do," Clotho gave her a searching look. "And I know that the ground control at NASA would love to get their hands on our system. Some of them would die for the chance to spend an hour here. Better than a computer with the power of a calculator."

Her tone quieted, sobering. "C'mon, my sisters are getting impatient. You really aren't meant to be here for very long. It complicates the variables."

Variables, right. Hecate rubbed at her eyes, trying to ease the ache behind her temples. "And that means…?"

"I know about Daniel and his illness," Clotho shrugged. "It was one of the equations I created for him."

Hecate swallowed back on the dry, faintly nauseated feeling in her mouth. "Daniel isn't a mathematics problem for you to solve, Clotho."

She looked at her unreadable through dark, nearly black eyes. "Isn't he? Mortals are made up of organic code. A, U, G and C. If you know the right equation, you can follow them from birth to death and predict how their lives go. It's a bit more complicated than that now, with so many different paths to follow but I can usually find the one thread that follows through their lives."

The young woman shrugged, half turning away. "My sisters, if it pleases you."

Lachesis and Atropos weren't as young as their sister but that was of little comfort to her as she looked from one to the other. Lachesis was in her early thirties, holding a dark eyed child in her arms. The infant boy squirmed, nudging at her chest before quieting.

Atropos was the oldest of the three, somewhere in her mid fifties, silver just beginning to thread its way through her dark hair. Hecate took a brief breath, steeling herself at the sight of the three. "Maiden, mother and crone."

One with blonde hair, one with red and the last with black, all with the same dark eyes. She opened her mouth and closed it a moment later, quailing under their collective gaze. What did one say to the fates? "Your child?"

Lachesis lifted a shoulder in a shrug. "If you like, yes. The father was a doctor volunteering in Sierra Leone. Ebola claimed his life. It was his time, and he went without regret."

"What's his name?" Hecate asked.

Lachesis tilted her head to the side, pensive. "One hasn't come to me yet, but I expect it will soon."

That was… comforting. Hecate sighed and sat down on the living room's couch. "Business then, I guess. I'd like to change the fate for a friend. He's ill, dying and he needs more time."

"No," Atropos' voice was flat. "What Clotho and Lachesis decide is set and must not be altered."

"But-"

Lachesis held a hand up, silencing her for a moment as she shifted the weight of her son to the other arm. "Enough, Hecate. What Clotho calculates on her whiteboard is often the path their lives take. Daniel's thread has been measured out and is coming to an end. He was never meant to see much longer than twenty-seven."

Her expression softened under Hecate's dismay. "I understand wanting to spare a mortal from Atropos's scissors, but his life was set at birth. All you can do is help Daniel make the most of the time he has left to him."

"Father said I could bind his shadow if I wanted to," Hecate said.

Lachesis's expression flickered. "I suppose it would be one way to circumvent us and still obey the letter of what we wrote for his life. Shadows are only the reflection of the mortal, not the mortal themselves. You would have to put a few pomegranate seeds in his pillow or a pocket and neglect the coin our brother expects for his passage. But Daniel may not welcome lingering in the mortal world as a shadow of himself, Hecate. His faith is strong but isn't the one we knew in Athens. He will want peace, not an existence lost between the physical and your father's world."

"I'll take that chance," Hecate said.

"So be it," Lachesis stood, passing off her son to Clotho and walking over to the apartment's front door. "A word, one out of my sisters' hearing. I may be persuaded to grant a period of grace to your young friend if you give me something in exchange."

Hecate bit down on her lower lip, remembering the warning her father had given her about Charon. He hadn't mentioned anything about the three sisters to the best of her knowledge. "What is it?"

Lachesis glanced away, thoughtful. "One mortal for another. You gave up the life as a goddess for a mortal one. I could… grant Daniel a few months more than what I measured for him if you willingly sacrifice a portion of your own life for it."

"A year," Her answer came before she fully thought it through.

"Six months," The Fate's expression cooled noticeably. "No more than that. And you sacrifice a century or two from your own. It seems a small price given how long our kind live."

"Done," Hecate found a box cutter knife lying abandoned on the nearby desk and sliced shallowly across her left hand. The blood oath wasn't strictly necessary, but it would be evidence of her deal.

Lachesis clasped it, looking down at the black blood streaking their hands before she traced a fingertip through the blood idly, delicately licking the dark liquid from the tip. "Done then. Your friend has the six months promised him. Use the time wisely, Hecate."

The apartment door opened under her touch, seeming not to require key or turning of the doorknob for the latch to unlock. Hecate looked into the hallway, uncertain. "Thank you,"

Lachesis gave her a thin smile. "I wouldn't, little one. Gratitude is unnecessary and a mortal concept, you might find your oath coming due sooner than you expected though."

"And you aren't going to tell me?" Hecate asked.

"Ruin the surprise? No," Lachesis frowned, looking into the apartment. "I've often thought mortals are less likely to fight us if they don't know what their futures hold. Hm, I believe I can comfort you somewhat with a name after all."

She was thrown off guard and her gate back to her father's realm fizzled midair. "What?"

"My son," Lachesis' tone was dry. "I have one for the boy after all. Nikandros, Nik for a pet name. I expect he'll do well in any army or air force he chooses to adopt as his homeland before dying in service of them to protect his men."

Her expression sharpened, focusing once more on Hecate. "You have your bargain and my word, that should be enough to satisfy your greed, Kate."

It was though she wouldn't have described it as greed to ask for the life of a friend. Hecate nodded wearily, accepting the other woman's words. "I don't suppose I'll find you in Calais at any point then?"

"Me, no. My duty is here, not in the mortal world." Lachesis looked past her. "My son, perhaps. One day. The boy will have the seer's gift enough to find you."

"Alright," There seemed little else to say and she was already itching to check her phone for voicemail or texts that wouldn't arrive until she returned to a place with decent cell service. Clotho's Delphi operating system looked powerful but lacking in anything resembling a network or internet connection. "I'll wait for him, I guess."

However long it took.

CHAPTER EIGHTEEN

K ate answered the voicemail he'd left for her two hours after he had sent it, sounding harried. "Daniel?"

He swallowed, looking down at the medical report still open on his folded legs. "There's something I need to tell you. And I'm probably going to have to give my notice as well. Bars aren't what I'd call clean places to work in."

"I see," Her end of the phone cut out for a moment before she spoke again. "Stop by the bar, I think that would be easier than over the phone. I just heard the voicemail you left me."

He nodded even though she couldn't see him. "I thought you were usually prompt in returning calls. I waited two hours for you."

She sighed. "It's complicated, I had some family stuff to take care of first. My father, my aunt and a taxi driver who overcharged me fifty dollars for going three blocks. Technically also family but I try to think of it more as an employee of my father's. His... sisters are a bunch of mathematicians-slash-theoretical physicists who could probably predict the length of time left to the human race. They don't think longer than a thousand years on the current path. Gods, they even mapped out the extinction of the Neanderthals and Deniso-vans once and that was before they had a computer on hand."

Sometimes Kate was hard to follow even when knowing she wasn't as human as she pretended to be. Daniel pulled the phone away from his ear, switching to speakerphone. "Did they really?"

Kate's laugh was hollow. "Given their occupation and how long those three have been around, I wouldn't be surprised. They might pretend to be human but the three of them are more a... personification of a concept than a shapeshifter or god. Gods, at least, you can sometimes under-stand them when they want you to. Clotho and her sisters operate on their own view of things."

Daniel rubbed the back of his hand across his eyes. "I hope you're talking about a metaphor here because if the mythology is real, I'd rather not know."

"Sure, go with the metaphor," Her voice was resigned. "I would too if I had the good fortune to. Unfortunately, I needed something of theirs and I had to sign away a little bit of my life to get it. Look, just come over to the bar and we can discuss whatever you want in more privacy."

"Alright," That was as good as any reason to and he needed the few minutes of alone time to try and get his thoughts into order. Or at least, resist the urge to let a few tears out. "I'll see you in a bit,"

He closed the laptop and set it aside, blocking out the website he had been scrolling through for an apartment in the Augusta area that would let him make whatever appointments he needed to at the hospital without a three-hour drive involved in the trip.

Haydee had her head bowed at the kitchen table, marking someone's language arts test as he passed by her, backpack over his shoulder. At least until she caught sight of him out of the corner of her eye and absently shook the pill bottle he'd left behind.

He grimaced, looked away and pulled the cap off, swallowing the bitter pill with a bite of the chocolate chip cookie she had left behind. The sugar probably wouldn't do anything for him under the circumstances, but it made the little tablet go down easier. "I won't forget next time."

She nodded, running a hand through her hair mussing it. "Milk would be better."

"Hate the taste," He brushed a hand over her shoulder before turning away. "Want anything on the way back?"

Haydee dropped the red pen onto the tabletop and leaned back, drawing a leg up to her chest. "A nap? I feel like I've been at this for three hours already and I have to have it in by tomorrow for class. What about you?"

Tell her or not? And how soon was Kate expecting him at the bar? He sat in the chair next to hers, wishing the walk down two flights of stairs hadn't left him as breathless as he was. "I'm going to have to... move out and find a place in Augusta. I can't keep making a three-hour trip to the hospital on your mom's money and gas fare."

"And you'll be taking Jocelyn with you, I guess." Her eyes blurred and she swore as she blotted at the wetness on her cheeks, ignoring how he flinched at the words. "I- I know this was coming- that you need somewhere closer for treatment but shit, I..."

"No," He glanced away. "I already asked Jocelyn if he wanted to go with me. He was rather... rude and threw his teddy bear at me when I brought it up. I think he wants to stay in Calais with you."

"And the wedding? I know we haven't really gotten anywhere in the planning but..."

Daniel closed his eyes, pained. "I want to do this right, properly but I don't know if there's time for it. My parents had to have several meetings with a parish priest before he decided they were a good match for each other. And Dad never remarried after Mom died."

Her hand covered his and she cupped the side of his face, giving him a gentle kiss. "I don't know very much about how Catholics do things, and my parents will probably kill me for converting but I think I can handle any church service you need to make the wedding real."

"You should probably avoid the wine and bread then," Daniel looked down at their hands, tracing the pattern of her ring. "It isn't much different from a normal wedding except for the mass and the prayer. I can't remember what the rules are for a non-Catholic marrying in a Catholic church other than the historical laws against it."

Her smile was wry but kind. "That's a little bit of a relief. I don't have to get splashed with water just to marry you. Think the priest will be willing to do a shotgun wedding?"

He had to flush and look away. "No, if you want that, we might as well go to the registry office."

Haydee went pink with shame. "Sorry, that was a… bad joke on my part. I wish I had your faith, but I don't, I wasn't raised like that. We can have the wedding here or in Augusta when you feel better or you're well enough that the doctor to say it's alright to go ahead with it."

She bit down on her lower lip and tore a blank sheet of paper from her notebook, scribbling addresses and phone numbers on it as she scrolled through her phone. "Do what you need to at Kate's. I'll see what I can rush through for planning."

Daniel tugged the pencil from her grip and set it aside. "Leave that for the priest when he says something. You have school and I have an apartment hunt to start. Neither of us have time to do this ourselves."

She sighed, chewing on her lower lip until it bled. "Saves a little time, I guess but sounds like it could take up to three months to arrange. I'm guessing you would prefer the dress to be white and modest then? Nothing strapless?"

"In winter?" He gave her a brief look. "It's your choice if you want to shiver but I'd… prefer it if you had something spaghetti strap wise at the very least. My parents took a year before they ever got down the aisle."

She laughed, though a tinge of emotion clung to it. "So we'll still get the shotgun wedding after all, if your parents' wedding was an example of a Catholic service. We might not have a year, Daniel."

"Or we might have five," Daniel said.

"We don't know that." Her voice dropped. "Think we can get this done within three months or is that too fast for any priest to like?"

Truth be told, he wasn't sure but that was something the priest could handle when he was in a position to ask. Right now, he had to go before Kate's impatient text message arrived. "I won't be long, I hope."

He didn't intend to be long in any case.

Kate was waiting for him at one of the few tables in the bar's common area and from the slight lemon scent clinging to the surface, she had recently used some sort of cleaner on it. Daniel sat down, pulling the file from his knapsack and slid it over to her. "I thought you had a right to know,"

She looked down but made no move to read it. "I don't need a medical report to see what's going on. I'm a witch, same as you. I can sense what's happening in your body as well as you can."

"Then,"

"I already guessed at the anemia, yes." She pushed the documents back at him. "It wasn't hard with a little help and a few thousand years experience. I've seen a lot over that time."

Daniel rubbed a hand across his eyes, briefly coming in contact with the mask over his mouth and nose. "You're not telling me everything, but I'll let that go for now. I mostly came tonight so I could give my notice. I can't risk infection or germs here because some of the medication the doctor gave me, crushes an immune system."

That caught her by surprise, and she drew back, worry crossing her face. "I expected the resignation, I didn't know about the medicine's effect on you, personally."

"Yeah, well, it does," Daniel sighed, grateful he didn't need glasses. They would have fogged up under the breath he'd taken. "Until they find a bone marrow match and cure this for me, I can't afford to get sick. I'm not even sure if I can risk getting a flu shot while on this."

Her expression clouded over. "Forget it, I'm not letting you quit on me. You're too good at running the bar but I believe what you say about your immune system. So I'll give you leave with pay until this is over."

"That's nice but-"

Hecate cut him off with a shake of her head. "Humor me. I went to a lot of trouble getting the answers I needed, the least you can do is let me keep paying you even if you can't make it into actually work here."

Her mind sounded like it was set, and she wasn't about to change it despite his protests. Daniel looked away. "Thanks,"

"No problem," Kate's smile looked a little strained but she hid it well as she stood, offering her hand to his. "I washed, don't worry. The trick is getting Malachi to do it more regularly. He's brilliant in his own way but he still thinks hot water is enough to kill germs. Soap is a waste of time to him."

Daniel looked towards the bar's entrance, hesitating and accepted her touch. "Thanks. I should probably start thinking about packing up the car in the next day or so. Not that I have much to begin with."

She nodded, wistful. "Hope you find a place in Augusta,"

He did as well, truth be told and Kate's words were as good as any formal farewell. Preferred, truthfully. Saying a real goodbye would have hurt more than he was willing to let on. "Thanks,"

He'd thrown his new phone, used an expletive Daniel hadn't expected him to know and eventually cried himself to sleep until the stupid, smelly alarm clock rang in the morning for school. Now he was staring unhappily at the soggy cereal in the bottom of his bowl. "Not hungry,"

Haydee glanced at the contents and sighed, shoulders dropping. "Me either, Jocelyn but you have to eat something, Daniel wouldn't want you starving for his sake."

Jocelyn sneezed, wiping his nose on the sleeve of the black shirt he wore. "It isn't fair. Dani had to get sick with anemia, not me. I was the one sick at birth, not him."

His voice trailed off into sniffling. "Should be me,"

The three or so boxes of Daniel's things were already piled by the door, waiting the time when Daniel was feeling good enough to put them in the back of his car. Last night's errand to miss. Kate's bar had taken a lot out of him apparently and he was still asleep upstairs.

"He doesn't want you thinking like that," Haydee's voice

was trying to be encouraging. "C'mon, get ready or we'll both be late."

Jocelyn bit down on his lower lip until it bled and trudged to their room, digging through the suitcase for a pair of jeans instead of his pajama pants while trying to touch as little of Dani's things as possible. Haydee had told him about the necessity of wearing a mask and washing while his brother had been out. Anything at all could make him sicker than he was already.

He found his jeans and tugged them on, fumbling with the zipper and little metal button on the waistband, trying not to look at Dani, still asleep in the other bed. Daniel's expression was less stressed than it was in daytime, but he didn't look like a happy sleeper either, sprawled on his stomach with one forearm underneath the pillow. The other was partially visible under the coverlet, old silver scarring still evident on the skin. Jocelyn whimpered and gently brushed a hand over the blanket, pulling it over Dani's shoulders. "Don't go on me, please."

Dani's soft moan and the brief stir of motion was all the response he got in answer before Daniel drifted off again. Jocelyn brushed wetness away from his eyes and turned away, closing the door behind him. School wouldn't be any better but at least he was ready for the day in real clothes, not pajamas.

Haydee looked at him but didn't seem like she wanted to comment on his choice of a black shirt and equally dark washed jeans. "C'mon, let's just go, Jocelyn."

"Okay," What else was there to say to that? Nothing, so far as he was concerned. Dani was sick and it was all his fault for not doing something earlier or using his magic to help his brother.

He barely paid attention during math and language arts or

science, just counting down the time until lunch hour. Luck willing, his quiet little place in the corner would still be unoccupied.

It wasn't but it was also a little bit of a relief to find out that his place was taken up by Brittney and Brendan. Those two were at least, relatively nice. "Hi…"

Spoken tiredly for fear that his girlfriend would leave him alone at the table. Brittney looked over at him and edged to the side, making space for him to sit. "Who died on you?"

"Nobody yet," Jocelyn put his tray down next to her, staring at his food instead of eating it. "But Dani- he's sick. It would be nice if it was a cold or a flu bug but it's worse than that. He was always a little on the little iron deficient side, now it's turned into anemia. The kind of thing that needs a similar treatment to my mom's cancer. Now he's going to have to find a place closer to the hospital in Augusta."

Sympathy crossed Brittney's face while guilt showed on Brendan's. "Sorry,"

"Me too," He pushed his food out of the way, tired of pretending to eat it. "I want to help him, but he says it isn't my job to. Even though I think I can,"

"That sucks," Brittney said. "How'd you want to help him?"

Jocelyn looked down, unsure. Daniel hadn't said as much or in so many words, but he probably wouldn't be happy if he found out he'd told the only two in this school who were his friends. "The same way I tried to help him during that double date. Using my magic."

He leaned back against the chair tiredly. "I think you're still able to come over, but we have to be careful around him. Chemotherapy or his pills crushed his immune system, so we're doing a lot more handwashing and masks there."

Brittney and Brendan exchanged looks with each other; Brendan shrugged. "Homework date? The three of us?"

"Yeah," Despite the bad things were going, he couldn't help a slight bit of cheer at the agreement. He hadn't lost his friends yet even after the long time not talking with them. "Anyone have a car? I call shotgun for the ride."

CHAPTER NINETEEN

H e wasn't surprised to find Jocelyn and his brother's friends around the kitchen table, papers, and textbooks scattered across the surface when he finally ventured into the dining space. "Study night?"

Jocelyn looked up, blinking as he shoved a shoebox out of sight behind a glass vase. "Yeah, Brittney drove us back here."

Daniel pulled the worksheet towards him, skimming it. "Name the parts of the diagram below?"

Jocelyn nodded briefly. "Review for a final exam but I'm going to kill that test, just helping Brendan and Brittney out. How's... you know, your thing."

His expression went pink with discomfort. He would have been lying if that wasn't a concern for him as well but helping with a basic biology assignment was preferable to the effort of dragging boxes out to his car and spending the next half hour after it, sitting on the couch as he tried to catch his breath. "It's fine, want help or do you think you have it under control?"

"We're fine but thanks for asking anyway." Jocelyn said.

Daniel sighed, turning away as he climbed the stairs to their- Jocelyn's room now, technically since he had managed to find an apartment on short notice. Moving day would be in the next couple days or so. He had to pause for a moment on the landing, trying to catch his breath before continuing. Once, he could have made this climb without being winded, but it seemed like those days were long past him now.

He knelt in front of his suitcase, rummaging through the clothing to the very bottom of the case where his kit was. Indecision about what to take or leave behind in the case of running away had nearly stilled him in packing but in the end, regardless of its dubiously intended purpose, he hadn't been able to leave the 'gift' behind. Alain was still his father, however else he felt about the man. Even if the intended purpose of the little medical set lay more in the way of anatomy lessons and not for any true medical use.

A set of scalpels, some suture thread and scissors as well as a couple needles specially designed for sewing the cuts up afterwards. Jocelyn's expression was difficult to read but he seemed to appreciate the gift of the kit as it was set down by his elbow.

Haydee briefly made an appearance in the kitchen but left just as quickly once the frozen corpse of a rat was defrosted on an old sewing mat. From the retching noise coming from the locked bathroom, she hadn't expected a literal diagram to be made of a dead pet's corpse. Daniel did his best to ignore the shame he felt at causing that reaction and let the little group gather around him as he pulled on the gloves.

The first cut parted fur and flesh to show what was underneath. Brittney leaned closer, watching in fascination as he pointed out and removed the lungs and heart, placing the small organs next to Mouse's corpse. The stomach and intestines were next as the three made notes on pieces of paper, labeling each on the diagram as he explained their location and purpose.

Brittney filled out the last line on the rat diagram before putting the sheet back into her binder. "Easiest eighty I'll ever get, Jocelyn, Thanks."

He nodded, trying not to let disquiet show as he stitched the cuts back up over the hollow shell that had been Mouse's internal organs. She might have called this fun and him a better teacher than the man at school, but he was trying to erase the memory of Alain giving his brother the same lessons at fifteen and expecting better than a ninety in that class. "What are you going to do with that lesson?"

She gave him a brief, hurt look. "I want to be a doctor, Jocelyn. Help people or animals or something. You might not be as happy about the lessons your dad taught you but they're useful."

That was something of a relief that she wanted to put his lesson to good use, to help people instead of using the miniature class as a way to hurt or wound another. "That's nice,"

Haydee came back a few minutes later, pale but recovered from her illness. "Is it over? I mean, I don't mind you helping your classmates, but your anatomy lesson was... very thorough. It was creepy, honestly. Even knowing in retrospect what the family was like."

"Believe me, I know it's not what most people learn after school," Jocelyn said dryly. "How's Daniel? I haven't seen him since he dropped his kit off for me. Last I saw, he was still carrying boxes out to the car."

"In the living room, catching his breath, I think," Haydee twisted the engagement ring around her finger with a sigh before her mother called her upstairs.

Jocelyn tucked the notes back into his binder, getting up

from his seat. "Thanks. Daniel? Need help loading the last boxes into your car?"

"I'd like that," Daniel looked down at the long sleeve shirt and sweatpants he wore as pajamas, one hand resting lightly over his chest.

Jocelyn knelt, hauling one of the cardboard boxes onto his knees before standing. "Oof, what's in this one? I didn't think we had more than a suitcase worth of stuff with us."

Though maybe with the time they'd spent here, things had crept in over the time. "I'll take this for you. Just rest."

It scared him to see how thin, tired his brother had become over the past few weeks, mirroring their mother's decline before the cancer claimed her life. "I wish you would let me help, Dani…"

Either with his illness or with the wedding plans. There was still no telling when that would happen, but it was some-where in the future. Daniel wasn't the kind of guy to leave a girlfriend or fiancée at the altar. He turned away, heading back into the house. "Call me when you get there. And take it carefully, I heard there was ice on the highway."

"I will," Daniel pulled his jacket on, accepting the keys Jocelyn offered him. "And thank you."

It didn't take long to transport his boxes to the fully furnished apartment, pay the first month's rent to the landlord with an apology for not making it an actively lived in home before he was left deciding what to take with him to the hospital and what to leave behind. And to ward it against any potential invaders with a thin line of salt by the threshold of the door.

With luck, the salt alone would be enough to protect the space or act as a warning. There was no power in the little rite this time, nothing he could afford to shed blood for anyway.

From the apartment to the hospital only took about twenty minutes, fifteen minutes longer to check in and acknowledge Persephone Sotaira before he was sitting, shoulders slumped, on the edge of the bed in his room. This was the last place he wanted to be, anemia notwithstanding.

His last memory before he drifted off to sleep that night, was the heartbroken look Haydee had given him hours earlier as she had helped him load the last box into the trunk of his car and watched him turn the corner of the street before the taillights vanished from her sight. But it was better this way, wasn't it? Safer for her and for Jocelyn if they spent the next couple weeks apart.

If in the unlikely event, family was hunting them, they'd only find him, not his brother or fiancée. Their lives were worth more than his, as ill as he was.

Divination was a worthless art under the best of circumstances, so easily fooled or misdirected by blood and its owner being in two different places but from time to time, it was the only tool available when tracking a runaway cousin, or in the old days, a slave. Delphine had known something of the skill and passed it down to her children and grandchildren before they in turn taught it to their children just in case something so lacking in immediate use came in handy. Jared closed his eyes, sitting cross legged in the hotel room's living room, a pencil in one hand and a map spread out on top of a hard surface. He was closer than he had been in days but it was the matter of sorting out the messy tangle of lives and paths around him to focus on the one he wanted more than anything else.

Daniel had been in Augusta for a little over a weekend and then vanished out of range, now it seemed that his cousin was back, though the trail was thin, weaker than it had been before. Less easily traced through a sympathetic bond. That meant something but he wasn't sure what, nor did he particularly care after the first attempt at tracking had ended at the door to a shop known for its unmentionables. He'd burned the place down and watched the fire as it consumed the building from across the street. It would have been a waste to use his magic on it so he had simply resorted to gasoline and a lighter for that one.

Jared frowned at the unexpected itch in the back of his mind and shook it off in an attempt to continue the search for his wayward cousin but the sense of... power remained, persistent and irritating. This wasn't Daniel, it lacked the right scent or sense of his cousin's wasted gift but whatever or whoever it was, had several times the power. And was well worth investigating even if he had to abandon the hunt for his cousin for the time being.

He sighed, tossing the pencil onto the map and standing, stretching out the ache of sitting for two or so hours on the floor before reaching for his coat and gloves. It seemed that this unknown stranger took precedence over Daniel. At least for now.

The newcomer wasn't hard to find or had deliberately let him seek them out. Jared took the dark-haired man in with a snort, noting the plain gray shirt, jeans and as strange as it was, lack of shoes despite the icy temperature outside. "Interesting, either you're insane or you simply don't care about frostbite and losing a few toes to cold. Which is it?"

"I'll let you guess," The man's voice was tinged with a noticeable Russian accent, fair hair loose to his midback. Not a local though his English was well spoken enough.

Jared smiled coolly, regarding the stranger. "Like that, friend? I think I can guess at who or rather what you are. Unlike my wayward cousin, I have some belief in the ancient spirits. So, tell me, are you as easily bound within a circle as Uncle Alain's stories say?"

The man snarled softly, eyes flickering wolf amber for a split second.

It only made him laugh to see the brief loss of control evident in the warning growl. "Divination may have failed to find Daniel. Yet. But I will eventually, I only wonder what will happen if I kill that body of yours. Sieh, is it?"

His smile turned from cool to something uglier now, more of a sardonic smirk than anything warm or relaxed. "Certainly, it didn't fail to provide me your name. You're far from your land and nature in this city, spirit. Not as strong as you could be outside of a place built from concrete and steel."

Sieh blurred, moving faster than the human eye could follow and he laughed despite the stars that formed upon the back of his head connecting with the brick wall of the alley behind him. "So that's how its going to be?"

Sieh's voice was low, made inhuman by the subtle shift of his vocal cords to whatever shape was his natural born one. "Still strong enough to freeze your lungs or choke you with ice before you had a chance to bind me, pup."

Jared snorted, contemptuous. "Strong enough, maybe but not so focused as you might have been otherwise. It distracts you, hurts you to linger in a human city for more than a few days, yes?"

The pressure of Sieh's arm against his throat lessened and he met the ancient spirit's gaze for a moment, long enough to pull the sheathed knife from his waist and drive it into Sieh's midsection, twisting the blade hard enough to slice through liver and kidneys, to do irreparable damage while making it a slow death. "Let me make your death a little longer then. I can't destroy you for good, that's beyond any human witch or shaman but I can make you suffer as your body fails on you. I wonder how long it'll take your chosen form to die."

Sieh snarled, sinking to his knees with one arm pressed against his middle, black blood staining the gray of his ruined shirt and shirt sleeve. "As if I'd give that to you,"

"Ah," Jared dropped a knee next to him, draping an arm over Sieh's shoulders in a mockery of friendship. "I doubt you would have a choice if I bound you to that circle I mentioned. You would have no choice but to obey me and with your power in my control, I could easily hunt down my cousin. I daresay you could follow any scent, any weakening blood trail without much effort."

Sieh's voice was thin, tight with pain as he spoke. "I'd never give you that chance, human. And you forget that a knife once unsheathed can be used against you."

Jared drew back with a laugh that turned into a string of foul expletives as his hand closed on empty air and as the spirit put the hunting knife across his throat, slashing deep enough to be fatal. More dark blood stained Sieh's throat and shirt collar as he- it went to all fours and shifted to a smoke pale wolf. One that proved to be as insubstantial to the touch as the mist it resembled before it faded away.

He was alone in the alley now and he'd lost his best chance of tracking his cousin unless he got another small sample of Daniel or Jocelynn's blood to use. That seemed... unlikely at best. And one credit card transaction was only enough to narrow down the location to Augusta itself. Daniel was too careful when it came to leaving a paper or cyber trail. "Damn it!"

His knuckles came away raw, bloody from the punch delivered to the brick wall. The strike did a little to clear his head. "You won't be able to hide forever, Daniel."

CHAPTER TWENTY

The trips to and from Augusta were taking their toll on her but they were worth it if meant seeing Daniel, even if only for a few hours at a time. She'd made the trip twice since he had gone into the hospital, leaving as soon as school let out and coming back to Calais on Sundays.

This was the third trip since Daniel had moved out and the first one that Jocelyn had asked to come along with her. She had agreed reluctantly, worried about his reaction. Last week's trip had been harrowing, coupled with an argument with a nurse who hadn't been convinced by her explanation of being Daniel's fiancée. He looked thin, dark circles under his eyes, and she had noticed new bruising on his arms. New to her at the time anyway, they had faded from black to an ugly purplish-blue in between her trips. Marks left behind by the IV needle. "You don't have to do this, Jocelyn."

Jocelyn fidgeted with the mask covering his mouth and nose, holding his hands out under the hand sanitizer dispenser before rubbing the liquid into them. "You're family,"

"I know, but..." She dropped to a knee in front of him,

looking at Jocelyn in the eye. "Daniel's not how you remembered him two weeks ago. Some of his medicine doesn't look like pills. It's given through a IV now."

"I remember," Jocelyn looked down at his runners. "I might have been little when mom died but it isn't hard to remember everything she went through. I was eight, Daniel was sixteen. We've seen this before. You don't have to hide anything from me."

He turned away, pausing just long enough at the hospital room door to slip the mask over his mouth and nose and ignore the quarantine sign pasted beneath the patient records. Haydee stayed a step or two behind him, grateful she had decided against makeup today. The sight of Daniel like this would have made her lightly applied mascara run. He was just as thin as she had told his brother, exhaustion barely hidden on his face, the wrist where his allergy alert bracelet and the paper band rested was little more than skin and bone. "How are you feeling?"

Daniel slumped against the pillow, averting his gaze from the IV needle placed and taped into his arm. "Like everything hurts. I've thrown up three times already this morning."

Jocelyn hesitated, crept forward a step or two and put a plastic wrapped pair of gingersnap cookies on the bed before he retreated. "I brought cookies,"

"Thanks," Daniel's smile was wan though. "I don't think the nurses would approve of you smuggling cookies in here."

"What they won't know, won't hurt them." Haydee looked over her shoulder and discretely dropped the treat into the bedside table drawer. "Is there anything else I can do?"

He shifted position and winced, sucking in a breath before the pain left his face. "Our text messages, have you had a chance to talk with the priest yet?"

The wedding plans. Haydee sat gingerly on the edge of

the room's only chair. "Father Allan wasn't sure at first, but I think I convinced him to go through with it. I told him about your illness if that's alright. He was the one you went to for that little confession moment earlier, right?"

It might have been, he'd never asked for the priest's name at the time though he had looked to the man for advice about Jocelyn's conflicting feelings. "I think so. What did he say?"

"He asked if marriage was something that we both wanted," Haydee said. "I mean, you're Catholic, I'm not. You wanted it in a church. He... asked me if I was willing to convert to do this."

She bit down on her lower lip. "Let's say I'm... considering it if means getting rid of another barrier in front of us."

Daniel lifted his free hand as though to brush a lock of her hair out her eyes before dropping it back to the pale blue coverlet. "I'd never ask something you weren't comfortable with, Haydee."

"I know," She looked away. "I'm not comparing two different things together here; gender identity isn't the same as struggling with the decision to get baptized but it's still a big step for me. Other than that, I think I convinced him that we don't need a year to make a decision about getting married."

Her eyes met his for a moment. "Have they found a matching donor yet?"

"It's only been two weeks," Daniel reached for the glass of water on the tray table and took a swallow of it, coughing as it went down the wrong tube. "Persephone said it could take at least a couple months, six weeks if there is a donor to begin with."

"At a minimum, spring," Haydee sighed. "Well, at least that's one less thing to worry about but I'm still scared by how sick you are."

He quieted, twisting the silver band around his finger and wishing that it wasn't as loose as it had become these days. Two weeks shouldn't have cost him a few pounds in weight but apparently, they had. "Honestly, so am I. Between the headaches and the throwing up into a basin from the medicine, I haven't been keeping much down."

Haydee's unhappiness was apparent but Jocelyn didn't seem to notice it as she shooed the eighteen-year-old boy out of the room. "Mind picking up a hot chocolate or coffee or something for me?"

It was a long moment before she spoke again. "I hope this doesn't happen but- but have you considered what'll happen if this, uhm, kills you?"

He had, and he'd had a few talks with his doctor over it as well. "Unfortunately, yeah. The anemia probably won't kill on its own, that's more likely to be an infection or the donor's transplant rejects my body."

She swallowed, looking around the room for a clean coffee mug or glass and failing to find one. "That was one of Father Allan's worries, the…"

"The funeral before the wedding?" He couldn't help the slightly bitter laugh at that and regretted it when Haydee flinched. "Sorry. You don't have to think about this, I have nothing but time to dwell on the situation. I hope nothing comes of this, but I've been on the phone when I can, talking with people. I want to give… you custody of Jocelyn and I've been fighting the bank woman in trying to get your name added to my account. At least that way, you won't have to struggle with student debt anymore."

She tried for a smile of her own though it wobbled and faded. "You sure that stress won't hurt your chances for getting better?"

"Better stressed than bored," Daniel tugged tiredly at the

paper bracelet on his wrist and lay back against what was frankly, a pathetic excuse for a pillow. "I'm starting to lose track of the days in here."

His request went unsaid, but she seemed to guess at it regardless, finally standing as a nurse walked inside the room, casting Haydee a dirty look for any perceived germs she had brought with her. Daniel sighed, looking towards the woman. "It's alright, we kept our distance and she's my fiancée."

The nurse snorted but cleared the abandoned 'breakfast' onto her cart and wheeled it out for disposal, calling over her shoulder as she left. "And you should be resting, Daniel."

Haydee reached for him and caught herself, flushing awkwardly. "See you again next week, I guess."

"Yeah," Truth be told, he was more tired than he had dared to let on and even a couple hours sleep would be better than a night interrupted by pain or the tugging of the IV needle in his arm. "Next week,"

He sat up, wincing again at the dull ache in his joints but he needed to brighten the already stressed visit. "I know I'm not supposed to know what the dress looks like but if you could text pictures of what you want for your wedding dress, I'm... well, desperate for any sort of news here."

She smiled shyly, expression going pink. "I'll send you three of my favorites but you'll have to guess which one I settled on when you see me at the altar. I'm not telling."

Haydee lingered at the door, one hand on the doorframe. "Just for the record, I don't care what you decide to wear on that day. It could be jeans and a dress shirt, and I would be happy with the result."

Maybe she would be, he was going to try to do better than wearing a pair of jeans to the wedding day. "You're so..."

"Informal?" She smirked, teasing him.

"I was going to say casual but that works too," Daniel said.

Haydee laughed and ducked out of sight, calling for Jocelyn until she was out of earshot.

Sleep was always hard to find these days and when he did manage to get an hour or two out of a nap, dreams didn't come with it. Usually, he was woken by the nurse or doctor's gentle touch and a word or by nausea and joint pain from the medicine.

This time it was the doctor's hand on his shoulder that forced him into alertness. Daniel winced, rubbing his free hand across gritty feeling eyes. "What now?"

If Persephone Sotaira had anything to say about his irritation, she kept it to herself and the pale blue medical mask over her mouth and nose. "I heard what was said about your fear and your faith. There is a small chapel next to the patient lounge if you need a moment or two to pray."

He snorted, lifting the arm with the IV still in it. "Not much I can do with this here, can I?"

Her mouth thinned but he couldn't read her feelings behind the expression. "I never knew you to give up, Daniel. You want to protect your brother, yes?"

"Yes," He flushed, feeling the barest hint of warmth on his cheeks. "But..."

"No buts," Persephone looked away. "Whether you believe it or not at the moment, you're a warrior, Daniel. Had you been born two thousand years ago; you would have fought any illness-"

Her mouth quirked in something that could almost have been a smile despite her reserve. "Or the gods themselves to protect your family. I knew a young man like you once in Greece, you and he could have been kin yourselves for the similarity between your faces."

Daniel forced himself to sit, drawing one knee up to his chest. "What was this guy's name?"

Persephone lifted a shoulder in a slight shrug. "Not all mysteries need an answer, Daniel but if you must know, I was thinking of Philoctetes. He fled, in his own way rather than betray a friend or family."

Apparent physical appearance aside then, there was less in common between them than Persephone thought. Daniel snorted but accepted the jeans the doctor tossed onto his bed. "That sounds more like a story meant to make me feel better than truth. He didn't want to betray a friend; I've done nothing but that when I ran away from New Orleans in the middle of the night."

She arched a delicate eyebrow at that. "Then what was your choice of Calais? If not exile after a fashion? You hate the Maine cold according to my niece's mention of you."

He sighed, hating her logic. "It still doesn't make it anything more than a good story, Doctor."

It was awkward pulling the jeans on one handed and even trickier navigating the IV pole from its corner by the bed but somehow, he managed it. "I don't suppose you know anything more about that donor yet?"

Persephone skimmed the patient records at the foot of the bed before placing the clipboard back where it belonged. "I came to speak with you on that. There is a match and pending a few more tests, we should be able to do the transplant soon."

He sensed rather than heard her hesitation in the words. "You're still worried?"

She looked away. "In truth, yes. Even a good match can have minor differences, enough for the donor tissue to reject your body. This is a high-risk procedure, Daniel."

High risk or not, he had to take the chance it meant for his life. "We're running out of options here and if this is the best one that I have, I'll do it."

"Very well," Her voice was cool, professional now. "I'll speak with the specialist this afternoon and we can begin getting things prepared for the transplant."

Daniel swallowed, sitting down on the bed harder than intended. "I'm going to have to go through chemo whether I want it or not?"

"I'm afraid so," Sympathy briefly crossed her face. "However, you will be able to return to your job if you so choose to. Ideally, though, you will stay in Augusta until it comes time for the transplant."

Daniel pulled a zip up hoodie over his shoulders, leaving one sleeve hanging limp, loose at his side rather than mess around with the IV needle and tube in his arm. "I- alright but I'm scared, honestly. Mom went through it and it cost her her hair. I was the one who ended up cutting it off for her."

The look she gave him was brief, just as unreadable as the one before it. "Not everyone loses their hair, Daniel."

"I know," Not everyone did but he wasn't optimistic about the prospect either. "Luck willing, Haydee'll get her spring wedding. What else do I need to worry about? It's already anemia so my blood counts are already low."

"There's still hope, Daniel," Persephone said.

He lifted his gaze to look at her and shook his head. "Doesn't often feel like that when I've been sick for over two weeks and throwing up two or three times every other day because of the medicine."

She quieted, moving to the side. "I think the hospital chapel will be good for you, little one. Surely it won't hurt to attempt finding a little peace somewhere?"

Maybe, maybe not but he was already dressed in a manner of speaking, wearing the jeans if not a shirt of his own. Daniel sighed, looking down at the pale blue short sleeved pajama top. "Alright, I'll try."

At the very least, it couldn't hurt.

The small chapel space was empty when he entered, noting the basin of water at the entrance and the paintings mounted to the walls. They weren't the stained-glass windows of the church in Calais or in New Orleans, but for a place enclosed by a brick and concrete exterior, this would have to do for now though it didn't leave him with as much peace as it might have done in another place. He closed his eyes briefly, murmuring the familiar prayer under his breath before crossing himself and sitting in one of the small wooden pews. "Whatever I did against you, I'm sorry for it. It was wrong and I failed, I should have been there or done better to protect my brother and if you'll forgive me, I'll try to do better if you're willing to help. Just... have mercy on me, please. Help me get through this."

"There's no need for the prayer,"

Daniel started, the words of the Salve Regina slipping from his thoughts as he turned to see the dark-skinned stranger sitting behind him. "Maybe not for you but it usually helps me."

The man smiled sadly, running a hand over his bare scalp. "I spoke badly. I meant that you don't have anything to be contrite about or for the Salve Regina prayer. You did nothing wrong."

Daniel drew back bracing himself on the IV pole as he paused long enough to catch his breath. "And how would you know that? No offense meant but you don't look much like a doctor, a visitor or a Catholic."

His new 'friend' briefly touched the copper pendant at his throat. "Maybe not but I'm familiar with the holy texts. As for knowing whether or not you did anything wrong- you didn't, your guilt is needless. You're doing all you can to protect your family, I'm sure."

Daniel sighed, sitting down on the wooden bench. "You're better at psychology than you look like, I'll give you that but I'm a little reluctant to trust strangers who say there's no need for prayer and refuse to give their names."

The man offered him another smile, this one shorter lived than the first and resigned. "Rashid, at least for the time being."

"For the time being?" He couldn't help the skepticism at that part of the answer. "What does an…Arabic man know about Christianity?"

That earned him a brief laugh as Rashid leaned back, draping an arm over the back of the oak bench. "More than any western born man or woman, I think. Not everyone in the Middle East is Muslim. And I'm Egyptian, not Saudi. I thought you might want a more honest talk than anything your doctor could offer you, as well as a conversation that didn't involve speaking to an empty room."

Daniel bristled at that before forcing himself to relax. "Who said the room was empty?"

Rashid shrugged carefully. "Once again, I meant no offense by my remark. Just that any of His answers might come hours or days later than hoped for."

He leaned forward, resting a hand on the top of the pew in front of him. "If it helps, I know a thing or two about fear and trying to protect family. I lost my father, two of my younger sisters and kin not tied through a close blood relation."

His mouth tightened at whatever he remembered. "And almost my own life before then, at my father's hands. Family can be difficult, Daniel. Particularly when you don't feel like you're good enough to save them. You failed no-one and you won't fail them either unless you decide His or her mercy for yourself. Whatever God or god is out there, I'm sure they'll be kind to you."

Daniel opened his mouth to speak and shut it again, at a loss for how to answer Rashid's words.

Rashid graced him with a wry smile. "Let's just say I've had some time and a religious education of my own over the years. Just not one solely confined to Christianity, Daniel. I've also been a soldier in my time as well. It's... given me a lot of time to consider the nature of faith and mercy."

He stood, putting a gentle hand on Daniel's shoulder before he could object or pull away from the Egyptian man's touch. "But-"

Anything he could have said was lost in the gentle warmth washing the joint ache from his body. Daniel swallowed staring up at Rashid. "You...?"

"No," Rashid's voice was dry but kind for all of the irony in it. "Best just call me a psychic. Not unlike you but not with the same gift. I learned my own lessons in anatomy and biology years ago but was taught a less... destructive path."

He dropped his hand back to his side, taking the few strides to the chapel's door. "You're far better than you give yourself credit for, but you still have a lot to learn about forgiving yourself and holding yourself to an impossible standard, Daniel."

Daniel dropped his gaze to the scuffed hardwood floor under his runners even as his free hand closed around the leather cord and copper pendant that had somehow been placed in his hoodie pocket. He frowned, lifting it to eye level and let it dangle, studying the rounded loop placed where a single bar would have been on a crucifix. "Wait, Rashid."

And again, because he couldn't tell which direction was more likely for the Egyptian man to have gone. "Rashid?"

It hadn't been that long; he should have seen Rashid's

retreating back as he turned a likely corner but the hallway was as empty as if he hadn't been there in the first place. As if they'd never had a conversation in the small chapel. "Rashid?"

It was Persephone who answered him once she dismissed the nurse with a brief gesture. "Did you get your answer?"

That was hard to say for sure. Daniel looked away, hoping for a sign or hint of Rashid in the meantime. "Honestly, I don't know. I'm not even sure how he knew my name without asking me, but he helped, I think. At least the joint ache's gone for a little while now."

He let out a resigned sigh. "Guess you were halfway right; some mysteries don't need an answer but people kind of like them. I don't suppose you saw anyone calling himself Rashid leave here, did you?"

She shook her head, a little furrow creasing between her eyebrows. "I'm afraid not. I spent most of my life in Greece and Athens until recently. My path never crossed with anyone named that though Hecate may have. Why? What did you talk about?"

"He said I was too hard on myself sometimes," Daniel looked away. "Maybe he's right about that part but he also called himself a psychic, a healer."

His attempt at a smile at his own expense was short lived. "Everyone says they appreciate my faith in things, but it isn't blind or literal to the bible. I just…"

He trailed off, running a tired hand through his hair. "Jesus of Nazareth and the one in the bible probably weren't the same man. It's just…"

"Odd," Persephone was watching him with an unreadable expression on her face. "I may not have lived among the Middle Eastern tribes, but I can assure you your… guest was not him."

Her gaze drifted downwards to settle pointedly on the leather cord and pendant half hidden in his hand. "That's no Christian symbol you hold, Daniel. It's Egyptian, an ankh."

Something shadowed crossed her face at that, a mixture of sadness and something else not so easily defined. "It means life, I suggest you hold onto that until its owner asks for it back. Might bring you luck despite the circumstances."

He needed medical help, not luck or hope but he wasn't going to offend Persephone or her beliefs by rejecting the apparent gift. "Maybe. Whatever he said or did, I don't feel like going back to bed again. I'm well enough to get a little walk down to the cafeteria."

Persephone's nose wrinkled slightly at the mention of the place. "I'm not certain it's my place but let me get a small thing from a local deli. You might find it more appealing than spaghetti with a meat sauce of an unknown origin. Just wait in the patient lounge, I shouldn't be more than an hour here."

Daniel glanced away, relieved despite himself. Truth be told, the cafeteria fare was pathetic and anything that could have been brought in from a deli or small grocery store would have been more appealing. "Fair,"

CHAPTER TWENTY-ONE

The bleach and cleaner smell made him want to sneeze and rub at his eyes, if it wasn't for the too big rubber gloves on his hands but the bathroom work needed to be done. Jocelyn bit down on his lower lip, scrubbing hard at a stubborn soap spot on the counter before it vanished under the sponge. This mattered if Dani was ever going to come home again. Things needed to be sterilized as best they could be for him.

"Jocelyn?"

Haydee's voice made him freeze, dropping the toilet bowl cleaner into the water. "Uhm…"

She held a copy of the room key up, sighing as she knelt next to him. "It isn't really your job to clean the bathroom and make the bed yourself. My parents will do that while we're at school."

He quieted and sniffled, blowing into a face cloth she offered him. "Have to grow up at some point, right? Why not now, maybe? I found a couple decent recipes that fit the vegetarian bill and won't trigger my allergies. I want to try them tonight."

She sighed, pulling him close and wrapping an arm around his shoulders. "I'm just as worried as you are, Jocelyn but you're still only eighteen. At least take a couple more years before deciding to grow up."

"Dani doesn't have a couple years," Jocelyn said.

"I know," Haydee looked away, glancing down at the tile floor they were sitting on. "Good job on mopping the floor though, Jocelyn. Most eighteen-year-olds wouldn't even bother with more than the sink."

"Not like most," He wrapped his arms around his legs, averting his gaze. "Mom died, my sister's in an institution and Dani's really sick. Kind of have to learn, right? I'm eighteen but I'm not legal yet. And I don't have a job to afford rent on some shit rattrap of an apartment."

"Yeah," She sighed, flipping through her phone's calendar and considered the money she'd set aside. Most of it would go towards paying off her debt but there was a couple hundred she could use for Christmas shopping. "C'mon, if you promise no more credit card fraud in an attempt at helping me and Daniel, I'll take you shopping. Maybe you can tell me what he likes as presents?"

She frowned, glancing at Jocelyn. "What does your family do for Christmas anyway? All I know here is that we like to spend too much money and there's a big ugly race for the latest tech toys."

Jocelyn shrugged. "Text Dani? He knows more 'bout what grandma and grandpa do in Paris."

Haydee managed a weak laugh at that. "Are you making fun of his accent because it isn't completely American?"

"Maybe?" He peered up at her through his glasses. "Dani doesn't sound completely Louisianan, doesn't bother to try, I think."

She stood, helping him to his feet. "I don't know about

that, but he did tell me once that he spent summers and winter vacations in Paris with your grandparents. I think that might have had some effect on his accent. He can't completely help it."

Their first stop at the mall was to the food court, just long enough for her to send a text or two off to Daniel and wait the fifteen minutes it took for him to answer. Jocelyn picked at the cheese pizza slice in front of him as tinny music sounded from the speakers. "What do you think he'd like?"

Jocelyn shrugged, dropping the pizza crust onto the plastic tray. "Dad got him that combat knife when he was eighteen, and the scalpel kit. Also, a car – the old Lexus he used to drive before Dad traded it in for his Audi."

"Anything a little less morbid or pricey?" Haydee asked dryly.

Jocelyn ran through the mental list of things Daniel might like and bit down on his lower lip. "How about a memory box? He can put things inside it for later. Or a laptop backpack?"

His expression brightened. "Oh, a coffee cup as a stocking stuffer. You can wrap it up instead."

The memory box felt like the best potential gift option of the three he'd listed. "What do you want?"

Haydee looked over her shoulder, wistful like, at a dress shop before turning away. "Maybe, but I don't know if it's in my budget."

"Oh," Jocelyn bit down on his lower lip, following her gaze. The wedding planning even if he wasn't completely a part of them. That was the priest's job apparently. And since he'd promised not to steal Dani's credit card again. "Maybe you could try a few on, just to see what they're like."

She still hesitated and he chewed on his lip again before tugging her after him, rummaging through the layers of silk and other less well-known fabrics. One was too pink, another in a strapless style that Daniel wouldn't like. A third that was too frilly and an alarming shade of yellow. "Uhm…"

He looked back at Haydee and went back to his digging through the hanging gowns. "This one?"

It was a lot of cloth to bundle in his arms, but he carried it back to her as if it was a baby. "Please?"

Haydee swallowed, reaching out for the ivory cloth, tempted by it and grimaced at the price tag. "Six hundred?"

Jocelyn felt his shoulders slump. "No? I guess I'll go put it back then."

"Wait," Haydee sighed, holding the dress against her body as she looked into the mirror mounted on the wall. It wasn't a strapless gown at least; Daniel would consider that a welcome plus if he had been here to see it. And she did like how the lace straps made a Y shape at the base of her neck. "Help me with the zipper?"

She was counting on Jocelyn's physical presentation not to cause questions though it was also a little unfair to him as well. Who outside his family would see him as the boy he was and not the girl he looked like? Certainly not the sales-woman hovering a few feet away. Jocelyn pulled the delicate little tab up and took a step back as she gave an experimental little spin in the ivory dress. "Pretty,"

"Isn't it?" Haydee smoothed her hands over the skirt, already half in love with the gown despite the price tag attached to it. "But I can't afford this one and Daniel might have few reservations about how much of my shoulders it shows. He asked for modest."

"Huh," Jocelyn took that under advisement and walked away, browsing the racks nearby before vanishing out of sight.

The saleswoman was quick to take advantage of his

disappearance, swooping in like a big like bird of prey like creature. "Your sister has good tastes."

Haydee flushed, looking away. "Oh, well, she's not my sister- she's my boyfriend's and she's a boy. It's complicated but thanks."

The woman regarded her warily for a moment before offering a half-hearted attempt at a smile. "Well, they always say that the gay boys are always better at finding dresses for women than any straight man. I'll be around if you need more help."

Jocelyn's return came back just as the older woman was leaving, his arms full of what looked like more ivory lace and silk. "These two?"

"One minute," She put the first dress on its hanger and snapped a quick photo of it with her phone, taking in both front and back for later. Daniel would want to see this even if he couldn't be here in person. "Okay, now for the other two."

The second of the two dresses was definitely more modest than the first with its Y neck pattern and cheaper but she blanched a little when she got a good look at the open back. While it covered more of her shoulders, it didn't leave her back to the imagination though the slim line of the skirt appealed to her. Haydee hesitated, torn. "Will Daniel like this one? I mean…the back shows a lot…"

Jocelyn blinked, looking at it wistfully. "Dani won't care, maybe. He likes you, not what you wear and it's pretty."

"Number three?" She put the lace sweetheart dress into her maybe pile and turned to the one she hadn't tried on yet.

Of all the ones Jocelyn had found, it was the most modest in its bodice, a V cut and short sleeved with a lace back to it but the long slit from her hip to the floor. "Uhm…"

Jocelyn's nose was wrinkled in either disappointment or unhappiness. "Nope, Dani's not going to go for you showing your legs off like that. Back maybe if you wear a scarf but not so much down there."

He glanced away again and ran off, careful not to step on any hem with his wet runners before coming back with one more. "This one?"

It fit with Dani's preference for modest and ivory as well as being long sleeved while still leaving Haydee's figure to be seen. She looked doubtful for a moment, holding it up and taking in the deep V that left her back visible. "Are you sure?"

He nodded, barely daring to breathe. "Nobody'll see your back with the veil over your head."

If she objected to that, he didn't hear her – already across the shop and biting down on a fingernail as he debated the veil length. It couldn't be too long, no one needed a tripping risk, and the wedding was supposed to be a small affair with Haydee's parents and the cat involved. "Mhm…"

Maybe a headband would be better instead? But then Dani took faith and marriage seriously. Jocelyn looked over his shoulder and gently pulled the nearest midlength veil free before bringing it to Haydee. Her saleswoman could handle to the arrangement and fitting, he was only the hunter in the dress search.

A formal dress was gathered up soon after that, something she could wear during the likely small reception. Dark blue with sleeves.

The small area of the shop devoted to wraps and jackets distracted him, bringing back to mind the first of the three dresses he'd insisted Haydee try on. Maybe a lace jacket or shrug or something? He grabbed one at random, hoping it would suit the dress he wanted to see her in. "Miss. Haydee, Miss, Haydee!"

True, adding the accessory meant that they'd have to

ASH

consider something strapless and against Daniel's wishes but maybe the lacy look would cover that up and make it look more modest than it was. But then his brother would get the white he'd asked of Haydee. "So many things…"

Her uncertainty turned to relief as she spotted him. "Where'd you go?"

He held up the lacy little jacket on its hanger, comparing it to the light blush pink dress off the clothes hook. "That one, and this."

"It's strapless-"

"Nope," He wasn't going to let her refuse this one, not when they'd already spent over an hour trying to find something that satisfied everyone in the small party. "This one."

She sighed, rubbing a hand over her eyes as she checked the price tag. "Well, at least it's under two hundred this time and not a pure white."

Jocelyn grinned sheepishly and went back, retrieving the dark blue reception gown he'd found for her. The little lacy jacket wouldn't suit it, but he wasn't about to let her run out of the store without the dark blue sparkly number.

He waited, bouncing impatiently on the balls of his feet as she paid for the garments and garment bags to store them in and then caught at her hand where the engagement ring rested on her finger. "No pickpocketing here, Haydee. Dani used some of the time he said he was apartment hunting to get a wedding ring each. It's real, I didn't borrow his card this time."

Haydee let out a sigh of relief, though it was tinged with exasperation. "Did you drink coffee this morning or are you always this hard to keep up with on a normal day?"

Jocelyn slowed down, trying to restrain his anxiety. "Bet on the coffee because I don't know how much time Dani has

207

left and I want the wedding to go off as something everyone will remember."

"Years, I hope." Haydee sat down on a nearby bench, trying to arrange the two dress boxes, a shoe box and the shopping bag containing her new purchases into an order that let her carry them easier. "Your wedding planner skills better be great, or I might just take off to the registry office after all."

Thankfully, he seemed to be as true as his word on that as the saleswoman deposited the two small velvet boxes into the shoebox bag. "Want to peek?"

She was a little bit curious but worried as well. "Isn't there a rule against seeing the rings before the wedding day? Which I might add could still be months away yet. We haven't even gotten through Christmas yet and from what the priest said, it could be spring before the wedding actually happens."

"I don't think so?" Jocelyn blinked, nose wrinkling in concentration. "I think that's just for dresses, and you aren't showing Dani it until the day."

Haydee sighed again and frowned, distracted. "Wait, what are you planning to wear? And what's your role in this as the brother to the future husband?"

Jocelyn looked down, rubbing the hem of his t-shirt over the lenses of his glasses. "I think I'll have to suck it up and go as his sister for the wedding. It's just one night for that. Wear the dress and look girly for one night but I give you the rings when you're up at the altar, right? It's just for a few hours, I think I can tolerate wearing a dress for an evening."

"Oh," She was quiet for a long moment before pulling him into a hug. "It means a lot that you'd go against how you feel inside but it isn't necessary, Jocelyn. You don't have to wear the dress if you don't want to."

When they pulled away, her shirt was spotted with wetness and Jocelyn's glasses were blurry with tears again. He sat kicking a runner out in front of the bench. "Dani won't insist, no. He'd tell me to do what makes me comfortable, but he wants a church service and wedding. I- I'll wear the dress and go with Jocelynn for that time but there's still no boy to carry the ring, so I'll be doing that instead playing bridesmaid or flower girl."

So that was the ring bearer flower girl portion taken care of albeit in a rather unconventional blending of the two roles, but it still begged the question of who was going to be the bridesmaid and maid of honor in the wedding. Haydee groaned, pinching the bridge of her nose tiredly. "I don't have a female cousin or two leaping at the chance to participate in this. My parents were only children. What about you?"

Jocelyn hesitated, uncertainty and a bit of fear crossing his face. "My sister's in an institution, she can't come. There's Jared's sister, I think. Maybe. But Dani doesn't like her any more than he does our cousin or Dad. Asking her might just tell them where we are and Dani doesn't want to get them involved, protecting you- us."

"We'll think of something," Though she was at a loss for what exactly. If there were no eligible female attendants around. "Well, lucky this is supposed to be a small wedding. Let's just get this stuff home before the snowstorm hits and my parents freak out over the fact that I'm about to marry a Catholic in a church in just a few months."

She couldn't dwell on the immediate reaction to her news but she was dreading it regardless. "They always hoped I'd get married, but I think the general idea was going to be some nice… Wiccan boy from their circle, not a Louisianan born Catholic who turned out to be a real witch. Not that they know the last part. They'd really freak out if they knew his magic was more of a destructive psychic talent. Everything… will be alright. Just got to tell them I'm about to marry someone who may or may not survive his illness."

"Haydee?" Jocelyn was peering at her now, concern evident on his face.

"I'm fine," She took a breath and stood. "Better than I was, let's just go before we have to drive home in the middle of a snowstorm. I… have pictures of potential dresses to send Daniel, never mind that it's been picked out already."

"Really?" He sounded doubtful but reluctant to ask further. "Okay,"

Her mother looked dubiously at the boxes and bags in the living room. "What's all this for? You didn't win a lottery, did you?"

"No," Haydee sat down on the couch, rubbing at her shoulders tiredly. "Some of it is Christmas shopping, Little things for you, Dad, Daniel and Jocelyn."

Those were already wrapped and under the tree in the corner, except for the memory box which was still hidden in the trunk of her car. Everything else would remain unmentioned.

"Then… the dresses, the shoes and the lacy looking jacket?" Anna asked, sitting down next to her. "I've been to my share of Christmas parties and arranged them. You never struck me as that sort growing up. You once skipped a New Year's celebration to study for a test."

"That New Year's celebration involved a magic circle greeting to your goddess," Haydee said. "I would have taken any test over the Wiccan thing you believe in."

She looked down, twisting the engagement ring around her finger in her anxiety. "It's a... wedding dress and a dress for afterwards. Jocelyn thought that instead of a big reception thing, we'd go out to a nice restaurant instead. Daniel's really not up to dancing lately."

"Oh, honey," Her mother pulled her close, wrapping an arm around her shoulders. "So you... want to go through with this then? He's... well, the boy is Catholic."

"So?" Haydee glanced away. "That shouldn't matter to you. He's nice and I love him. Who cares about what he believes in? You're just as fond of him as I am and his faith never bothered you before."

Anna bit down on her lower lip, a flicker of hurt crossing her face before it passed. "Well, true, I admit but I never thought you would agree to marry him, as little as you like to have with religion and faith."

"This- he's different," Haydee sighed. "You were always worried that I wouldn't find anyone and that your only grand-child would be the family cat. Now that I have, you're concerned about his religious upbringing?"

"I'm worried about how quickly you're going into this," Anna's voice took on a sharper note. "You never were the impulsive one, not like your father and I. Now..."

Her tone softened and she sniffled, blowing into a tissue. "Are you... pregnant? Is this why you're planning things so soon?"

Haydee flushed pink, grip tightening on the hem of her faded university t-shirt. "Mom! No, I'm not pregnant. Daniel's not that kind of guy and even if I was, it would have been ten years ago with my last asshole boyfriend. He's never going to take advantage of me even if I asked him to do it. Besides, he's sick. Sex, and germs are kind of out of the ques-tion right now. If anything, I'm agreeing to this so that

Jocelyn doesn't have to declare whatever it is they call it, lawfully an adult when he's only eighteen."

"I see," Anna swallowed, crumpling the tissue up in her hands before dropping it into the nearby wastepaper bin. "Well... whatever else you need, I'll support you. Your father and I both will. Now, I expect we'll be meeting with his parents and family then?"

"No," Haydee winced as she bit the inside of her cheek. "He's... not really on good terms with his family, to be honest. They're kind of transphobic and he wanted Jocelyn to have a better chance away from them. It'll probably just be you two, Jocelyn, Malachi and whoever else Daniel thinks is a friend. He doesn't talk much about his life in New Orleans."

Her mother almost looked disappointed by that. "I'm sorry to hear that,"

Anna's hand folded over hers, warm, comforting and a reminder that there were still good things to look forward to. "At least he has good taste in engagement rings, I like the Celtic design he chose. It suits you."

"That was Jocelyn's idea at first," Haydee said. "But thanks, anyway. Mind helping me take this stuff up to my room. It's a lot and I'm tired."

She scrolled through her phone for text messages and barely managed to hide the smile as she read them. Daniel almost never used smileys in his answers so seeing one or two in response to her dress choices was a pleasant surprise. "Yeah, I miss you too. Hope you're feeling better soon."

Judging from his next answer; a little green smiley face, he wasn't feeling great. Haydee sighed, sweeping a strand of hair from her eyes and answered him. "Sorry about that. The smileys are just because you can't type anything out in full?"

His answer in turn took a full five minutes before it showed on her screen and she winced, covering it hastily.

"Yeah, I guess chemo makes you feel like shit. Can't swear in person but it sure as hell doesn't stop you over the phone."

She pocketed the phone and was asleep within minutes, not caring about its hard shape against her hip or that she hadn't bothered to get changed into the cotton tank top and pajama pants before then. There would be time later to deal with any messages or voice mails.

CHAPTER TWENTY-TWO

Crying wasn't something he usually let himself do, in front of other people or in privacy – Alain had discouraged anything that might hint at weakness as he had perceived it and so, he didn't let anything streak his face. Though his eyes burned with the tears either way. Jocelyn was at home, tucked up in bed with something that might have been the sniffles and a couple boxes of tissues, unable to visit this time.

"Hey," Haydee knocked on the door and entered, setting a box like object wrapped in red and silver paper, a bit of green ribbon tied around it. "At least the IV's out of your arm, does that mean you're getting better?"

"Depends on better," His voice was acidic, a moment before he flushed, running a hand through his hair. "I thought the medicine before was bad, this is worse, somehow."

She set the box on the foot of the bed. "We could always talk before. What changed, Daniel? Apart from the fact that you're looking on the little shaggy side."

He tightened his grip on the plastic cup, resisting the urge to throw it across the room. His hair had never been on the longer side for a guy but weeks without a haircut had left it just shy of his chin. His father never would have approved of the look. "It doesn't matter,"

"Hey," She slipped a hand over his, glancing at his face. "Whatever happens, I'm not going to give up or leave on you so we might as well talk now. And before you snap at me again, I washed and used hand sanitizer, short of leaving myself with chapped skin there, I'm as clean as I'm going to get. So... talk, please."

"Fine," He stood, steadying himself on the foot of the bed as dizziness threatened and subsided before looking into the bathroom mirror where a spiderwebbing crack showed itself. He'd thrown the hospital's ancient hairdryer at it several days earlier.

She traced lines delicately, looking back at him with a look of concern. It was an effort not to be reminded of similar but different damage done to his arms. The old scarring hidden underneath the sleeves of his pajama top. "Ouch, okay. What happened during the week I wasn't here?"

Daniel slumped on the toilet, passing his arm over his eyes. "I need your help."

Haydee bit down on her lower lip, taking both his hands in hers as she tasted something bitter in her mouth. "Anything, Daniel. You know me."

Behind the ugly taste in her mouth was fear. The past weeks had cost Daniel a pound or two of weight, she'd seen it in his wrists and hands, now the V-neck pajama top showed his collarbones against the cloth. "You haven't been keeping much down, have you. It's the chemo?"

He nodded, looking away from her. "Yeah."

"I'll help," She said. "Just tell me what to do."

Daniel held his hairbrush out, handle first. "Just help me get rid of this mess."

Haydee swallowed, accepting it like the weapon it almost was. "Okay,"

He sat on the floor as she knelt next to him, trying not to wince at the first brushstroke pulled a hank of dark brown hair free. When he looked up again, it was Haydee who was crying, wetness trailing down her cheeks. Daniel glanced away, taking her hand in his and trying not to notice the pallor of his skin against hers as he rubbed a thumb over the back of it. They were both naturally fair skinned but his skin against hers, made her look like she had the beginnings of her summer tan. "I can finish if you want me to."

She'd only managed to brush out the one hank after all.

"No," She took a breath, hiccupping a little. "I'm not much of a hairdresser but how do you... feel about military short? I think the drawer might have scissors or an electric shaver around."

"Good guess," Daniel gestured at the left most drawer under the sink and she pulled the thing out, plugging it into the wall socket though it stayed still, silent for now.

She ran the hairbrush through his hair, pulling loose strands free from it to form a small pile on the floor between them, occasionally sniffling. "Is this... how it was like for your mom? I mean when you did it for her?"

Daniel let out a breath, catching her hand in his for a moment. "She had red hair, so I guess so. She cried when I shaved it off for her. Wouldn't let Dad touch it or do the honor of cutting it off."

He sighed, wistful. He hadn't intended to dwell on his mother again, but it couldn't be helped under the circumstances. "She had the pretty kind of red, not carrot or ginger.

It was a nice auburn color. My sister was the same way, I got the brown from Alain, same as Jocelyn."

Haydee was quiet for the longest moment, save for the occasional quiet little whimper until she set the hairbrush down on the floor with a click of the wooden back against tile. "I have a compact mirror if you want to look at yourself before I turn the razor on."

He hesitated but accepted the small mirror she offered him before tightening his grip on the circle of glass. Haydee wasn't done yet but with as short as his hair was for now and the way it had been brushed out, it was a younger version of his father looking back at him. More innocent, kinder but still his father apart from the hazel eye color. That belonged to Delphine LaLaurie through her possession of his father's wife. Corinne had been red haired and green eyed, classically Irish according to his grandmother.

"Daniel?"

Haydee's voice intruded on his thoughts and he focused on her again, distracted. "What? Oh,"

He'd been holding onto the little mirror harder than intended and she was watching him anxiously. "Sorry,"

She squeezed her eyes shut tight for a moment, looking like she was about to steel herself for what was about to happen next. "Ready?"

"No, but I want this over with," Daniel said.

"Okay," She took a breath and pressed the razor's on button, filling the small bathroom space with a soft buzzing before she ran it up and over what little remained. Daniel stayed still; his expression so remote she couldn't tell what he was thinking about. It could have been anything or he was concealing grief or anger from her. However his magic worked, emotional control seemed to be a part of it. Lose a temper, lose control of whatever power a witch had. "Hope this is more of a short military cut and less a convict look."

His smile was unreadable. "You've been doing a bit of research, sounds like."

Haydee shrugged helplessly. "You'd be surprised at what a badly written romance set in the eighteenth century will tell you. Don't know if you would call that research exactly but at least I now know that short hair of any kind back then equalled someone off to the gallows or the hangman's noose. And then there's Malachi who might as well copied the hair-style from one of those books. He refuses to cut his hair shorter than chin length on a good day. Says short hair on a guy is a sign of his old age or ungentlemanly."

She turned the razor off, silencing its little buzz. "What do you think?" He glanced into the little mirror with a sigh, noting how short the new haircut was and how little remained under his touch. "It's fine, you did a good job even without experience."

"How hard is it to shave my boyfriend nearly bald?" Her voice was dull. "You did most of the work already, brushing your hair out for me. I liked your shade of brown."

She gathered up the scraps of hair into a paper towel, looking towards the garbage can before tossing it into the container. "I told Mom about the wedding plans, she didn't freak out exactly, but she did, uhm, ask if we were going into this because I was pregnant. I said no, you weren't that kind of guy. She seemed relieved though still a bit concerned I wanted- want to marry a Catholic."

"What did you say?" Daniel asked.

Haydee swallowed, rinsing the hair choked brush off in the bathroom sink before setting it down on the countertop. "I said I didn't care, Catholic or not, you're the one I want."

She stood, offering her hand to him. "C'mon, cutting your

hair wasn't what I had planned for today but maybe we still can do something else instead. I bought you something as a Christmas present since I wasn't sure if you would be able to make it to the family dinner or not. Jocelyn misses you."

"I didn't get you anything," Daniel said.

Her smile as she turned to him was rueful. "Getting married is the best Christmas present you could offer even if Jocelyn manipulated us into it. I don't need anything else. C'mon, open it."

Daniel pulled the ribbon free, unwrapping her present so that the brightly colored paper didn't tear to pieces and set it aside, looking down at the carefully crafted box in his lap. "This is like the box Dad gave Mom one year for her birthday. She used it for jewelry up until she died and I never knew what he did with it afterwards."

Haydee blushed, pleased with her choice. Jocelyn's hunch had apparently been a good one after all. She had worried over the choice until it was too late to take it back. "It's a memory box, you don't have to store jewelry in it."

If he could have given her a chaste kiss, he would have. "To be honest, I wasn't expecting anything at all this year, so this is nice."

He gently folded the Christmas paper up into a square and stuck it into the box, latching it closed. The ribbon he kept, running it through his fingers before slipping his engagement ring off and onto the narrow strip of green silk. There was no way as it were, for the ring to stay on his hand. The small little circlet was already loose on his finger, more weight lost from retching or the medicine and it would come off completely. "Help, please?"

She seemed to guess at his unspoken request and tied a knot in the loose ends of the ribbon, slipping it over his head so that the ring rested under his pajama top. "Think you'll be able to come back to Calais for Christmas dinner?"

"Maybe?" He glanced at her and away again. "It depends on what the doctors say I can do."

As much as he tried to push the feelings away and ignore them, the lack of hair made him feel self-conscious and exposed, more vulnerable than expected despite the haircut only having been minutes before. "Least I can do is ask."

On one hand, his brother was back. On the other hand, he barely looked like Dani anymore. Too thin, too tired and the familiar nearly chin length haircut was gone, shaved off in favor or a short army haircut. Jocelyn knelt in the window seat, watching as Haydee's car pulled into the spot outside the house and the two got out of the vehicle. She wore a dark red jacket and a fluffy white scarf with matching mittens. Daniel had the hood of his sweater up over his head and another jacket on top of that.

It was an effort not to race out of the living room and give his brother a hug. Whatever medicine he was on now had wrecked his immune system or something. Jocelyn skidded to a stop a few feet from him, "You came."

"Yeah, I did." Daniel shrugged out of his jacket but kept the fleece hoodie on.

Jocelyn bit down on his lower lip. "Still cold?"

"Still cold," Daniel glanced away. "And not well enough for turkey or vegan chocolate cake."

Haydee took his hand in hers before releasing it. "Mom has a list from the doctor about your diet restrictions, I emailed it to her while we were on the road. Luckily my parents are vegetarians."

Her smile was wry. "I think the end result was chamomile tea and some sort of rigatoni mushroom dish. Probably best if you skip the dessert though. She always makes her chocolate fudge. It's good but really sweet."

Jocelyn bounced on his feet, daring a look over his shoulder and down the hallway. "They're here!"

Anna came out of the kitchen, drying her hands on the apron tied around her waist. "Dinner's just about ready, you two. Come into the living room."

Jocelyn went a step or two ahead of them, barely able to contain his excitement at the thought of opening presents tomorrow morning, Dani and Haydee had probably already done their gift exchange at the safety of the hospital but he'd seen a few things from Haydee's parents under the tree with his name on it.

His gaze dropped to Daniel's bare hand. "Where- where's the engagement ring?"

A small uncomfortable feeling filled the pit of his stomach and he swallowed, hoping it didn't mean what he thought it did.

Daniel sighed, pulling a cord made from a green silk ribbon out from under his shirt with the ring threaded on it. "It wasn't fitting as well as it used to, thanks to how much I've thrown up lately. At least this way I won't lose it."

The feeling of lightness returned, and he breathed a sigh of relief, one followed by a sneeze. "Sorry, sorry."

"Dinner's ready!" This came from Anna as she hung the apron off the post to the second-floor bedrooms.

"Yay!" At this point he didn't even mind that Anna's idea of a turkey or duck was a vegetarian like imitation of one. All that mattered was that the family was all together like it should have been. He happily polished off his meal within twenty minutes, trying not to notice how Dani picked over his own meal and pushed the plate out of the way, only half eaten.

If anyone else noticed, they didn't comment on it. He was too keyed up to care for longer than the ten minutes it took to clean the dining room table up and start the movie for the night before at last, it was time for bed.

Prayer wasn't usually the first thing he turned to, not like his brother but this time he did it, looking out the window. "Please, please let it snow tomorrow."

It was the only thing that could make Christmas even more perfect in his mind.

CHAPTER TWENTY-THREE

"Y ou're leaving? On Boxing day?" He couldn't help the hurt in his voice at that, blocking the front door with his body. "You promised, Dani. You said you'd stay."

"I promised Christmas, Jocelyn." Daniel dropped to a knee in front of him though he kept his hands to himself. "I'm still sick and this was all the time I was able to persuade my doctor to give me. I have tests, appointments I need to make, and I can't do them from three hours away."

It was a girly thing to do but he looked away, putting his foot down. "You're always leaving me alone, Dani. One day you're not going to come back on me and- and…"

He couldn't finish, pushing past Daniel without caring about potential germs or risks. "Fine, go then. I don't care."

Dani's stricken expression didn't matter to him when all he could feel was hurt. It wasn't fair that the tests and things had to take his brother away from him. They were family and that stuck together, no matter what.

"Go, do what you need to. I'll talk with him," Haydee said.

Daniel hesitated for a moment before pulling his jacket on and closing the door behind him. A dull thud about the third of a way down the door hinted at Jocelyn's kick against it, followed by a muffled argument. He sighed, looking down at Haydee's keys in his hand. Borrowing her car wouldn't take long but it was necessary since his was still in Augusta. Kate had called instead of texting and from her tone over the phone, wasn't happy with him.

That needed to be dealt with before any planned trip back to his apartment.

She greeted him at the entrance of the bar, stepping aside with an unreadable expression on her face. "Got the haircut after all, I see. Looks good on you."

Daniel snorted at the biting tone in her voice. "I can guess at the rest of that sentence, Kate. Cancer patient or autoimmune disorder?"

Kate gave him a pointed look and went behind the bar, pouring a couple drinks into the nearby glasses before taking a swallow of one. "I was trying to be polite despite the circumstances."

"And you thought polite would be pouring me something," Daniel gave the amber liquid a look and shook his head. "I can't drink, Kate."

"I wasn't offering," Her mouth thinned as she set the glass down a little harder than intended. "My friend is dead because of you. It took me the better part of a month to figure out why he didn't come back after he left us the first time, now I know. I thought it was random, some accidental shooting or something at first but he wouldn't have let something so mundane stop him even despite how easily distracted he can be."

Kate pulled a coffee mug out from under the counter,

running tap water into it and slid it across the counter instead. "That's yours,"

Daniel grimaced at the faintly metallic taste of the water and pushed it aside. "I'm not sure if that's just me or the apparently ancient plumbing you have in here but I'm sorry about your friend."

She snorted, dismissive before resignation colored her expression. "So am I, so am I. But judging from your sympathy, you didn't have anything to do with his death. So to speak."

"So to speak?" He frowned, attentive this time. "What's that supposed to mean?"

Kate shrugged, looking down into her glass before taking a swallow of the one that hadn't been touched yet. "One, that he's older than I am by a few thousand years and two that he has the kind of power I do, or did, anyway. I gave that up for a mortal life. He never did. But it still counts as murder even if it was only his body that died."

Daniel flushed, reaching up to run a hand through his hair and sighed, dropping his hand back to his side. "I'm still not sure I understand this but I'm trying to. Mind if I put this in a way that makes sense to me? Your friend died but he pulled a...err,"

He looked away, uncomfortable with the bit of blasphemy involved. "Let's just say he's almost a god. I'm not sure I can actually compare whatever he did to the resurrection. There was only ever one and it wasn't within your friend's abilities,"

Kate sniffed, once more dismissive. "Christians, fine. It was like that and he's almost a god, yes. Be that as it may, someone killed him a month ago and sent him back to the place he was born from. It's taken him this long to reclaim any sense of self and come back to me."

A month. Daniel sat down, contemplating the water in the coffee mug rather than sipping at it. The metallic taste had been in his mouth rather than the plumbing but that didn't make the prospect of choking the water down any more pleasant. "Why didn't you tell me earlier?"

She grimaced in response. "You were sick in the hospital, in no position to do anything about it and I wasn't sure who killed him then. Now I-"

"Now she knows who my murderer is,"

Kate's eyes narrowed as she looked past Daniel's shoulder to the newcomer. "Sieh,"

Daniel glanced in her direction, a dry taste in his mouth at the stranger. Russian accented, shoulder length white-blond hair and a fading line of scarring across his throat. "That's it? Sieh?"

"I never needed anything else," Sieh considered the remnants of the abandoned beer and downed it like it was water itself. "Daniel,"

That made him hesitate, regarding the newcomer warily. "I'd remember anyone with a Russian accent and I'm pretty sure we haven't met before."

Sieh regarded him for a moment. "You thought I was Malachi's father when we first met. Said you couldn't trust anyone you didn't know well, even if they offered to help."

"I- that was weeks ago," Daniel said. "Anyone could have learned about that…"

"Then I'm worse at discretion than I thought I was after nearly twelve thousand years," Sieh glanced at him, tilting his head to the side. "Louisianan, New Orleans if I'm not mistaken, with a touch of French to it. Paris, yes?"

Daniel went still at that. "You're good with accents, traveled there?"

"No," Sieh's voice went flat, toneless. "But I've met my

share of Frenchmen over the years. Spent a season or two in Quebec and left after the horror their language became. Farmers, the lot of them."

He was still struggling to keep up with what he'd seen then and what he was seeing now. "You were different, Native American then. People can't change their whole physical appearance just like that."

"I'm not people, exactly," Sieh's tone was more dry than toneless now. "And how is that more impossible than what you call witchcraft? You could kill with a touch if you wanted to, bind a spirit or shadow in a circle or set something on fire with just a word and a gesture."

"Point, I guess," Daniel looked down. "So, I owe you an apology for whatever happened a month ago?"

Sieh snarled softly, his eyes flickering amber for a moment before the color faded back to a blue gray. "You don't, your kinsman owes me his life for what he did. The two of you share a scent."

There was only one guy that fit that description. Daniel winced, wishing that this wasn't what he had to deal with now. "Not that Jared doesn't deserve whatever you want to do to him, but is killing him really the answer?"

If he was being honest with himself, Sieh scared him. There was something in the ancient shapeshifter's gaze that wasn't human, hadn't been that for a very long time. Jared was only a pale shadow of that look.

Sieh's mouth tightened slightly before the glass clouded under his hand, thin cracks fissuring across its surface before it shattered into so much sand on the countertop.

Kate sighed, stilling him with a light touch on the arm. "You owe me a glass, Sieh. Daniel's right, after a fashion even if I can see your point of view. No need to lose your temper and break my things."

Her look towards Daniel was more apologetic than angry now. "I won't lie and pretend to you that Sieh isn't dangerous, and yes, he has a taste for blood but once he decides something, he isn't likely to give it up."

"He's a hunter," Daniel said.

"Quite," Hecate nodded briefly.

Sieh cleared his throat, drawing their attention to him. "I wasn't cautious, but I won't make that mistake again, I think. One way or another I'll have his life."

Daniel swallowed back on the nausea that threatened and slumped. "I don't like Jared much, but I can't be a part of whatever hunt you need to go on."

He looked back at Kate and stood, reaching for his jacket. "If that's everything, I should go. I borrowed Haydee's car, and she needs it back. She's driving me back to Augusta later today."

"I understand," Kate said. She pulled a dustpan and brush from underneath the scarred counter and swept the remains of the glass into it before dumping the contents into a garbage can. "Sieh can see you out,"

So, he wasn't entirely forgiven yet. Daniel shrugged half-heartedly and pulled his jacket on, fumbling with the zipper before it joined both halves together.

Sieh was watching him as unreadable as ever. "You're dying, I can smell it on you."

Daniel paused, unhappy with the acknowledgement. "Yeah,"

"Does your mate know?" The question was blunt but soft despite it.

"My fiancée," Daniel corrected. "And she knows I'm sick. Still hoping that there's a cure though. There's still blood work and tests, the doctor's scheduled the bone marrow transplant for later this week. If I'm lucky, that's what will save my life."

"Luck then," Sieh glanced towards the sky, expression pensive for a moment before a soft light surrounded him, growing brighter and then dimming as a silvery gray wolf took his place.

It looked over its shoulder and padded into the alley next to the bar before vanishing from sight.

Haydee met him at the front door, holding a hand out for the keys he dropped into her mitten. "Done what you needed to?"

Daniel glanced over his shoulder, still wary of the ancient shapeshifting creature's presence despite the unlikelihood it- he had followed him. "Kate only called to yell at me but it... turned out we're not as alone as we thought we were."

He shoved his hands into his jacket pockets. "I thought I'd lost my cousin in Baton Rouge; I was wrong apparently. How's Jocelyn?"

The smile she gave him at the question was bleak. "Still mad at you for leaving, won't talk to me now either. I'm sure he'll get over it eventually."

Daniel forced a laugh. "I wouldn't count on it; my family is well known for holding grudges or remembering insults long after the incident happened. Jocelyn's no different. He'll forgive you in time, just don't expect it for two or three months and a decent bribe. He likes animals."

Haydee pinched the bridge of her nose and sighed, slip- ping into the driver's seat of her car. "I'll be sure to keep my eye out for a puppy somewhere then. A puppy's better than a couple rats anyway. Now... what breeds does he like?"

A puppy, it wasn't the worst topic of conversation to carry them through a three-hour drive back to Augusta. Daniel shrugged, absently scrolling through his phone in an attempt to ignore the small but growing sensation of car sickness in the pit of his stomach. "Something small, I guess."

"Small, stubborn and loyal to his family," Haydee rolled her eyes at that. "Well, that rules out all but one breed in the entire Maine state area. Looks like he's about to pay a visit to a Lhasa Apso breeder or two in a few weeks."

Any irony she intended was quickly lost as they pulled into a nearby gas station to refill the tank. "Are you feeling alright?"

He shook his head, swallowing back on the bile as he pushed the gas station door open. "I'm going to throw up."

The woman behind the counter blanched and hastily slid him the key across the plastic covering a display of lottery tickets. "In the back, just opposite the storage closet."

They barely made it in time before he ended up on his knees, retching into the toilet. Haydee stood behind him, waiting until he emptied his stomach. "I think I saw Gravol in the corner behind a magazine rack."

Daniel wiped his hand across his mouth, sitting back on the balls of his feet. "I've got prescription stuff I can take, might as well use that up first."

She sighed, offering him a plastic bottle of water minus the cap. "Here,"

He fumbled with the medicine bottle cap, finally managing to pull it open before dumping the right dose into his hand and swallowing the little pill with water. The bitter taste of the medicine didn't cut through the unpleasant taste of the water as much as hoped. "Thanks."

Haydee flinched as her hand brushed across his skin. "You're burning up, Daniel. Like really warm this time."

She lifted her gaze, worry crossing her face. "Lucky we're only half an hour outside Augusta. Think you can hold on for that long?"

That wasn't an answer he could give, between the nausea and the sweat dampening the collar of his jacket.

Haydee swore under her breath, wrapped an arm around his shoulders and cursed again at his weight as she staggered under him. Even with the five or six pounds he'd lost between his regular medicine and the chemotherapy, he was still heavy. And at five foot ten, a good four inches on her. "Move, damn it!"

She skidded on a patch of ice in the hospital parking lot, nearly forcing her second-hand Toyota up on two wheels as she made the turn, cutting off a Ford truck in the quest of finding the nearby stall. The driver of the truck flipped her the middle finger; she ignored it as Daniel went white and then retched again in the foot space on the passenger side. That too, would need to be dealt with but it wasn't on her list of priorities for the moment. The puppy problem as well, seemed inconsequential. "I need help here."

"Yes?" The receptionist looked up, a bored expression on her face as she gestured towards the waiting room. "Take a seat and wait to be called, Miss."

She gritted her teeth, wishing briefly for some of the same power Daniel had. Maybe then the woman would listen to her. "Can't afford time, lady. My boyfriend's feverish and spent part of the last three hours throwing up. He's on chemotherapy, damn it."

"He'll still have to wait to be called." The woman glanced back at her computer screen. "I'm sorry, Miss."

"Not that sorry," Haydee said. "Just call a doctor, okay."

The woman sighed, irritation crossing her face. "Look, kid, I don't make the rules around here. And we have others here with more serious problems than a fever."

"Which part of he's on chemo did you not understand?"

Haydee said flatly. "I'll pull the fucking cancer card if I have to, but he needs medical attention now."

"Alright, alright," She ran her hands through artificially blonde hair and dialed the phone by her computer screen. "Who's his doctor?"

"Persephone Sotaira," Haydee said.

The woman sighed again, wrapping the phone cord around her fingers. "Paging Doctor Sotaira to the visitor waiting room. Adult male with a fever and vomiting. Code gray; adult woman."

Could the receptionist get any more cynical or frustrating? Haydee pushed away from the desk, glaring at the pair of security guards as they arrived in the waiting room. Persephone was only a moment or two behind the men with a nurse and a couple interns. "You can help, right?"

Persephone put a gentle hand on Daniel's forehead and pulled away as if she had been burned. "For the love of all the gods, Edith Martin. The young man here should have been declared a code blue from the start. Get me a gurney. Now!"

Edith had to be the receptionist then. Haydee ignored her as she tried to edge a step or two closer to the newly arrived gurney. "Will he be alright?"

The doctor's mouth was a thin line. "Wait here, girl. We'll call you when we get him into the ICU unit."

"But-" Haydee opened her mouth to speak and shut it again as the apparent code team made their exit. There was just enough time before the doors closed behind the medical time for her to see the odd balloon mask thing put over Daniel's mouth and nose.

She slumped on one of the hard orange chairs, tasting something sour in her mouth. "Please be safe, Daniel."

Her last memory of him couldn't be the brief sight of the thing used in so many medical drama shows for respiratory arrest. "It was only a fever and throwing up. He was fine three hours ago."

At least he hadn't complained about chest pain or breathing problems to her, though it had seemed shallower than she remembered it being before. One hour passed and then another and she went through two mint dark chocolate bars before Persephone returned, looking harried. "Is he alright?"

Persephone looked away, towards the closed doors, seeming to choose her words carefully. "He's... fine now but I feel I should tell you that he seized before we got the fever under control. He's on fluids now but unconscious. It wouldn't be wise to permit visits right now."

She bit down on her lower lip, looking down at her boots. "The fever, this isn't because of the chemotherapy, right?"

"Fevers can be, unfortunately but we may never know the source of this one," Persephone said. "There can be tests done to try and determine the bacterial or viral source, if there is one but it could just as easily have been a result of the chemotherapy medicine, yes."

"And the balloon thing?" Haydee asked.

The doctor sat down on the chair next to her, a hand on her shoulder. Haydee sat reluctantly, Persephone's touch was gentle, but she was stronger than her delicate build suggested. "Just as a precaution, Haydee."

She nodded, rubbing at her eyes. "He was fine when we left this morning, I swear it. All he had to do was an errand for Kate MacKinnon and come back afterwards. The only thing that I can think of is that Jocelyn had a cold the week before Christmas. He got over it, he wasn't contagious."

Persephone's eyes narrowed for a moment before she touched the arm of her glasses, looking weary. "He might have gotten better but Jocelyn could have spread it for some time after recovering. And with Daniel's compromised immune system. It was a foolish risk you took; I never should have allowed the visit home, had I known beforehand."

Haydee's voice dropped, meek and tiny. "I'm sorry, It was an accident. Whatever or however he got it from, none of us knew what would happen."

"Sorry," Persephone glanced at her briefly. "You shouldn't be apologizing to me but to Daniel. Intentionally or not, you put his life at risk."

"So, what do I do now?" Haydee asked.

"Go home, go get something to eat," The doctor stood, looking away. "Doing anything at this point would be better than waiting in a visitor's lounge. I'll call you if and when he's ready to have visitors."

What else could she do but follow the doctor's advice? If she was lucky, an hour or two would be long enough to distract her from her boyfriend's condition and from her own fears. "Thanks."

Impulse and a poor GPS map ended with her parking in the small lot of a coffee shop before entering it. Inside was decked out in bright red and green streamers and buzzing with conversation, someone's game night apparently.

She leaned against the counter, wishing Daniel was here with her. The ridiculous character sheet discussion and dice aside, this was the kind of café he might have liked seeing. From the set up and the counter, this might have been a real bar once.

"Coffee for the pretty girl?"

"What?" Haydee blinked, glancing at the server behind the counter. "I didn't order anything."

The guy flushed, sliding the drink across to her. "On the house apparently, or at least a surprise from that guy over in the corner with the Huxley book. He called you pretty. Thought you shouldn't be alone on Boxing day."

"Oh, okay," Haydee glanced in the gestured direction and reluctantly sat down at the table with her coffee. "You got this for me?"

He looked up at her, putting his book spine upwards. "Yeah, saw you come in earlier, alone. Didn't think you were a part of the elf and half orc crew."

"I'm not," She took a swallow of her coffee, savoring the hazelnut and cinnamon flavor in it. "Might have been, back in high school but that was a while ago. Outgrew the games. Honestly, never would have found the café if it wasn't for the stupid GPS insisting that I take the long way around."

His gaze lingered on the engagement ring on her hand and she colored, dropping it below the level of the table. "I'm engaged,"

"Must be a piss poor fiancé if you're here alone instead of with him," He said.

Haydee drew back, offended. "It's not that, Daniel's the nicest guy you could meet. It's…"

She sighed, wrapping her hands around the tiger striped mug. "He's in the hospital and I feel like its my fault for it. I should have taken more care, worn a mask or encouraged his brother to do it more often after getting over a cold but now…"

Her new friend looked pensive, folding a corner of his book over, dog earing it to mark the page. "If it isn't too personal to talk about, I'm willing to listen."

"Maybe," She was hesitant. This was Daniel's business not a stranger's. "I don't even know your name."

"Lucas," He shrugged like it didn't matter. "Talking helps sometimes."

"I guess," She turned a stir stick around the edge of the

mug for the whipped cream. "He's sick, the kind of sick that means taking chemotherapy and killing his immune system. I don't know when he caught it or where, but he was more or less alright this morning. Just a little bit a bad taste in his mouth, tired but that part was usual for him. Two, three hours later- he's throwing up and running a bad fever. Next thing I know, he's admitted to the hospital's ICU unit. They won't let me see him."

Haydee blew her nose into a paper napkin and crumpled it up onto her plate. "They're saying he had a seizure as well."

"That sounds rough," Lucas glanced at her. "I'm sorry,"

She slumped, tipping the mug over onto its side. "It feels like he's only getting worse, not better and I'm just standing here, watching it happen."

"If there's anything I can do to help, I'll do it." His smile was brief. "I can't help with Daniel's health but you, I think I can do something for. Just give me the name of the hospital."

Something made her bit down on her lower lip at his choice of wording, but he hadn't hurt or touched her in anyway, so he seemed alright. "Augusta General, why?"

Lucas considered his coffee for a moment. "Just curious."

He slid a scrap of paper over to her with a number written on it. "Just in case,"

Haydee looked down, memorizing it and folded the scrap up into her sweater pocket. "Thanks,"

"No problem," Lucas dropped a five onto the table for his coffee as the barista arrived with a cloth and spray.

She waited a good five minutes after he left before dropping the phone number into the abandoned coffee mug. However nice Lucas was; something about him made her mouth feel dry, uncomfortable. "Sure, no problem."

Her memory alone would be good enough to retain the number, she didn't need any piece of paper of his or want it, truthfully. She looked back, snagging her phone just as the plastic shell vibrated against her touch. "Hello?"

"It's Doctor Sotaira here, I just wanted tell you that Daniel is out of immediate danger but he's still in intensive care."

It was a relief to hear the doctor's voice, less so to hear the bad news about Daniel's health condition. "When will he be out of the unit?"

There was a sigh on Persephone's end. "It could be hours or as long as two weeks if he doesn't respond to the antibiotics."

Haydee swallowed, looking down at the ring on her hand as she switched the phone from one hand to the other. "Antibiotics? Are you sure that's a good thing? He's allergic to penicillin, doctor."

"I saw his medical alert bracelet, yes." Persephone's voice was patient. "I'm aware of his allergy, as are the rest of his team. He's receiving a different antibiotic."

She could breathe a sigh of relief at that though it was still tinged with fear. "Is he awake yet? I know I can't see him yet, but I'd like to know."

"Not yet, I'm afraid." Persephone said.

"Didn't think so," Haydee said tiredly. "Just wanted to check."

She had a key to Daniel's apartment anyway, she could spend the night there if she wanted to. It was a better choice than curling up in her car under a sleeping bag and wasting gas by keeping the vehicle running overnight. "Doctor, thanks."

Chapter Twenty-Four

The news channel on the TV held little interest to her that morning as she turned it on and turned it off ten minutes later. This wasn't her apartment but even so, it felt cold, lonely and absent any personal touches of Daniel's beyond a few leather-bound journals, a pair of worn runners on the plastic mat and the folded pile of cardboard boxes in the recycling bin. Everything else could have belonged to a previous owner or held over to make it a fully furnished home.

Haydee glanced into the fridge and felt hope fade at the empty shelves. Food would have been a waste of money and effort, given how little time Daniel had spent in the apartment but it would have been nice to see something other than a pathetic excuse for a tuna casserole in it. What remained in its bowl stank and was growing a coat of blue fur on its surface. "Daniel,"

She sat down on the couch, turning her phone over in her hands before setting it down on the coffee table. Like the TV and the dime store paperback in her backseat, it held little interest to her. Only one thing mattered, and Persephone hadn't called with an update yet.

Between her boredom and the lack of anything of interest to do, she fell asleep on the couch, curled up under a brown fleece blanket until the irritating ringtone on her phone woke her. She squinted at the number; half tempted to ignore it before pressing the answer button. "Yeah?"

"As polite as ever, I see." The doctor's voice was bland. "Your fiancé is out of the intensive care unit and in his own room, should you want to visit him. I do suggest keeping it short however, he's still easily tired."

Haydee nodded abstractly though the physician couldn't see the gesture. "What time is it?"

"Just after four," Persephone said.

That meant she'd slept through the night and then again after the tuna casserole adventure. Haydee pinched the bridge of her nose between two fingers. "Shit,"

"Excuse me?" Persephone's voice dropped a note or two, cooling noticeably.

"Not you, just... something else," She flushed, looking out the doors onto the balcony deck. "I didn't get much sleep last night. Maybe overslept. I'll be at the hospital soon."

It was an effort to remember that she wasn't driving on ideal conditions and that the roads underneath her car were icy as she navigated her way back to the hospital. Haste would only get her killed and then she would be less than no use to Daniel.

Once inside though, she nearly ran for the elevator, catching it just before the doors closed. "Third floor please,"

The intern holding a carton of coffee cups gave her a long-suffering look and hit the button for the right floor. Haydee tried for a smile as the door opened. "Thanks,"

She stuck her hands under the hand sanitizer bottle

mounted on the wall, rubbing them together to work the liquid in before entering the room. "Daniel?"

He stirred briefly at her voice, turning his head to look at her before sitting up and pressing his hand against his forehead. "Yeah,"

"How are you feeling?" She had to bite back on the feeling dismay at the sight of the thin oxygen tube at his nose and looped behind his head as well as the new IV line in his arm.

"Better than I was," His voice belied his words though.

She winced, digging her nails into the crease of her opposite arm. With the sweater on, there was little chance of damage, but she wasn't interested in hurting herself for Daniel's sake. "Not so well, I take it."

Daniel glanced at her tiredly. "The fever's gone at least, that's something. The antibiotics worked and I didn't have a reaction to them. Everything else, well, I feel like it's an effort to breathe here. The tube is supposed to help."

"Does it?" Haydee asked.

"Kind of," He sighed, looking down at the IV line in his arm. "Thought I was free of this."

"You will be, soon." She tried to be encouraging. "You'll get the bone marrow transplant sooner or later. No reason to delay, right?"

"No, no reason," He bit down on his lower lip, slumping with his back against the headboard of his bed. "You feel... sparky, like you had a cup of Italian coffee and are trying to keep yourself from crashing."

She laughed despite herself and the strain she felt at that statement. "Is that a psychic thing or just yours? I thought using your magic was dangerous."

He forced a smile before it faded. There was no easy answer to her question or one he found comforting. "I wish I knew. Maybe half and half. It's not something I've wanted to risk exploring without supervision."

In the meantime, he needed to know for posterity if nothing else. "What happened earlier? All I remember is the nausea, throwing up and then the dizziness before waking up in her with the tube in my nose and a new IV in my arm. And…"

He frowned, struggling to remember. "Something about a gray code and shouting. Everything else just fades to black after that."

Haydee blushed pink, scuffing her foot across the tile floor. "I might have gotten into an argument with the receptionist and almost arrested for it."

"My fiancée, the rebel." Daniel managed a weak laugh at that, only to have it turn into coughing for a few moments. He subsided, panting a moment later until he caught his breath. "I appreciate the visit, but you look and feel like you're about to crash on your feet. We'll have a chance to talk later if it's allowed."

She nodded, gaze drifting over to the memory box and opening it for a peek. It was still mostly empty but some well meaning nurse or doctor had removed the silk ribbon and ring and placed it into the space rather than cut the ribbon from around Daniel's neck. "Tomorrow, promise."

Leaving him felt like the hardest thing she could have done but if he was to ever have a chance of recovery then it would have to be done without her hovering over him. Constant attention could only hurt more than it helped. And truth be told, Daniel had been right about the coffee, she couldn't remember eating or drinking anything else beyond that since the other night. It probably meant she hadn't in the end.

A good Chinese dish and an even better bed would be the

best things to look forward to once she got back to the apartment. Worth it if she could sleep without worrying over Daniel's physical wellbeing. Persephone was a good doctor and Daniel had a team behind him to support his recovery after the transplant. That was all that mattered.

He had maybe fifteen minutes before Daniel's worthless girlfriend showed up but it didn't matter, fifteen minutes was enough time for a short conversation with his cousin. Jared wrinkled his nose at the bleach and antiseptic smell of the hospital, quickly checking yesterday's visitor's log for the room and floor number. Chances were he'd have an easier time of a visit than she ever would. He was family, she wasn't even if the bitch was engaged to Daniel.

Last night had been informative to say the least and she had been too easily manipulated into giving the name of the hospital to him. Give any name other than Jared and a coffee to the "pretty girl" looking for someone to talk to. The rest came from the semester's worth of theatre arts classes he'd taken one year. Aldous Huxley's book had been a touch to set the scene and the stupid girl hadn't even noticed the irony of his choice. She might have been a touch more intelligent than his own girlfriend – she was a schoolteacher after all-, but it wasn't by much.

It took a moment longer than hoped for but he found Daniel's room in the end, more by his magic than reading the numbers or the names listed on the cards by the doors. As weak as his cousin's presence was, it was stronger than it had been in over a month, their proximity to each other through the sympathetic bond.

Jared smiled briefly, pushing the door open and pausing in the space as the beeping of a machine or two reached him. The sound itself was irritating but made tolerable by the sight of Daniel asleep on his side in the bed, a faint expression of unhappiness apparent on his face. "So the family price finally caught up with you, hm."

He'd come here fully expecting to see Daniel awake, alert and much less vulnerable than he looked now. Now, well, Daniel was barely recognizable as the man who had scraped up the paint job on his car and left in the middle of the night so long ago. He looked too thin, too weak to be a challenge in any fight between them. Bruising marked his skin where old scarring wasn't and at some point, recently, he'd had his hair cut and shaved into a more army style. Jared sighed, almost disappointed as he glanced at the IV line running to Daniel's arm. "I thought this would be fun, cousin but it looks like chemo and whatever this is, beat me to it. I can't even bring you back to face uncle Alain now."

He closed his eyes, resting a hand on Daniel's forehead for a moment before calling on his magic. His cousin was too far gone or too exhausted from the medicine to put up much of a fight against him as he went deeper, searching for the answers he wanted. It came after a few minutes effort and he pulled away, pensive. "So you're not just ill, you're dying, cousin. I would have thought the strongest witch of our generation would have beaten the odds. Disappointing. Aplastic anemia's a bitch, isn't it? Just like that girlfriend of yours."

"Not everyone feels the need to take a life to fuel their magic, you know."

Jared started, grip tightening on his hands so that his knuckles whitened against skin. "I would have thought a doctor or nurse might have been polite enough to leave me alone with my cousin."

The stranger shrugged idly, crossing the threshold of the room. "I might have, yes but Daniel doesn't seem inclined to welcome any visits from family of late. And I'm always concerned when someone threatens Persephone Sotaira's patients. She doesn't take kindly to her wards being crossed."

Jared glared, crossing his arms over his chest as he took in the dark-skinned man's face and body. "What the fuck would you know about that, black bastard?"

"A lot more than you would expect, I think." The man took a step closer, seeming unconcerned by the language or the slur used. "Jared, is it?"

Jared swore again under his breath. "I dealt with you once already, Sieh. Don't make me do it again."

"Sieh?" His laugh was dry. "Hardly, he might be vulnerable to your family's binding magic. I can assure you, I'm not. I already gave my life and oath to one man, you would be hard pressed to take it from him."

He gave more credence to old mythology and legends than Daniel did but that didn't mean he enjoyed them either. His reach was wary, testing as he went searching for any crack or weakness in the medical student's guard. "What would an intern know about a dead goddess's patients or wards? Persephone is just a name now, something a New Age wannabee would name her brat."

"Perhaps, if their surname was anything but Sotaira," The other man glanced away. "But she's very much alive, Jared."

Alive or not, the woman was no threat to him. She wasn't here. Jared ignored the medical student's words, still searching for a weakness in the young man's guard. He'd broken others before him, with words and manipulation before finishing with organs and tissues. Usually by the end they were begging for death. He preferred giving it after a few hours or a day or two. This man's composure was... unnatural and frustrating. "Why won't you give in? Everyone else does. They can't help it. That shapeshifter in New York did when I finished with him."

And it had been a pleasant reward to see the creature's natural shape afterwards. "The black panther was beautiful in its own way; too bad I wasn't able to keep the pelt afterwards."

"I remember," The intern's eyes narrowed with dislike. "I patched the pup's sorry ass up on request from his sister. He was my sister's child."

"Ah," Fascinating if true but he doubted the statement personally. The shapeshifting kind rarely told a truth if they could help it. Their lives were built on lies and stories after all. "So tell me, what's your story? No one is this good at guarding their thoughts."

He found a minuscule crack and fought to break through it, not caring about the physical damage he was doing to the young doctor's heart and internal organs in the process of battering the mental wall. Stress affected the mind first and then the body itself. "Show me,"

The crack widened, the last of the protection falling in front of him but he was the one to stumble and swear under his breath at the assault on his own senses. A desert place with the heat of the sun baking fresh blood on the sand, a smell of iron in his nose. A young man similar in appearance to the medical student standing in front of him, dressed in a white tunic. The bones of so many dead...

Jared choked, sinking to his knees in front of the other man as he wiped wetness away from his upper lip. His hand came away bright scarlet with blood from the unexpectedly bloody nose. "You..."

Century after century followed that scene or memory. Egypt, Greece and then Rome. Countless wars and battles after that, some as a soldier, more often as a field doctor and healer. A few, much later as a physician tending to the ill and dying. "Who the hell are you?"

"I think you can guess by now," The stranger's voice was cool, nearly cold in its tone. "And the only reason you got through enough to see those memories is that I let you see them. Maybe your father neglected to mention this, maybe he doesn't have the power to do it but the connection you tried to make goes two ways, Jared LaLaurie. You saw my past; I know what you're more afraid of than anything else. Sieh doesn't have the interest or the gift for that, I do. He's part of nature, I'm not."

"Not... afraid of some doctor," Jared spat the words out, forcing himself to stand.

"No," His voice was tight, barely holding onto the fury in it. "But you are afraid of being judged for what you do. That's your hunt, searching for a way to avoid judgment, isn't it? You want forever."

Jared gritted his teeth, backing towards the doorway. "Damn you,"

"Already been done after a fashion." A slight shrug at that. "I could have joined my sisters and father in rest, I chose to serve Osiris instead. A penance for failing to protect them in life."

He frowned, looking at Jared and shook his head, breaking the connection between them as if it was an ancient thread. Jared went to his knees with a gasp, one hand pressed against his chest as his heartrate slowed to a normal pace. "Enough, you're a child trying to play my game. You haven't earned my real name, but I'll give it anyway, maybe then you'll reconsider challenging or killing the gods."

Jared spat a mouthful of blood onto the gray tile in front of him, still in no position to stand yet as a soft twilight light grew and turned into a circle big enough for a person to stand in front of. Persephone stepped out of it, regarding the medical student for a moment before looking at Jared. "Security is on its way, little one. I trust you won't kill them on your way out."

Little one. He bristled at the name and stood, bracing himself on the doorframe as the two guards cuffed him and led him out to the main lobby. "This isn't over yet, doctor."

She sniffed, glancing at him as her eyes flickered from the same twilight gray as her gate to a falcon's gold and back again. "A year from now or an age of your time and you will answer to Anubis, Jared. Count on that fate."

He pulled away from her, scowling as the police car showed up at the curb. "This isn't over."

CHAPTER TWENTY-FIVE

"This isn't over," Haydee gripped his hand in hers before letting go, looking over her shoulder. "You're going to get through this, Daniel. The transplant is tomorrow and then you'll be free to go home."

He turned his head to look at her, reaching up with his free hand to brush a lock of her hair out of Haydee's eyes. "I don't know." She bit down on her lower lip, pressing her mouth to

his hand briefly, hoping this wouldn't affect his health more than the fever and the seizure already had. "You will, Daniel, you will. Don't give up now,"

If he wouldn't, she would even if it hurt her to see the new IV line in his arm and the little oxygen tube in his nose. Or how thin and tired he looked to her. "Remember the little teddy bear Jocelyn got you for Christmas?"

Daniel tried for a weak smile, finding the little bear under the blanket. "I remember, yeah. Hard not to forget a panda who had its white fur dyed blue in the washing machine."

She laughed despite herself though the sound was strained, holding the little toy in her hands before placing it on the pillow next to his shoulder. "I think it looks cuter now than it did."

Cuter and much less stereotypical in her view. Black and white pandas were nice, a black and blue one was unique and well worth putting in the memory box for later. "I wanted to mention before I left, I'm not going to convert to Catholicism, but Father Allan's been teaching me what to expect from the wedding service."

She made a face. "You would have been the better teacher, I think. Less boring or... err, cringeworthy. I don't have your faith, but I did do a decent amount of history in school. More than most of my classmates anyway. They barely knew the Korean war, I at least tried to look further and research the original Martin Luther. Jesus, he was a bastard by the way."

"I think he knew his parents," Daniel's voice was dry albeit pained.

Haydee rolled her eyes at that, trying to crush the rising tide of panic she felt. "Wrong kind of bastard, Daniel. Old Martin was like the fifteenth century version of a Nazi. He hated Jewish people and Catholics even more. Said he'd love nothing better than burning their homes down and everything they owned with it."

Daniel's smile was tight, pained as he sat up in the bed, bracing the pillow between his back and the headboard. "I know. Dad has a few... books from that time. Journals so old he wouldn't let me touch them until he was sure I wouldn't spill juice or tear the pages accidently."

"Theology?" Haydee blinked. "I didn't think he was interested in the Protestant thing. Or spoke that period's German."

"Witchcraft," Daniel's tone went flat. "And he doesn't, unless he decided old High German was one language too much for my reading list and decided not to teach me that one. Those are in Latin, mostly. Women who were too educated for the priests' liking and died for it. Martin's German didn't come around for a few centuries afterwards."

"Oh," She quieted, glancing away, torn in how she felt on that particular subject. It was always... disconcerting to hear about the kind of education Daniel had had as a child. In some ways, utterly useless, in another, well worth it if one was to end up a biblical scholar or antiquarian studying ancient books. "And those women? Do I want to know what happened to them?"

"Burned at the stake, probably," He glanced down at the bear lying on the coverlet. "There isn't a lot that the New Age religion gets right, there was no unified feminist movement but the I'll be the first to admit that some men really don't like it when women prove them wrong or get an education."

Haydee sighed, standing. "I'm going to say it again, your lessons are a lot more interesting than Father Allan's but if I don't go now, I'll be driving home in the dark and I'd rather not risk that."

"Good luck," Daniel said.

She nodded, leaving him alone in the room. Daniel watched her departure until he could no longer see her. Sleep didn't come as easily as hoped after an hour of trying and he sighed, ignoring the jeans thrown over the back of the chair. The pajamas would be enough for now.

The room three or four doors down from him was open, he paused unable to tear his gaze away from the scene in front of him. Rashid was sitting by the bed of another patient, hand clasped around hers as he murmured something in an undertone to her. The elderly woman smiled weakly, nodding and subsided; eyes drifting shut as the heart monitor flatlined. "Who was she?"

Rashid turned, expression clearing before he pulled the

coverlet over the woman's face. "Mrs. Stanton. She didn't have any children and her husband passed away ten years ago."

Daniel looked down, pulling the ankh from his hoodie pocket and pressed it into Rashid's hand. "I meant to return this earlier, but you weren't around."

Rashid glanced briefly at the copper pendant before folding Daniel's fingers over it. "It was a gift, keep it. I'll need it back eventually, but it won't be right now."

Daniel let out a breath, reluctantly pocketing the necklace again. It didn't feel right to keep the piece, not least when it didn't belong to him but if Rashid said it was a gift, he wasn't going to insult the Egyptian medical student by refusing it. "Persephone told me what it was, the Egyptian cross. If it didn't belong to a saint, I have no right to keep it."

Rashid sighed but he didn't seem upset by his answer. "I'm not asking you to believe in the old Egyptian gods, Daniel. This was a gift only."

What could he say to that? Daniel closed his eyes, giving in for the moment. "Who are you, really?"

"Who do you think?" Rashid's voice was gentle.

Daniel bit down on his lower lip, unsure how to put his words into a logical order. "You answered my prayer and offered a little advice when I needed it but you don't seem to be employed here. Or at least I've never found any public record of your employment in the hospital."

His gaze drifted over to Mrs. Stanton's covered face. "You spoke to her; she smiled at you and took your hand. She was at peace afterwards, but you don't dress or look like a priest."

He sat, needing to continue despite the carefully unreadable look in the other man's eyes. "I've had a lot of free time on my hands and a relatively stable internet connection. I didn't find employment records and I doubt I'd be able to without getting into trouble for it but I need to ask. Vietnam and Korea?"

Rashid hesitated and nodded. "Yes, I was... there both times serving as a medic."

"World War Two?" Daniel forced himself to look away from the elderly woman under her coverlet.

"Yes, though I try not to dwell on that particular war over-much." Rashid pinched the bridge of his nose before dropping his hand back to his side.

"The Spanish flu? I found a couple articles about the negro doctor in New York treating victims of it. At a time when African Americans didn't have much in the way of rights." Daniel said.

Rashid sighed again. "It wasn't easy, but yes. I witnessed that outbreak."

"The same man or his grandfather was in New Orleans on the night they burned Del- my mom's house to the ground for the treatment of her slaves," Daniel said quietly. "They called him a friend to slaves once, a black freedman who saw the attack."

He held out the printout of a clumsy looking sketch to Rashid. "Boston, 1775. The same man again, his companions were unknown but..."

Rashid accepted the photograph wearily, running a hand over his bare scalp. "Ah, yes. I knew these men and women. Malachi, I believe you may have already met and know some of his past. The dark-haired Spanish woman is my surviving sister, the woman you would readily name an angel for her wings and her uncanny eye color, came from a world unlike ours. Her name was Elizabeth. The other man was Malachi's companion at the time. He and Elizabeth died in battle during the war."

"How far does it go back?" Daniel asked.

The Egyptian medical student looked away. "Centuries, in truth. I've seen the crusades, fought and killed in them on one side or the other over the years. I saw Rome's rise and fall. And the deaths of my own kin."

Daniel opened his mouth and closed it again, briefly unsure of what to say to that. "Are you...dangerous?"

"Yes, but not to you," Rashid glanced away. "I'm not like the one who calls himself Sieh."

Daniel swallowed past the dry taste in his mouth. "I've seen the pictures painted on the walls and in any books on ancient mythology. It's the same image there, drawn over and over again. A man bending over the dead or dying and pulling the white sheet over them. Comforting them as they pass away. Who are you?"

His voice wobbled slightly at the question. Rashid glanced back at him. "Who do you think I am, Daniel? I won't deny any of what you just said."

Daniel bit down on the inside of his lower lip, wincing at the pain in it. "I- you... You're Anubis."

The little copper charm was warm from where he held it in his hoodie pocket.

Rashid ducked his head briefly, assent crossing his face as quickly as the sorrow before both vanished behind the neutral mask. "Yes, though for obvious reasons, I don't use that name in public and the dog headed theme was once intended as an insult, my father's fury at work against me."

His mouth tightened slightly at that. "Dog headed fool of a son, he used to say."

There was no doubt about it, the darkness swimming at the edges of his vision was real, not the product of standing up too quickly or from the exertion of walking a few yards from his room to Mrs. Stanton's. Daniel swallowed again and let the blackness take him, hiding in what little comfort it could bring for a time.

He woke again, this time with a pounding headache and in his own room. An anxious looking young nurse hovering by his bedside. "How long was I out?"

She blushed and stammered something before clearing her throat and trying again. "Just a couple hours but it was quite a nasty fall you took. Hit your head and managed to tear the IV from your arm with it. I imagine finding poor Mrs. Stanton in her bed like that must have been a shock. Poor lady."

Something in the girl's manner or words felt artificial, forced like she was playing a role in a movie and not a very good one but the headache behind his eyes made it too difficult to focus on the feeling for long. "Where... I was talking with Rashid before. He helped her, must have given her something for whatever pain she was in."

She blinked, looking like a not particularly bright goldfish and shrugged, pulling a tube of strawberry lip chap from her pocket. "Dunno where you've been but there's no one I know here named Rashid. Might have been one forty years ago, a doctor but he's probably retired by now or really old."

She was right on one count and off on the other, but she was still somehow way off on the entirety of what she had just said as well. Physical age was no measure for actual. "Thanks,"

The nurse gave him a lingering look, patted his arm just below where the IV line was placed and set a little cup of water and the pills on the breakfast tray. "Of course,"

There wasn't much else to do after that but attempt to sleep again and wait for Persephone Sotaira's arrival. And count down the hours until the time came for the transplant. It by itself wasn't particularly high risk- but the chances of infection afterwards were.

Truth be told, he was terrified and there was no-one around who he could talk to about this. His life depended on something so small, vital but getting sick again was his worst fear since he had been first admitted to the hospital.

CHAPTER TWENTY-SIX

Try as she might to focus on the lesson for her students, she couldn't and it was an effort to race out of the classroom alongside them at the end of the day. Fridays were just as special to her as they were to the students in the class – though for a very different reason, likely. They looked forward to their video games and free time, she looked forward to the couple days a week she could see Daniel.

And this time, Jocelyn would be going with her. It wasn't fair to keep the two apart for much longer after all. He was looking antsy, looking up at the clock mounted above the principal's office door in a way that she couldn't let herself do until the bell rang for the end of day.

When the three o'clock bell finally rang, it was with an anticipating sigh of relief from the staff and receptionists, moments before the predicted rush for the door and the teachers parking lot began. She hung back, waiting a moment for the chaos to clear before retrieving her keys from her jacket pocket. "Ready?"

"Yeah," Jocelyn's hopeful expression couldn't be denied now. "Think he'll be able to come home to Calais now?"

Haydee managed a brief smile despite the faint pang of regret she felt. "There'll probably be tests and blood counts Daniel needs done on a regular basis, but he should be alright to be released from the hospital."

She glanced down at the box of medical masks in her hands. "Still probably best if we take this along with us and wear them. Feeling better or not, he's still going to be immunocompromised. So, no germs if we can help it."

The trip from Calais to Augusta was one she'd taken so often now that she barely remembered the three-hour drive beyond the taste of anticipation in her mouth. And this time there was no Edith Martin to hold her back from seeing him or to deny lifesaving medicine. Rumor had it that the receptionist had recently lost her job for incompetence or a lack of interest in doing what she had been hired to do in the first place. Either way, good riddance to her.

This time she parked carefully, mindful of the space between her car and someone's white Mazda before stepping out onto the icy pavement underneath her. It was still only January, but it had rained instead of snowing the night before and the frozen concrete was treacherous.

Jocelyn wobbled and she caught his arm, steadying him before they picked their way across the parking lot. "Ready?"

Jocelyn bit down on his lower lip and nodded, pausing for a moment in front of the sliding doors and stepping through them. "Honestly, I'm scared, a bit."

"Yeah, me too." She put the mask on, holding her hands out under the little sanitizer bottle on its stand before rubbing the liquid into them. "It's a big step for everyone. Why don't you wait here in the lobby and I'll check first? Too many people and all that."

Jocelyn looked down, fidgeting with the zipper on his jacket before nodding and settling down in one of the chairs. "Okay,"

Daniel's room was empty, and she couldn't help the fear that overwhelmed her excitement. What if something had gone wrong during the week and he was back in the ICU or... or worse? "Daniel?"

She tasted the coppery flavor of fear in her mouth and smoothed a hand over the recently made bed. He couldn't be, could he? He had been alright, if not what anyone could have called one hundred percent.

There was no-one around to ask about him and the janitor sweeping the floor probably wouldn't know much more than she did. Haydee glanced away, letting out a tired breath and retraced her route back to the visitor's lobby. Jocelyn noticed her and went very still in his seat before rubbing a shirt sleeve across his eyes. It came away slightly damp as he lowered it. "Oh..."

"We don't know anything yet," She was trying to be reassuring despite the fear in the back of her mind.

"Haydee?"

She started, lifting her gaze from the tattered magazine in her hands at the sound of the familiar voice. "Daniel?"

He still looked too thin, and his hair was as short as when she had shaved it for him but the backpack was slung over his shoulders. Haydee stood, wrapping her arms around his waist. "How are you feeling?"

Daniel cupped the side of her face before dropping his hand back to his side. "Better than I have been, honestly."

Haydee smiled shyly, resting her head against his chest. She could feel the leanness of his body through the fleece hoodie and cotton t-shirt. "You're finally allowed to go home now? I'm glad."

It was a relief in more than one way as she took a step back, giving him some space. "How about dinner first?"

His smile was rueful. "I'm still on a restricted diet, Haydee. There's a lot I'm not supposed to eat right now."

She shrugged, running through a mental list of restaurants before settling on one. "How about Greek? That's mild, right? C'mon, I'll pay. My treat for tonight."

Jocelyn spoke up now, glancing at them. "And you'll come home to Calais soon?"

"Maybe," Daniel looked away. "I still have follow-up appointments and tests that I need to be here for. I can't make them if I'm three hours away."

"Oh," Jocelyn quieted at that and scuffed a booted foot across the tiled floor. "Okay,"

Haydee was as good as her word though he took things carefully, cautious with his meal. He was better, but it would take a while for his appetite to come back. Jocelyn and Haydee by contrast, seemed perfectly happy to polish of their meals. He set his knife and fork down after a few minutes, the dish still only half finished.

"Take it home?" The waitress asked.

He nodded, leaning back in his seat and trying to ignore the other customers in the corner of the little Greek restaurant and the small girl pointing at them. "Please,"

She inclined her head, setting a Styrofoam box in front of him and turned to Haydee with the bill. "Split the bill or...?"

"I'll pay," Haydee pulled her card out of her purse and set it on the table as he stood, pushing away from table.

She made a discrete gesture and he nodded, making sure the face mask covered his mouth and nose. There was no choice if he wanted to use the bathroom, he would have to pass by the table with the little girl and her parents.

The girl giggled, pointing at him and wriggled free from her place, ducking out from under the table. "That's scary."

Her parents exchanged looks with one another before the father sighed, reaching for the girl's hand. "Sorry, she's only six. She doesn't know about masks. I work at the hospital as a security guard. Claudia, it's rude to point and say scary when there's a reason for wearing the mask. People with them are getting over really bad colds."

"Oh," Claudia pouted but didn't resist her father's hold. "Okay. Can we go for ice cream now?"

"It's January," The other man's voice was resigned. "But-"

Claudia stamped her foot and followed it up with a sneeze. "Want ice-cream."

Her mother blanched, hastily pulling the girl back away from Daniel. "Sorry, really I am. Her grandmother spoils her rotten, especially when she has a cold. There's no talking with my mother about this though we've tried to."

Claudia's father looked away tiredly. "Don't ever have kids, unless you already do."

"We haven't even gotten to that point yet," Haydee's voice was wry. "Engaged through a bit of manipulation, sure. Sex and kids, no. Not yet. It's been... complicated."

"I can imagine," The man's voice was resigned. "Let's not get in your way then,"

"We were just about to go, to be honest," Haydee held up the plastic bag holding the leftover Greek food. "Just celebrating Daniel's release from the hospital."

"Congratulations then," Claudia's mother tucked a strand of hair behind one ear and picked the girl up in her arms.

"Maybe," Haydee fumbled one handed for her keys and pressed the unlock button on the little fob. "There's still a ways to go yet. Recovery wise."

"And then the wedding," Jocelyn said brightly.

Haydee flushed, tugging the younger boy towards the door. "Yeah, the wedding. That too."

She'd almost forgotten that it was only two months away now, with everything else going on, it had felt like they had much longer before then. And now there were more than butterflies in her stomach at the quickly approaching date. "Thanks so much, Jocelyn,"

He somehow managed to plaster an innocent look on his face. "Welcome."

If he hadn't been her student, a few years older than he was or Daniel's brother, she would have flipped him off for blurting that out to virtual strangers. "Let's just go, please."

"I'm happy here if you guys want to go out and do something else," Jocelyn held his book out and let it drop onto the apartment's coffee table. "Fun stuff,"

Haydee glanced reflexively towards Daniel, noting the way he had gone pink and averted his gaze from her. Apparently fun things in Jocelyn's book didn't equate to a movie and popcorn somewhere. "Uhm, I don't know who you've been hanging out lately but that's not exactly an appropriate thing to ask, Jocelyn."

Jocelyn blinked as a look of dawning realization came over his face and then he bit down on his lower lip. "Oh. Sorry, Haydee, Dani."

His voice was smaller than it had been. "It just slipped out before I could think about it."

Daniel sat down on the couch, dropping an arm across his

shoulders and pulled him close. "Don't bother, just so you know not to say that again."

Haydee's expression was bewildered as she looked between them. "For anyone who doesn't know how your family is like. What's with the soap?"

He forced a rueful smile at that, recalling the memory. "I was eight, maybe nine when I told Dad to... well, go away but it wasn't particularly polite. He had Mom find the lavender soap and warm water and rinsed my mouth with it. And then spent half an hour after that on my knees in church praying for forgiveness. Never swore again after that. Jocelyn's too young to remember but he must have heard the story from somewhere or guessed at it given how our family is."

"Our sister," Jocelyn's voice was still meek. "She told me it was what bad kids deserved. She didn't swear either." Haydee dropped into a crouch next to the sofa. "Not one to spoil you,

huh."

"Not particularly," Daniel's tone was dry. "Though he stopped well short of abuse. Dad wasn't one to hit any of us or use his belt when we did something wrong."

She paused, considering that. "You know, you don't actually talk much about your childhood in New Orleans. The soap incident is the first real story I've heard from that time. That and..."

Haydee shivered in discomfort. "A disturbing semester involving a medical examiner's skills."

"And that's why I don't talk about it," Daniel's irony turned to toneless. "It wasn't until high school that I realized most people don't watch as their parents preform an autopsy on any stray cat or dog they recently put to sleep."

"Fair," Haydee glanced away, putting the leftover Greek into the refrigerator. Jocelyn's unsubtle hint towards allowing them sex aside, and Daniel's reservations about any such thing before the wedding. "What do you want to do, anyway? I don't think a club would be in your interest and probably too risky as it is."

"A movie," Jocelyn's interjection was hopeful. "The Hobbit?"

He had a copy saved from home stashed in his backpack just in case.

"It's as good as any," Daniel said.

Haydee bit down lightly on one fingernail before nodding. "Sure,"

She could use a little escape for the three hours or so it took for the movie to run from start to finish. "Popcorn anyone?"

Jocelyn cheered a bit at that, scrambling from the couch to go in search of the treat. Daniel's mouth tightened briefly before he shook his head at the handful offered to him in a paper towel. "Persephone didn't mention popcorn as a risk but I probably shouldn't chance it. And I'd rather not have someone's grubby little paws over my food."

"Loss," Jocelyn's answer was lost amid the handful of popcorn he stuffed into his mouth.

Haydee sighed, taking a piece or two and half closing her eyes in pleasure at the buttery flavor. "I hate to say it but you're missing out, Daniel."

He snorted, shaking his head. "I doubt I'm missing anything at all. I wasn't a big junk food fan even before I got sick. The movie's starting."

She had expected Jocelyn to the one to fall asleep halfway through the three-hour movie but she wasn't surprised when it was Daniel. He'd had a long day after all and as well as he was now, the anemia and lingering medicine in his body had likely worn him out. Haydee smiled briefly, muting the film and pulled a blanket over his shoulders, fluffing the pillow against the armrest. "I don't think he'd mind too much if you took the bed. I'll go find a hotel room for the night."

Jocelyn looked at her sleepily. "Stay, one of Dani's boxes had a camping cot just in case. An' a sleeping bag. I'll curl up on that instead. Bed's yours, maybe."

As tempting as that was, she nearly refused until a yawn escaped. "Fine, bed it is."

She only woke long enough to see the bathroom light flicker on, hear the door close behind someone and the sound of that person retching into the toilet before she drifted off, dismissing it as nothing. There would be time to investigate in the morning, not at two AM.

Morning came before it and she woke first, dragging herself into the bathroom to tidy her pixie cut up and brush her teeth free of the lingering popcorn taste that coated the back of her throat. "Points for saying no, I guess."

The ice-cold water she poured from the tap cleared her head and rinsed some of the taste from her mouth. Mint toothpaste did the rest before the scent of coffee filled the air, tempting her with its scent. Coffee was good, was life and she really wanted a cup.

Daniel looked much less enthusiastic by the mug Jocelyn put down in front of him. "Decaf?"

"Uhm," Jocelyn sniffed at the contents before taking a cautious sip of his hot chocolate. "Dunno. I'm not a fan of coffee, so maybe?"

Haydee took a swallow of her own cup and discretely spat it out into the mug again. "Decaf. Where does an eighteen-year-old learn to make coffee anyway?"

Jocelyn shrugged, holding his cup in both hands. "The internet teaches everything. Couple guys at my own school had a theatre thing about making a coffee pot one year. School's one act play festival, think."

His expression drooped as he looked towards Daniel. "You don't like it?"

"I'm sure it's fine but the smell is kind of putting me off eating right now." Daniel said.

Haydee bit down on her lower lip, hiding her expression. So it had been Daniel throwing up last night, just when she'd thought he was over this. "It smells fine to me."

Then again, Daniel did have a faint expression of nausea on his face, whether or not he was aware of it, remained to be seen. She glanced away and reluctantly emptied the mug down the sink. Caffeinated or not, it would have woken her up better than without it but she would have preferred caffeine to not. "Anything around here that won't make you sick?"

"Oatmeal, maybe? Yogurt?" Daniel looked away. "I wouldn't mind a bit of toast. Something light."

Something light wasn't the problem, it was how little he was eating and able to keep down without throwing up afterwards. "I don't want to call you out on a problem that might not exist but…"

Haydee trailed off, uncomfortable with the direction the conversation was taking. "You don't think this is getting pretty close to anorexia? Not the eating disorder exactly, just in how you aren't eating much or keeping it down."

"You think I'm…" Daniel glanced at her tiredly before looking away. "Anorexic? I'm not counting calories or exercise obsessed. I can't go down a flight of stairs without being winded- it'll be months before I can go on a run again."

When he put it that way, she had to agree with him but it didn't make her any less worried about his health. "Alright, fair enough. Just… try to eat something for breakfast."

She was trying to reassure herself that there wasn't a problem, but it was hard to watch as he picked over the toast and yogurt cup in front of him. It was his medication, not any desire to lose weight here that was causing this. Wasn't it? "Please?"

It was easy to see he was trying for her, but it was still disappointing when he only finished a couple pieces of lightly buttered toast and half of the yogurt in front of him. "What's the plan next? After I go back to Calais?"

"Cleaning, probably," Daniel rinsed his bowl out and dropped the breadcrusts into the garbage can, "And then going to service. There's a church not far from the apartment."

Haydee quieted at that, taking the plate from him before placing it into the dishwasher. "You need time to think, I guess. I understand."

It wasn't that Daniel no longer wanted her, he just needed a little space to himself from time to time. And it was getting past the time when she should have been on the road home. "Daniel?"

He looked up at her and away, leaning against the kitchen counter. "Yeah?"

There was only one thing she could say now. "I'm glad you're alright."

CHAPTER TWENTY-SEVEN

The time in prison hadn't been for more than a night or two but it was still irritating, he'd barely laid a hand on Daniel. Certainly, he hadn't hurt his cousin. And yet it had earned him a security escort out of the hospital and into the waiting police car.

On the other hand, it hadn't been a long stay in the cell, just a night or two before release but it was a release he wasn't looking forward to. Uncle Alain might not have expected a return so soon. He was expecting a phone call though. Jared gritted his teeth, looking down at the phone in his hand before reluctantly dialing the number and switching to French. His father might not have been so strict with where and when to use the language, Alain was, unfortunately. Though it had the small advantage of covering his conversation from those who might overhear him. "Uncle?"

Alain's voice on the other hand was prompt, cool and as predicted, answering in French rather than English. "Yes?"

Jared glanced away, glaring briefly at a young woman crossing the hotel lobby. She squeaked and edged out of his way with a hasty apology. "I know where Daniel is now. It took a few weeks of looking but I found it."

Alain's voice took a harder edge at that. "And where is he? For that matter, where are you?"

He paused, glancing down at the phone again and looked away. "Augusta, Maine. And a shit forsaken place, it is. It's snowing."

"I didn't answer your call for a report on the weather, Jared." Alain's voice tightened with irritation. "Your call came just as I was negotiating a deal on behalf of another party. With a substantial benefit to our family."

Jared scowled, ignoring that remark. "Play at politics if you want to, that's your thing. It's not Dad's or mine. Daniel is in the hospital being treated for something he could have fixed himself if he had the sense to. Or avoided completely if he wasn't so stupidly obsessed with being nice. He was weak."

Weak and an idiot at that.

"Not as weak as that," Alain's tone turned towards briefly pensive. "He was as good as playing the game as his mother was, even if his... motivations were questionable. He should have been teaching Jocelynn, not trying to protect the girl."

Jared leaned against the wall next to the elevator, idly playing with the lighter in one pocket of his leather jacket. "From what I figured out, Jocelynn learned all on her own. And better than Daniel ever could. She pickpocketed his credit card, used it to make a purchase at a jewelry store and got away without raising very many questions. None, actually. If I cared about that, I might actually be impressed."

"Quite," Alain's voice was carefully neutral. "Jocelynn's quick grasp of manipulation aside, you said Daniel had been hospitalized. Did you learn why he was?"

"Don't know, don't care," Jared looked away, irritated.

"Apparently someone's more interested in protecting him than I thought. Some black guy getting off on using Anubis as a name and a lady doctor who calls herself Persephone. She sounds more likely than he does."

Alain's sigh was soft and full of warning. "You always lacked the subtlety your father hoped in you, Jared. A little more time in Paris may have helped, I think. You've always been the American in the family."

"So what?" Jared asked. "Just because I prefer going straight for things rather than running-"

"You lack patience as well as subtlety," Alain's words were nearly ice now. "Things expected here, nephew. You may be thirty-three, but you are a child in temperament. Always going for the immediate instead of waiting for the better prize. One day you will gamble, and you will lose it for the sake of a quick reward."

"I've waited," Jared said. "I could have tracked Daniel down sooner if he was a little less cautious. It took me weeks to find him. And I only did because his bitch of a girlfriend told me where and how to look for him."

"His girlfriend," Alain said.

"Yeah," Jared smirked slightly at that. For once he had a slight, small advantage here. For a few minutes, he was the one in control, not his uncle. "The jewelry store trip Jocelynn tricked her way into, she used the credit card to buy an engagement ring for Daniel's girlfriend. I can only guess that there's been a proposal, but I would put an easy grand on it. Daniel's too nice to refuse that. More than that, the slut isn't even Catholic. Her parents are make-believe witches. I looked briefly just before. Not a scrap of our power in them."

There was no way to see Alain's expression, but he was willing to bet on fury even if it was hidden behind the ice. "How's that for patient? I could have killed her weeks ago if

I'd found her then. I haven't because I want to see the whole family's misery. Daniel isn't just ill in the hospital, he's dying."

"You would be wise to hide your pleasure, Jared." Alain's voice dropped again, becoming toneless. "Regardless of my feelings on his escape and theft of my daughter, he is my son and your cousin. A little loyalty and respect matters."

"I won't pity someone dying from anemia," Jared's tone was tight. "He brought it on himself by using his own life instead of another. Weak, just as I said. Not strong enough to take what he needed."

"And yet, his skills are better than yours," Alain said dryly. "At thirteen, he managed to shatter bis bedroom windows and drive away a ghost intent on hurting him. By the time he was eighteen, he was already binding the dead to ask questions of them, and he was at least proficient in using his magic to delay an aneurysm if he wanted it. You struggled to master even the basics of Latin, a language they once taught in school, much less work anything with as care as he does. He's only improved since then. You, nephew, can barely light an emergency candle when it's right in front of you."

Jared bristled at that, offended. "I don't need to do anything with fire when I have a lighter and a can of gasoline at hand, uncle. My skills are elsewhere,"

"Clearly," Alain's tone had returned to cool if not outright cold. "Save it for when you need someone dead of a particularly messy knot in their intestines, Jared. It's all you're good for."

He hung up with a soft click, leaving Jared fuming at the phone in his hand before he pocketed it. "Damn him."

Alain's words and the tone behind them were clear enough; it was past time to return home to New Orleans. Whether or not he wanted it.

Persephone put the file down, glancing at Daniel as he took the seat in front of her desk. "I've been going over your tests and the medical history again. There's been some improvement but not as much as I would have liked to see."

Some improvement was better than nothing at all. Daniel looked away, trying to follow the faint woodgrain printed on the door's surface. "It's a start, isn't it?"

"It could be," Her gaze was carefully neutral. "But I was reading the medical history your general practitioner sent me. You neglected to mention the medication you take."

Daniel went still, a dry taste in his mouth at that before he let his shoulders drop. "I didn't mention it because I haven't had an episode in five years. The doctor in New Orleans tried phenytoin and phenobarbital first. Neither of them worked for me. It was Tegretol or surgery and Dad shut that down when it was suggested."

She sighed, pinching the bridge of her nose before dropping it back to the desk. "I thought the anemia was idiopathic, now… one of the side effects of carbamazepine is an adverse effect on the production of blood cells. It's rare but it does happen."

"I understand," He looked down at the desk between them, biting down on his lower lip. "Look, I'll keep coming in for any test you need but this doesn't have anything to do with the anemia."

"Daniel, you had a seizure after being admitted to the ICU unit," Persephone said. "The fever and its effects may have been because of your exposure to a cold or germs but I cannot ignore your medical history either."

"So, what then?" The question needed to be asked regardless of the ice making its way down his spine. "The wedding's in six weeks now. It's too late to change the date and postpone it."

She sighed again, pushing her glasses back up to the bridge of her nose. "So long as you're careful then. Do try to remember that."

"I will," It was all he could promise under the circumstances. The wedding and its date were set, and he wasn't going to back out of it just because of his illness. "Maybe we'll see more of an improvement in the next few days?"

He was hoping anyway. A slight rash across his shoulders and arms had appeared and then healed within a few days, a day or prior to the follow up appointment. "I mean, the nausea's gone. I'm feeling better now."

"So long as you're sure," Persephone said.

He nodded, standing. "Thanks,"

Groceries were the first thing on his list of errands to run and then it was back to the apartment for a nap. Just because he wasn't throwing up anymore, didn't mean the fatigue had faded as soon as the rash had. And he wanted to run a little test or two of his own. It didn't take long after the groceries were put away for him to clear a space in the living room and spread out the cheap navy-blue rug over the hardwood floor. It was already marked with a white line of paint but that by itself wasn't enough for what he wanted to do. The white paint was only to make tracing out the salt line easier, connecting the candles at the four corners. He could have lit the candles with just a gesture, but it seemed wiser to use a lighter this time around. A fifth candle was set in the middle, unlit as he closed his eyes and cast the warding. It showed itself as a slight shimmer in the air around the edges of the circle.

He held a hand out, calling a little ball of fire to it and drew back, tossing the flame against the warding. It splattered against the barrier, fizzling out into nothingness. Daniel sat back, glancing at the unlit candle at the center of the circle before extinguishing the four at the edges of the salt line and scuffing part of the white marking out. The warding vanished a moment later, no longer needed for its purpose. Daniel managed a brief smile, relieved that his test had worked. He hadn't expected it to so it was nice to see that he still could use his power, if sparingly. At least until the gray sparkles started at the edges of his vision and threatened to

overwhelm him. Daniel went to his knees, bracing himself on the coffee table before the darkness closed over his head. The dark time felt like forever but when his vision cleared enough for him to look at his clock, it had been less than a minute and a half though his head hurt. Daniel forced himself to sit up, briefly touching the wet, sticky graze on the back of his head before lowering his hand. The fingertips came away stained with red, a few spots on the edge of the coffee table. "Oh…"

He squeezed his eyes shut tight for a moment before finding the little pill bottle in his backpack and swallowing the dose dry. Persephone could say what she liked about the possibility of the anemia and his medicine being connected, he disagreed. As… uncomfortable as the fainting spells were, they weren't the episodes he'd had as a child.

The graze on the other hand, he sighed and dialed the phone number in his contact list. "Persephone? I don't know if you have the time for a home visit but I think I fainted again. I definitely hit my head."

"I'll be over as soon as I can be," Persephone's answer was abrupt.

"Thanks," Daniel said.

CHAPTER TWENTY-EIGHT

The wedding was as small as anticipated, with her parents and grandparents in the front pew. A couple of her closest friends from university next to them. Haydee took a breath, smoothing down the skirt of the lace sheath dress she wore as the first notes of the song started. Father Allen had reluctantly agreed to a simplified version of a Catholic service since few of the people she knew were familiar with the rites.

She swallowed, taking one step and then another down the aisle. Her gaze was fixed on Daniel standing by the altar rather than the priest. He had shaved his hair again rather than deal with the itch and look of hair just beginning to grow back.

All that mattered today was that she was about to marry Daniel. It didn't matter that all he wore was a dress shirt and pants. He still looked perfect to her. His eyes widened at the sight of her dress and the little lacy jacket, but he seemed to approve despite the wedding dress's strapless state. "It suits you…"

"Thanks," Haydee blushed, looking down and tuning out

the service portion of the ceremony in favor of admiring Daniel. "It's still hard to believe that I'm two years older than you."

He kept his voice to a murmur, looking over at the priest for a moment. "You read too many romances, Haydee."

Daniel was teasing her in his own way, she wasn't the kind of woman who read romance novels. Most of the female protagonists were silly, shallow characters. Still, she was close to having her own dream filled. Even more so when his mouth met hers in a brief, chaste kiss. His touch was just as gentle as he slipped the wedding band onto her hand. She reciprocated after him and at last, the service was over.

The hours afterwards were a blur. Dinner at a nice steak-house and a short reception afterwards. Haydee rested her head against his shoulder as they turned in a slow spin of a dance before stepping off the floor for his sake. Daniel's stamina wasn't like it had been before he had gotten sick. "How are you feeling?"

He glanced away, sitting down on a nearby chair. "Tired, honestly. It's been a long day."

"We could slip away," Haydee said. "Mom booked us a hotel room downtown for the night since a honeymoon is out of the question and I still have a couple months left teaching for the school year."

Slipping away was easily the best idea all night and he was looking forward to it. "Jocelyn?"

"Mom'll take him home," Haydee glanced towards the boy sitting at the table, picking over brownie crumbs leftover on his plate. "It's our night, let's enjoy it."

She arched her back at that, wrapping an around Daniel's shoulders as she pulled him close against her body. The pleasure he gave her was greater than his lack of experience and she clung to him, in part desperation, in part love. Sooner or later they would have to return to the real world but luck willing, that wouldn't be for minutes yet.

Haydee straddled him, cupping the side of his face in one hand and sliding the other down across his shoulder and upper arm. Care? Not when the white spark of her climax was running through her like fire. Her first time hadn't been so engaging, so... perfect. It didn't even matter to her that Daniel had a fresh shallowly healed mark on his upper arm or that when she explored the lines of his body, she could trace out his collarbones and the smaller bones of his wrists. "M-mine,"

"Mine," He echoed her claim, brushing a lock of her hair out of her eyes before subsiding, pulling away and reaching for the pair of jeans inexplicably at the foot of the bed. Her evening gown was discarded in a heap on the floor, in a way that would likely leave wrinkles in the cloth if she didn't get it dry cleaned later on.

Haydee sagged against the bedspread, still feeling the warmth of him between her legs. "Told you it would be alright. You did better than I thought you would for a virgin."

"Not anymore," His voice was dry as he sat on the edge of the bed. "Have you thought about the surname problem?"

Taking LaLaurie was a problem? She sat up, pulling the hotel blanket over her chest to spare Daniel from discomfort. Sex was one thing; she'd noticed how his gaze had lingered on her and then hastily averted. Some things clearly hadn't changed, and he found the female body uncomfortable to look at. "Other than it sounding a little bit... alliterative?

Odd, anyway. I don't have a problem with it, if that's what you want me to do."

He glanced away, looking down at his hands. "No need to be officially tied to my family, Haydee."

She shrugged, pulling a loose-fitting tank top over her head for modesty's sake and sat next to him, tracing the old lines of scarring that decorated his forearms. "Haydee LaLaurie…"

On second thought, she could see why he had a reservation or two about that. His name didn't suit her given name. And given the reputation, the LaLaurie name had… little wonder he wasn't entirely sure about her taking it in place of Ashworth. "Mhm… okay, I see it. It doesn't sound that great when said out loud. But if we ever have a kid, she's taking your surname and people be damned about how funny it sounds."

That begged the question then and she sat next to him, bracing her back against his arm. "I know it's too soon and that pregnancy doesn't always happen on the first try but what would you name a baby if it was yours?"

He looked back at her, tangling a bit of her hair between his fingers before letting it go. "Lisette, Elizabeth if she's a girl. A boy… Marin?"

She was a little skeptical of his suggestion for a boy if they ever had one but willing to look past that for the sake of the way the usually faint trace of a Parisian accent in his voice was stronger than he normally let it be. It added a slightly more exotic flavor to his speech, and she liked hearing it. "I like Elizabeth at least."

"Good," He played with a bit of her hair before letting go of it and moving to put a little space between them. "What now?"

Haydee bit down on the tip of one nail, pretending to

consider the question. "Jocelyn isn't as good at holding a grudge as you said he was, but do you think there's still room in your budget for a puppy?"

Daniel glanced at her for a long moment, moving his arm away from his stomach. "Depends on the price, I guess. Why?"

She laughed, trying not to notice the flicker of pain that crossed his face. "We promised, didn't we? I try to keep my promises and his birthday is coming up, isn't it?"

"So long as he promises to take care of them, I think I can manage," Daniel lay back on the coverlet, glancing at her. "There's... another thing."

Another thing. She bit down on her lower lip at that, fearing the worst. His hesitation must have meant something bad, or the prospect of another impending hospital stay. "Daniel..."

He turned his head to look at her. "It isn't the latest results from my blood tests. I just thought you should have a vehicle after what happened to yours. It was second hand at best, and it was fifteen years old. It died on you."

"Oh," She blinked as the clarification hit her and then her shoulders slumped. "The offer's appreciated, Daniel but what kind of junior high teacher drives an Audi, much less can afford it. Don't get me wrong, I'm grateful but sometimes you don't really realize what money is worth. Not everyone has the ability to throw cash or credit out for the sake of a new car."

Daniel sighed, taking her hand in hers. "It isn't a brand-new car, Haydee. I just changed the registration and insurance so that we're both listed on it. For when-"

"If," She corrected him briefly. "If, Daniel."

"When," His voice was wan. "It's when the time comes. My blood count hasn't improved much since I had the transplant and the nausea's back. It was mild tonight, thankfully but…"

"Any other symptoms?" Haydee moved back, trying to take him in full. He looked healthy to her though still lean. "What do you think this is?"

Daniel subsided for long enough that he might have drifted off into sleep before he spoke again, looking at her. "Between the nausea, throwing up in the toilet again and the stomach cramping. Persephone…thinks I have graft versus host disease. She gave me cyclosporine just before the transplant, but I've been off that for weeks now. It's Prograf and hope for the best but it doesn't seem like its helping much."

He offered her his hand to take, and she accepted it numbly, turning the hotel room light on to get a better view of things. The space between upper arm and forearm was dry, peeling like a bad sunburn. Haydee swallowed, careful not to press too hard as she touched the new scarring. "You haven't… have you?"

"No," He sat up, retrieving his t-shirt. "Not since I tested things a while ago and fainted afterwards. Besides, knife cuts are clean. This… just peeled and scarred over."

"What exactly is graft versus host disease?" Haydee asked. "It's been a while since you've mentioned it and I'd rather hear it from you than the internet."

"The cells from the bone marrow transplant are… attacking my body," Daniel said. "But things are… inconclusive. She said she would give us a week of space for anything we wanted to do. After that, she wants to run a biopsy or two."

"I see," Haydee quieted at that, hating the prickling feeling in her eyes at his words. Just married and if luck wasn't with them, just as soon lost. "There's treatment, right? Some medicine or something somewhere. There must be, I didn't marry you so we could have the next couple months together – I want our whole lives ahead of us. Kids and grandkids or something like that. I want you to see Jocelyn's family when he's older."

Daniel's sigh was resigned, weary. "You're assuming Jocelyn will want kids, Haydee. He might not be as devout as I am but even, he'll draw the line at carrying someone's baby. Last I heard, when I asked me about surgery as soon as he was able to, he wasn't planning on anything down low. Too invasive or creepy, he said."

"He's a boy with a vagina," Haydee wiped the wetness away roughly. "So what? He can adopt instead. I just want you to live and get better again."

She tightened her grip on the pillow and held it close to her chest. "I'd be the last person to accuse you of anything here, but don't you think you're being a little bit too fatalistic?"

"Acceptance isn't fatalism," Daniel said.

"It is to me," She slumped against the headboard of the bed, not meeting his gaze. "You might not think you're giving up, but it sounds like you already have."

"So, I'm supposed to go out screaming and fighting the doctors until its too late?" His voice was tired. "I'd rather accept what happens and be… comfortable at the end rather than reject reality."

"That might be you, it isn't me," She hated the misery coloring her voice and looked away, trying to focus on the lamp light in an attempt to hold back on the tears threatening to fall. "I won't stop fighting, even if you have."

Under other circumstances, those would have been fighting words but Daniel was far more patient than most guys. Too good to her, in truth and far better than she deserved. "There has to be something out there, something else we haven't tried."

He opened his mouth to speak and turned away hastily, coughing.

Haydee blanched, all thoughts of the pleasure he'd given her, forgotten at the way the cough sounded. Harsh and laboring to breathe between it. "Daniel?"

She put a hand between his shoulder blades, hoping that it would help – however slight it would be. And tasted something bitter in her mouth at the tension in his body as he fought to breathe. "If I can help, I will."

The coughing seemed to subside after a few moments, enough for him to sit and wipe his mouth with a tissue. "You are helping, you know. I wouldn't be here if not for you."

Maybe he would be, maybe he wouldn't. It was hard to say but she held her hand out for the crumpled tissue. "Can I?"

He sighed, giving it to her. "I don't think you'll be happy with the result."

She bit down on her lower lip and smoothed it out, noting the blood spotting the white paper like cloth. "How long has this been going on?"

"Briefly, months ago but it cleared up then," Daniel looked away, something like shame coloring his expression. "I noticed the coughing just before the wedding, but it wasn't as bad then."

"That's blood," Her voice was tight. "Daniel, I don't think you'll agree with me right now but we're going back to the hospital in the next day or two. Please, for Jocelyn if not for me."

He sighed again, brushing a hand across her cheek before lowering it back to his side. "Alright, we'll go tomorrow."

CHAPTER TWENTY-NINE

Daniel's strength was to be commended but it was just as apparent that he was burning something up inside, just trying to hold his illness at bay. Persephone glanced at him over the rim of her glasses and folded them up neatly, placing them on a stack of paper. They weren't strictly necessary for her kind, but she had always found the fashion appealing enough to wear a set. And truth be told, her sight was weak after centuries of time spent in her kinsman's domain. Colors, shapes were blurred and faded around the edges. Fine print was nearly impossible without her twin's aid.

Demeter somehow had managed to escape that fate for which she was grateful for, though poor sight was less of a disadvantage when she had scent and hearing to compensate for her vision. As well as more unusual gifts. Things very few mortals were aware of, and certainly, only one of her patients.

Those, however, couldn't be spoken of while the young man's wife was in the office with him. There was a firm line between the shadowy world and the daylight one and only through accident or mischance would she step across it.

She squinted at the report in front of her and cursed the tiny lettering as she reached for a magnifying glass. "You had concerns?"

If Haydee had been one of her kind, the girl would have been a hedgehog or a porcupine for the way she bristled at the question. "Kinda, yeah."

Her voice dropped slightly as she looked at the hand Daniel clasped in hers. "He, uhm, was coughing up blood last night. I thought it was important enough to check out after-after…"

"After the rash and the scarring on my arms," Daniel said. "Doctor…"

Persephone set the magnifying glass down, distracted by the prickle in the back of her mind. This wasn't Anubis, she knew the scent of his presence even if he wasn't physically around at the moment. And if he were, it would probably be doing what he had for the past few thousand years. Tending to the dying and the dead. This was a different sense, something she hadn't felt since before the time she had bound her spirit to Hades. Life, or the beginning of it anyway. Humans rarely conceived on their first try so this smelled of fate to her, Lachesis and her sisters' interference long before these two had ever known of each other. Daniel's girlfriend was with child. "Yes?"

"You seem like you're distracted,"

Haydee's voice cut through her thoughts and she glanced away, focused on the present situation. "Just the child of a patient's wife, I think. Forgive me for that. This may not be the answer either of you want to hear but I think it best if Daniel were to be readmitted to the hospital. Simply for a test or two."

"But you've run every test you can by now," Haydee's

voice was tight, struggling to restrain whatever she was feeling. "Doctor Sotaira…"

Persephone sighed, running a lock of hair between two fingers before releasing it. "You should have been Hephaestus' child with that fire in you, Haydee. Or maybe Ares, though few in mythology liked the man."

And the man in question had a wildling daughter and a son of his own already. Ares had been a given name, not one he had adopted of his own will but then names meant little in the end. Ares or Fenris, it was still the same bear sized wolf she was grudgingly acquainted with through the man's now feral son. Fenris's daughter was only little better. To this day, she wasn't entirely sure if the black panther favored Alexander of Athens or of Kiev for a name.

"What?" That seemed to at least put Haydee off or distract her from her demands of more tests and hypotheticals. Things that didn't have answers yet.

"I was attempting to distract you," Her voice was dry despite attempts to keep a neutral façade on. "Clearly it was enough for now. If only you'll listen, little one. I can ask for the tests to be done but he will have to spend the time in the hospital for it. I know you would… prefer not to but this is the best place under the circumstances. Particularly with his compromised immune system."

Haydee slumped, looking defeated. "Okay, fine. I know I asked for it first, but I was kind of hoping it wouldn't happen."

"I am sorry," Persephone said. "But it is the truth, regardless."

The girl nodded, glanced away and stood before walking out the door. "Coffee break."

Perhaps it was for the best, she had some questions better asked when not in Haydee's presence. And coffee was a better alternative to asking for a cigarette and lighter. "What does she know?"

Daniel hesitated, gaze drifting towards the closed door before it returned to her face. "About you? Or me?"

It wasn't always clear what Persephone wanted or asked for. She had a habit of keeping feeling and expression masked around him but whether that was reserve or necessary as a doctor wasn't certain. "She... knows I'm a witch. It didn't seem right keeping that from her."

"And?" She was looking at him, still unreadable. "What about the things we spoke of last time? The episodes as you called them."

"I haven't mentioned that." Daniel said. "It's one more thing she doesn't need to worry about right now."

Persephone ran a hand through her hair, letting out a sigh. "She deserves the truth, Daniel. About your childhood and what you're attempting to do right now. I'm not a fool and I can sense it without even trying."

He glanced down, shamed. Maybe Haydee deserved the truth but he wasn't in a place where he could give her that. "It's complicated."

She arched an eyebrow at that, leaning back in her chair. "Tell me,"

What could he do but try to explain things to her? "You said it was my medication that was causing the anemia, I thought it was my magic. Maybe there isn't one particular origin but I've been trying to... slow my illness down, buy a little more time for myself." It was a delicate

balancing act either way, trying to slow the way the donor cells were attacking his body and using his magic without losing what little time he might have had left. "Haydee had a good point or two last night, I just didn't want to consider them at the time."

His voice dropped, quieting. "She's right, I don't want to die but at some point, soon, I will. I thought faith, maybe, acceptance but it's more like resignation. Like I'd already given up on a cure."

He lifted his gaze to her. "Even though there isn't one anymore. Everything we've tried so far hasn't worked or it hasn't been as promising as hoped for. And now I'm coughing up blood again. I don't need a chest x-ray to tell me that there's internal damage and scarring on my lungs. Much less a chance of pneumonia."

Persephone stacked the file folders into a neat pile, setting a pen horizontally across the top of the records before she moved around the side of the desk, taking a seat in the other chair before letting him rest his head on her shoulder. It wasn't strictly professional, but they were alone and the office door was closed to observers. They wouldn't be disturbed. "I know it seems inevitable, but people have beaten fate before, this may not be an end."

"I won't survive this," His voice was tired. "I know that much already."

She sighed, letting him cry onto the shoulder of her white coat. There seemed little else she could say or comfort him with beyond permitting him the small comfort of her touch for a few minutes. Any apology was weak at best, not worth the words the attempt at sympathy could bring. She was a doctor but one who preferred the clean, crisp nature of a medical report to dealing with people. Her sister was the one who liked the social interaction of dealing with patients. "Stay for an hour or two, I'll get the work done on admitting you again. Perhaps... you'll beat the illness after all, you're stronger than you give yourself credit for. As a witch and as a young man."

He snorted but didn't dispute her attempt at comfort

before snatching at a Kleenex from the box on her desk and coughing into it. When the crumpled tissue came away from his mouth, it was spotted with red, A trace of it lingering at the edge of his lower lip. "What should I tell Haydee?"

"The truth," Persephone said. "She deserves it in one way or another even if you refuse to mention your episodes to her."

Haydee had chosen a frozen hot chocolate from the coffee shop across the street than the hospital cafeteria's coffee, judging from the plastic cup and the rounded dome like lid when he found her seated at one of the tables. "Hi,"

She looked up at him, the tip of her nose pink from crying. "What did the doctor say?"

Daniel sat down gingerly, twisting the wedding band around his finger before quieting. "She thought it best if I told you the truth, at least once."

That earned him a hollow laugh. "You can't lie to save your life, Daniel. You're usually honest to a fault."

He tried for a smile he couldn't feel. "I omit things, Haydee. That's-"

"Not the same as lying to my face about it," She pushed the empty cup away where it teetered on its bottom rim and fell, rolling in a circle before going still. "You couldn't do that even if it killed you, metaphorically speaking."

"I know," He cupped her hand in his, looking away. "I don't need an x-ray or a scan to tell me that I have pneumonia and that the donor versus graft disease is damaging my lungs, I can sense it myself, even without seeing the blood on the tissues."

Haydee sniffled, brushing a hand across the side of his face. "But… what about everything else? Maybe…?"

"That might take another blood test or biopsy but…" He quailed before forcing himself to continue and put what he had sensed with his power into words. "My liver and kidneys are starting to fail on me even with my attempts at slowing the damage."

"So, what do we do then?" Her voice was subdued. "Do they know how- how long you have left?"

Not yet," He reached for the plastic cup and set it upright, rubbing a hand on his jeans leg. "I'm trying not to think about that, but Persephone said we should start thinking about palliative care. Or… end of life care."

"I don't want to," Haydee wiped a hand roughly across her eyes. "Daniel, please. I can't."

bit down on his lower lip, squeezing his eyes shut tight at her words as much as the pain that knotted in his abdomen. "Was the wedding a mistake?"

"No," Misery colored her voice. "It wasn't and I don't regret a moment of last night either, I just wish there was something we could do to help you get better." "I've been slowing

things, trying to anyway, with my magic," Daniel said softly. "I already told Persephone that this is a delicate balancing act. Using enough to slow things, using it sparingly enough to not tire myself out. I was stronger six weeks ago."

"And that's why you put my name on your car insurance and the rent for your apartment," Haydee said. "I remember what you said last night."

He sighed, shoulders slumping. "Yes, we're married now, I'd… hate to leave you without anything."

She chewed on her lower lip, drawing blood from the

small cut. "Is this something you talked about with Jocelyn? He deserves to know at least."

"I will, I just need time to figure things out and find a way to tell him." The words felt hollow, a lie even to his ears despite what Haydee had said about his inability to lie to another person. "I'll tell him, count on it."

"I hope so," Haydee said. "He loves you,"

"I know," What else could he say to that remark? It was the truth, however much it hurt to hear. Jocelyn would... grieve, whatever else happened in the next few weeks. "He's stronger than he looks though, he'll get through this."

Daniel glanced down at their clasped hands, not daring to pull away and break the connection between them. To do so would be like rejection of their relationship or a refusal of her unspoken offer of comfort. "I've already started talking with Persephone and- making arrangements for later. There's... things I want done." "I understand," Though her voice was dull as she looked at her phone. "School starts again next week but I'll be here for that weekend.

Just... don't decide that the middle of the week is a good time go on me. I want to be here for you. I promised you that, didn't I?"

"You did," Daniel said.

"Good," She stood, blowing her nose into her shirt sleeve and retrieved the empty plastic cup from the table for disposal. "Just so you know. And your doctor better call me as the next of kin or whatever if something does happen."

"I will," For what little it was worth, he would.

CHAPTER THIRTY

It was harder to remember the simpler things when the painkillers dulled everything else and made reaching for his power like trying to grab hold of water. There, easily perceived but much less easily held onto. The magic might have helped slow the progression of his illness if he could have found it. Instead, he was relying on medicine and what little he could keep down food wise. Little, truth be told, if it wasn't for the anti nausea drug, he would have spent a lot more time in front of the toilet. Or curled up in a shivering little ball next to it, for all the strength he could muster to get out of the bed.

He was always cold these days, it didn't matter that the sun was warmer than it had been a week or more earlier, heralding spring. The fleece hoodie and a scarf wouldn't change that truth for him.

"Daniel?" Rashid's voice was gentle, sounding from the hospital room door before the medical student crossed the threshold with a breakfast tray of orange juice, cereal and a small croissant. "You should try to eat something."

Vomit now or force himself to choke down the meal? One

would empty his stomach now, the other would only end in sorrow as he threw up in the basin by his bed. "Since when do you personally take care of food for patients?"

Rashid's smile was wan before it faded. "I persuaded the kitchen staff to part with something better than they usually serve. I won't be offended if you refuse, however."

For the young doctor's sake, he'd try to finish off the little pastry if nothing else. "Thanks, I guess."

He set the leather-bound journal on the bedspread, rubbing a hand across his eyes. The headache behind them was persistent now, stubbornly refusing to leave and at times, making his vision swim if not blur out of focus for seconds at a time.

"How are you feeling?" Rashid asked.

"Do you need an answer to that?" Daniel tore the croissant into pieces rather than eating it. "I feel like there's a knot in my abdomen, the headache won't leave and the rash looks like a bad sunburn across my shoulders. That's when I'm clear enough to think these days."

He slumped, wishing even that small effort of movement didn't leave him struggling to catch his breath. "H-Haydee's going to be mad. I promised her a year and I've already broken it."

"You've been fighting this illness for the better part of five months, Daniel." Rashid's answer was quiet. "I don't know anyone who could have survived this long and fought as hard as you have. Whether you regard it as I do, you're a warrior. One even my father would have respected."

His mouth twitched in something that might have been a wry expression. "And given Ra's temper, if not his disregard for humans – that's a generous compliment. He certainly never thought much of me."

"Sorry to disappoint," Daniel sucked in a breath, pressing

an arm against his stomach as the pain overwhelmed whatever medication he had been given to help a couple hours earlier. "Reminds me of Dad."

Rashid laughed despite himself. "Possibly but I doubt Ra would have ever gone as low as manipulating others for power. He was as blunt in his manner as a dull rock. No imagination to speak of. From what you've told me, Alain has more than his share of that, enough to get creative in how he... ah, hurts people."

"Thanks," Daniel said dryly.

"I meant no offense, of course," Rashid held a hand out for the journal, skimming the pages as a shadow crossed his face. "The ink, the faded sections are more than just a need for a new pen, aren't they?"

Daniel looked down at the blanket, tasting something bitter in his mouth. "Those are parts when I get tired and force myself to keep going. Haydee, Jocelyn deserve to know, right? I'm trying to teach Jocelyn how to control his skills but..."

"In case you leave him before he's ready," Rashid's hand was light on his shoulder, doing whatever the pain medication was failing to accomplish. "Is that why it's in English?"

"Yeah," Daniel lay back, turning onto his side towards the other man. "He doesn't know Latin or medieval... French and I wanted to be honest with him. Even if it risks disturbing anyone else who might read it."

"I'll hold onto it if you want me to," Rashid said.

That was kind of him. Daniel pulled the coverlet up over his shoulders, wishing it was warmer or heavier than it was. Linen and cotton were well enough and cheap, he would have preferred flannel. "You'd do that for me?"

The doctor snorted but there was no dismissal in the sound. "I'm a guardian, little one. May have failed in my duty where my own family and people were concerned but I think I can take care of a book or two without damaging them."

He was too tired to consider sitting up now but there seemed to be a story behind the remark. "What do you mean by that?"

"Ah," Guilt and something that might have been shame, briefly crossed Rashid's face. "Tutankhamun's tomb should have remained hidden, secret but Carter managed to stumble across it somehow. I failed the boy there when I gave my word I wouldn't. More recently, a New York museum archeologist managed to find and rob my father's tomb for science. The apparent story going around those circles is that Ra is an unknown, possibly predynastic pharaoh who fought against Narmer's attempts at unification and lost. Hidden away by a small priest sect and given a respectful burial instead of being left on the battlefield. I helped tend to his body in those days."

That must have been hard to deal with, maybe it still was but it was easy to understand being a protector at least. And the fear of failure. "Jocelyn,"

"Something like that, yes." Rashid looked away. "Though my duty was to the dead, not the living beyond using my medical skills."

He stood, brushing a hand over Daniel's shoulder. "Go on, get some sleep."

It was tempting but there was one thing he needed to know first before anything else. "Would you... know where to find a Catholic priest around here? I..."

The rest of the question went unsaid, unspoken through the coughing fit that tore at his chest. Rashid hesitated and shook his head. "I don't know Augusta as well as I know Detroit, Daniel. I'm sorry. I'll look but that's the best I can do."

"Then?" Though it was an effort to speak through the fit. "I'd... prefer it but I don't need him. So- so long as you're willing to listen."

Discomfort crossed Rashid's face at that. "I know what you want, it isn't hard to guess at, but I don't know if I have the right to do it for you. I'm... familiar with the Christian tradition, yes but Daniel, I don't have any faith in it. You're asking a pagan shapeshifter to give you last rites and absolution. I knew a priest or two once who would have named that blasphemy."

"Not in Rome," Daniel said.

Resignation followed the discomfort. "Lucky guess at the time period. It was sixth century Constantinople, however."

"Following the plague then?" Daniel asked.

"No," Rashid's mouth thinned. "Not in that sense, anyway. I could help people, so I tried to-"

He cut himself off with a bemused snort. "Clever for a human. Fine, I still can't say I agree, quite but I walked into that one for you. I'll give you what you want. On the condition you write a letter or two to Haydee before hand. She deserves that much, at least."

It wasn't uncommon for her period to be late by a day or two but a week was odd and worrisome. Haydee glanced into the bathroom mirror before turning away from the reflection. Her delay could have been easily from stress, nothing more than that. Anything other than that was more dangerous or unthinkable. "Ready to go?"

"No," Jocelyn said. "But... we have to, right?"

"It's Daniel, we owe him a visit," Even if she quailed at

the prospect rather than looked forward to it this time. "He's family."

And family stuck together no matter what, especially when they were sick. No matter how poor their condition was. She bit down on her lower lip, sticking a butterfly clip in her hair. Fidgeting with her appearance was easier to dwell on than Daniel's decline. The morning after the wedding and his readmittance to the hospital had been hard enough – Jocelyn hadn't been present to see it, the weeks after that just got harder and harder to bear seeing Daniel in pain. Or with the IV tube once more in his arm and a breathing tube in his nose. Last weekend, he'd barely awakened for her visit. Luck willing, this time would be different.

Even with the warnings about his condition – he had her biting on the inside of her cheek and wincing at the flare of pain. "Daniel?"

His expression went white with pain, sucking in a breath as he forced himself to sit up against the pillow enough to look at her. "Hey…"

"How are you… feeling?" It felt like a trite question, something asked only to comfort herself more than Daniel.

He slumped as his pallor took on a grayish look and he doubled over, retching into the plastic container next to the bed. "…Fine,"

Daniel had never been able to lie to her and his attempt now was at best, pathetic. Haydee sighed, sweeping a lock of hair behind one ear. "Daniel, please."

He quieted, wiping sweat away from his forehead and dropped his hand back into his lap. "I think I mentioned this earlier, how my liver and kidneys are failing on me. The donor cells decided my gut was the next best target."

She swallowed past the hard lump in her throat, taking his hand in hers and holding it. Daniel's skin felt thinner, the little bones of his wrist more apparent against the flesh than they had been earlier. "So... basically everything then? Stomach, liver and muscular? I've been doing... a little research in my spare time."

The research and what she could tell with her own eyes anyway. The rash had spread from his shoulders downwards across his arms and looked like a sunburn after too long on a California beach and his breathing was labored in between his words. It was hard to ignore the pain that crossed his face every time he shifted position in the bed as well. "How are you moving?"

He gave her a weary smile and lifted his arm, cupping her hand in his before releasing it. "Like a man in his seventies, not mid-twenties. Doctor Sotaira and the rest of the team think I've got a- a week or two left if I'm lucky. I get tired even going from the bed to the bathroom now. Can't imagine running like I used to."

"I'm sorry," Her apology felt as trite and worthless as asking about how Daniel felt right now. "Is there anything I can do for you?"

"I miss chocolate," Daniel said. "Don't know if I'll be able to keep more than a couple squares down but... I miss it. French chocolate more than the stuff they sell in the gift shop. Too sweet."

She wrinkled her nose in distaste but stood, reluctantly letting his hand go. "You mean the stuff that's so full of cocoa, it's nasty, bitter tasting?"

"Seventy percent cocoa isn't nasty,"

Daniel's protest was weak, but it made her attempt a smile regardless. At least he had a little strength left to argue with her over chocolate. "You can keep your French shit, I'm going for milk chocolate, the sweeter the better. Jesus, just find a piece of semi sweet baker's chocolate and nibble on that for a while."

"Please?" Daniel asked.

She squeezed her eyes shut for a moment, fighting back tears and nodded. "Don't know if any place around the hospital sells what you consider good chocolate, but I'll try to find it. Bernard Carlson?"

"Bernard Callebaut," He glanced away. "Or something like it."

Her smile wobbled, nearly fading but she nodded again. "Lucky I have my phone and an internet connection. You're picky, you know that. Most people would settle for a Hershey or Cadbury bar or something. Something... simple. You jump right to the French and apparently Canadian stuff. At least, that's not a shop I've heard of until I met you."

"Or spoiled," Daniel coughed, pressing his pajama sleeve against his mouth before looking away. "It's a lot I'm asking for, I know but American chocolate stinks."

Haydee bit down on her lower lip, wishing she hadn't said what she had. It was just one chocolate bar, something easy enough to get her hands on even if its source was far from the continental US. "No, look, even if I have to spend a day driving around the city for this thing, I'll find it, promise. There has to be some kind of French chocolate shop around here somewhere."

She hurried from the room before Daniel could see the tears streaking her face or continue the argument over the quality of American chocolate versus French. Spoiled was the last thing she would have called him for his request, not when his condition had worsened so quickly during the time when she wasn't around to visit him.

Her phone was already out of her pocket and she was anxiously scrolling through possibilities that fit Daniel's request as she collided with a doctor reading over his notes outside the small chapel space. Clipboard and her phone ended up on the floor, her phone's screen now black with a long, deep crack running down the front. "Oh…"

Now what was she going to do? That phone had been her lifeline to finding something for Daniel after all. "Sorry,"

The young doctor knelt, gathering up his notes and her phone before handing the newly created paperweight back to her. "Don't worry about it. Though, if you don't mind, you seem in a bit of a rush."

She colored, ashamed as much as anxious as she looked over her shoulder. "My boyfriend, he- he's got a taste for expensive French chocolate and he's sick, like the really sick kind of thing. I was looking for a place around here that might sell it."

Hope was better than fear, right? "Do you know anywhere?"

He shrugged, making the gesture careful. "Claudette Fortier's, maybe? A small family run thing; I think. May have inherited it from her father and never sold out to the bigger companies. They're a speciality chocolate maker and they might use the French style he's asking about."

"Thanks," She looked down the hallway towards the elevator. "I should-"

"Wait," The dark-skinned doctor caught her arm and released it, flushing a moment later. "I'm sorry, it was uncalled for but if your boyfriend doesn't mind waiting a little bit, I'd like to speak with you for a moment. If you don't mind."

Haydee hesitated and looked at her runners. "Sure, where?"

"The chapel, if you don't mind," The doctor gestured for her to go first, taking a step back for her.

Haydee swallowed, pushing the door open before sitting

down on the wooden pew. Daniel might find peace in such a place, she couldn't. "I don't even know your name."

"Rashid," He sat next to her but with a foot of space between them for courtesy's sake. "There's no need to call me doctor, I'd prefer not to, honestly."

"What is it? Are you one of the doctors trying to help Daniel?" Haydee asked.

"Not directly," He almost sounded apologetic at that.

His gaze was fixed on her face and she blushed, averting her eyes. "What's wrong? Do I have a runny nose or chocolate on my mouth?"

"No," Rashid shook his head, a shadow crossing his face. "I- it was your hair dye that caught my attention. I've only seen it once before. On a... woman who could have been your sister."

"I'm an only child," She stood, trying to hide her discomfort at Rashid's stricken look. "But what happened to her? The lady who had the interesting blue streak in her hair."

"She died a long time ago," Rashid made no move towards her for which she was grateful for. "Her husband passed away and she chose not to, well, live without him. I don't want that to be your fate. I heard how close you are with Daniel from Doctor Sotaira. It's..."

His voice dropped, something unfamiliar in the tone even as he looked back at her. "My father's curse."

"What?" She put her hand on the door handle, torn between calling for a nurse or two on Rashid or simply running away from him and his insanity.

Rashid grimaced, shaking his head. "It's nothing, you just caught me by surprise, that's all."

Curiosity was a stupid thing when it came to the unknown but some small part of her couldn't resist either. "What was the lady's name?"

"She called herself Laelaps, I never knew if that was something she was given or chose for herself but I was only a child when I met her and she passed away soon afterwards," Rashid's expression was wry. "You look just like her, down to the blue streak in her hair. Though she never would have chosen a pixie cut for herself. Too short."

"The fox and the hound story," Haydee's voice soured on that note. "I think it was in a museum when I was sixteen. No one could figure out how a Greek statue ended up in an Egyptian tomb, a couple thousand years before the culture existed. The Teumessian fox was too realistic looking."

She shifted from one foot to the other. "The... story was interesting, but I should probably head out and get that chocolate bar now. And maybe find Jocelyn as well. He'll want to see Daniel, I think."

At least that was the excuse she was trying to give. She had the age and maturity to handle seeing Daniel like this even if it hurt to look. Jocelyn, she was much less clear on. "I should probably go."

CHAPTER THIRTY-ONE

The message she had been dreading for so long finally came in the form of an uncertain looking eighth grader. "Miss. Ashworth? Uhm, the hospital called the office and the principal asked me to bring you the message. It's... it's about your boyfriend, I think."

"Right," She pinched the bridge of her nose tiredly, dropping her hand to her side. This begged the question of where she was going to find a substitute teacher for her class on such short notice. "Fifteen-minute study break, I need to take a call."

And maybe the next few days off as well if this was what she suspected it to be. She was already dialing the phone number, past caring that she would probably be interrupting of one of Jocelyn's classes midway through the lesson. "Jocelyn?"

She could picture Jocelyn's nose as pink and clutching a crumpled tissue in his hand. "Coming, I guess. I'll be out on the front of school's steps, waiting."

He grabbed his backpack, shouldering it and trudged out of the classroom. Haydee sighed picturing that as she switched her phone for the junior high's line.. The school's office had never felt so cold or impersonal as it did now as she held the receiver to her ear. "Doctor Sotaira?"

Persephone's voice was carefully neutral. "I think it best if you come to the hospital now."

"I know," Haydee twisted the phone cord around her fingers, tasting something bitter in her mouth as the hard lump settled in her stomach. "Can you... make it so that he holds on until I get there? It's a three-hour drive from Calais to Augusta."

"It's up to him," Persephone said. "But the boy is stubborn."

That was no answer at all, so far as she was concerned. Haydee bit down on her lower lip, tasted blood in her mouth and hung up on the doctor. "Thanks, I guess."

Thanks for nothing, really. For all her medical skill, Persephone was useless when it came to grieving family members or a bedside manner.

She was halfway to the car when she caught a glimpse of the stranger out of the corner of her eye. "What do you want? Daniel mentioned you, briefly but he never gave me your name."

"Kate MacKinnon," The woman's voice was resigned. "Daniel was one of my bartenders before he gave his notice. I know things are going to sound nuts and you're probably going to ask how I know this when it shouldn't be my business but there aren't very many secrets in my family. Patient confidentiality aside, Persephone Sotaira is my aunt. Look, if you can manage it, keep my aunt from slipping a coin into Daniel's pocket. It's important for both of you."

Haydee let her shoulders slump. "I don't really know what that's supposed to mean but sure, I'll try. I can't make any promises there though."

Jocelyn was looking up at Kate wide eyed. "It's a Greek thing, right? Coin to pay the guy or something? You don't want Daniel to go anywhere?"

"No more than you," Kate sounded tired. "No. Daniel's a good guy, one of the best I've seen in a long time. He doesn't deserve this."

She took a step back, glancing away. "I shouldn't keep you longer than needed to."

"Thanks," As weird as Kate's request was, there had to be some logic behind it as well. Enough to make her consider it seriously for a few minutes. This was Daniel after all. And if keeping a coin out of his pocket was enough to help, she'd do it. This wasn't as strange as Daniel's own abilities.

The IV line and the little oxygen tube were gone now, much to her relief. Everything else, had her swallowing back on something as she brushed a hand over Daniel's wrist. "Daniel?"

Things couldn't end this way, they just couldn't. It wasn't fair that a rash and shortness of breath had turned into this. Liver and kidney failure as the donor cells attacked his body, soon followed by the cells' decision to make his stomach and muscles their next target. Now everything was dying on him. "Please wake up."

He barely reacted to her touch and she slumped, dropping into a crouch next to the bed as the wetness made trails down her cheeks. "Please,"

All she wanted was some small scrap of acknowledgement from him, something to tell her that he was still in there somewhere. It didn't matter how thin, fragile he looked to her. "Hey, remember the first day we met? The principal just wanted me to make her coffee run for her and you came into the office with Jocelyn's transcripts. I thought you were coming in with your sister dressed in boy's clothes at the time. I didn't know how he really felt underneath his appearance. I do now."

If that wasn't enough to wake Daniel up, there was nothing else she could say. "Just, please… give me five minutes of your time. Just a chance for me to tell you bye."

"He won't wake, Haydee," Rashid's voice was gentle but tired, sounding from behind her. "He's too far gone for that now. I'm sorry."

Anger would have been easier, cleaner but all she could feel was numbness and cling to his hand tighter. "Dani?"

Using Jocelyn's pet name for him for the first time since they'd met. She'd never been comfortable using nicknames for people, preferring the name in full but now it was as good as any and she understood why Jocelyn did it. "Three minutes?"

Down from the five she had asked for moments earlier. "Or just one? I'd do anything right now."

"Haydee," Rashid's use of her name was enough to haver her turning to look at the dark-skinned doctor. "I know you don't want to but you have to let him go. He's clinging on for your sake. It isn't fair to either of you."

He reached past her, brushing a hand over Daniel's short haircut and lower across the side of his face before gently freeing a copper pendant on a leather cord from Daniel's grip and pocketing it in his coat. Haydee sniffled, in no mood to ask why an Arabic doctor carried a cross with him, or why the cross had a loop at the top instead of the traditional bar. "I don't want to lose him."

"No one does," Rashid looked away. "You've no doubt heard this before, but he was a better young man than most."

"So…" He looked blurry through her tears as she finally met his gaze. "What do I do now?"

"Let him go," Rashid said gently. "It's a mercy, not a death sentence, Haydee. I'll be outside if you need me."

Persephone Sotaira had been Rashid's quiet, discrete little shadow for the longest time, now she spoke up, holding a tarnished circle of silver in her hand. "Call it superstition if you wish to but I think it bad luck not to pay Charon his due, just in case."

The coin or equivalent that the doctor's niece had mentioned. Haydee bit down on her lower lip, cradling the ancient coin and shook her head, folding Persephone's fingers over it. "He's Catholic. I don't think he buys into the ancient Greek burial rites much."

Persephone went still, rigid at that and only relaxed when Anubis murmured something in her ear, too low to overhear before she took the coin back and walked out of the room with an "Of course," spoken under her breath. There might have been a word or two along the lines of heathen savage involved but she chose to ignore them.

Haydee swallowed past the hard lump in her throat, closed her eyes and tugged the wedding band from Daniel's hand. "I'm sorry, Daniel."

All she could do was hold onto his wedding band with her free hand and Daniel's hand with her other as the slight rise and fall of his chest slowed and stopped. Rashid's sigh was tired as he pulled her to her feet and offered her the nearby chair before laying the thin linen of the coverlet over Daniel's face.

Jocelyn's expletive was somewhere between angry and miserable as he held out a phone and the image on it of an

Egyptian painting and the jackal headed man depicted, standing over someone on a bed. "Is this... you, Rashid?"

Rashid hesitated, accepting the phone to look at the painting. "Sometimes a tomb painting is just a painting, Jocelyn. I think I would have too many questions if I went around wearing a mask like that. I'm Egyptian, yes and I respect my home's history, but I don't seek to imitate the ancient gods. Personal thoughts, they were jealous men and women who didn't take kindly to mortals dressing up as them."

"Oh," Relief seemed to cross Jocelyn's face. "Okay, I just... thought it weird and things. Like you'd done this before or something. And you feel funny to me. Kind of..."

He shrugged helplessly. "You've got a lot of stuff in your head."

Rashid handed the phone back to him. "I won't deny seeing a lot of bad things, no but I think it best if you guard your own gift, Jocelyn. And don't try to look deeper at mine."

Jocelyn quieted, rubbing a hand across his eyes and scuffed a runner across the floor. "Okay,"

The doctor's smile came out as slightly forced. "If I might talk with Haydee alone? Persephone, maybe you could take Jocelyn down to the cafeteria."

Persephone nodded briefly, guiding Jocelyn out of the room without another word.

Rashid sighed, sobering as he went over to the closet and opening it. Daniel's backpack sat at the back alongside a pair of runners and a couple changes of clothing. The memory box sat on the top shelf and he retrieved it, placing it in her lap. "He wanted you to have this before the end."

Haydee looked down, half tempted to throw the gift across the room but opened it instead, feeling her eyes burn at the memories the photographs brought to mind. Christmas and Jocelyn grinning as he held up a reindeer printed sweater.

A couple images from the wedding day. Another from earlier before that, captured when Daniel hadn't been looking, leaning over the bar counter- half turned away from the camera. A little bit of his hair saved and sealed in a sandwich bag from when she'd cut his hair for him. The green silk ribbon and the engagement ring nestled in a little cloth bag. "I miss you…"

There were letters or at least envelopes at the bottom of the box but those she left untouched, unopened for now. Things were still too raw to consider reading anything Daniel had wrote. "What am I supposed to do now?"

"Live, for his sake," Rashid said gently. "He wouldn't want you to dwell on his passing, Haydee."

She squeezed her eyes shut tight for a moment and opened them again to see the unopened box of a pregnancy test in her hands. "But…"

He sat next to her on the remaining chair. "It may not seem like it but that was his gift to you, Haydee. I won't tell you my past, I can't but at least know this, I have enough of the psychic talent to know when a young woman is pregnant."

"Then…" Her voice was weak. "Why bother with the test at all, if you know I'm already pregnant?"

"Just as a confirmation," Rashid's hand covered hers before letting go of it. "I'm a psychic, not infallible. I have been wrong before. And I can't tell the gender of the child any better than a ultrasound tech until they're born."

"If- if it's a girl in nine months," She had to force the words out, trying not to look at the bed or the sheet that covered Daniel's body. "Danielle Elizabeth Lalaurie, she deserves to have… something of her dad at least."

If it was a boy, she didn't have a clue what to call them. "Was there anything about the funeral mentioned?"

Rashid's expression was weary as he passed her a smaller envelope from his coat pocket. "Here, he dictated, I wrote for him. He asked for a cremation rather than a burial in New Orleans. He wants the ash scattered in Paris over the Seine."

She had to wince and close her eyes at that. "But… that's not something I can afford. Plane tickets are expensive at the best of time and this is Paris. Way across the ocean. I don't even speak French. New Orleans would have been easier to get to."

"I'm aware," Rashid said. "But would you deny his last wish?"

"No," Her voice was small, miserable. "I'm not like that. I'll do it somehow. Daniel did put my name on his vehicle insurance and the rent agreement for his apartment here. I wouldn't have put it past him to have left me a bit extra on top of that. I mean, he cleared my student debt for me." For which she was grateful for, but she would have preferred to have Daniel instead of the money. "If you don't mind, I just want to be alone for a while, thanks." "I understand,"

Rashid let out a sigh and stood, helping her to her feet. "Call me if you need anything, I'll do my best to answer the phone if I can. If you ask and give me the address, I could come over to the apartment."

She wasn't really in the mood for company, but his offer was appreciated regardless. "Thanks, Rashid."

He inclined his head in acknowledgement and let her go. Haydee wiped a shirt sleeve across her eyes and went in search of Jocelyn. With the apartment apparently sorted out and her financial situation seemingly set for a while, there was no reason to return to Calais – at least for the next few days anyway. But it was going to be a cold, lonely place without her boyfriend around. "We should probably get started on cleaning things up at home, Jocelyn. Even if he put my name on the lease agreement, there's still a lot of his stuff that needs to be put in boxes and- and storage or donated."

In a week or two, maybe she would begin to feel marginally better, but it wouldn't be now or anytime soon. There were just too many memories too close to the surface for her to take any comfort in the things he once had. "Let's... let's just go. The funeral stuff can wait for a couple days, right?"

Jocelyn was just as tear streaked as she was, holding onto the teddy bear Persephone had placed in his hands but he nodded bravely, clutching the little toy. "Maybe, I guess. Dad said that mornings were always brighter, right?"

It wasn't a sentiment she could share but she could appreciate the attempt at comfort anyway. "Sure, let's just say that and get back to the place before I can't drive anywhere at all."

All her plans for the remainder of the day involved curling up in one of Daniel's coverlets and a bowl of mint chocolate chip ice cream on his couch. And maybe cuddling one of Jocelyn's two Lhasa Apso puppies as well. People... just weren't creatures she was prepared to deal with right now. "Let's just go home, please. We can worry about normal stuff later."

Worrying about things later was a good plan but not one he was prepared to join Haydee in just yet. Jocelyn glanced away, still clutching his phone. "Could you wait for me? There's something I need to do first, if you don't mind."

"Sure," Who was she to deny her boyfriend's brother that? "Just don't be too long, okay."

"Promise," Jocelyn turned away, going in search of the doctor who called himself Rashid. Asking at the front desk was about as useful as trying to get a peek at the computer records and making sense of them so he did the next best thing he could think of. Making a physical and psychic search of things.

Rashid may have claimed to be a healer but underneath the skill and the honesty about that, he had been lying about who he really was. Only a witch or someone with the empath knack could have told for sure but there had been a less than... human edge to his feelings, something that took a distant view of things. Luck, or that maybe 'Rashid' was more willing to stick around than he had let on earlier, was with him tonight as he found the man in the hospital room. "You might have lied to Haydee, you can't lie to me. I felt it when I looked at you. You recognized the picture on my phone."

Rashid's mouth thinned, wary. "It would be hard not to, these days. It doesn't take a witch or psychic to see that."

"But it takes someone to recognize mythology and a pathetic attempt at being human," Jocelyn folded his arms over his chest. "I don't have the right to demand anything of you, *Anubis*. But I figured a bargain would be something you were more willing to talk about. I want in with whatever your people do."

Rashid's expression cooled. "You don't know what you're asking."

"I think I do," Jocelyn said flatly. "The past five months were spent searching for a way to save my brother's life as soon as he was diagnosed. I'm aware that there's a price involved but I'm willing to pay whatever it takes."

"No," Rashid shook his head. "I won't be the one to end your life when you have so much still ahead of you."

EPILOGUE

Anubis was a friend, but this was something she had
to do herself, whether he agreed with it or not. And
chances were he wouldn't. She had given up her
goddess given powers several millennia ago, he had earned
his through the bargain with Osiris. This was her business and
her business alone even if he was in the bar as a witness. "I
have to do this."

He leaned against the closed door, arms folded over his
chest and the little copper ankh just visible at his throat,
looped through the leather cord. "And you think this isn't
essentially a rape, Hecate? There's a reason your father
forbade stealing from him. The dead aren't meant to be in this
world."

She snorted, looking over her shoulder at him. "My father
permitted me this one. And it's not like vampires don't exist.
Those of the king your kin fought and the ones made by
psychics. If I recall correctly, you've cursed one or two men
with the vampire thing over the years."

"As a lesson and punishment for the blood they spilled,"
Anubis's voice cooled noticeably. "But you aren't trying to

make a vampire here, you're trying to bind the dead for the sake of cheating your fates. I think the punishment for that if you succeed is a century or two in your father's realm. Time taken from your own life."

He sighed, pinching the bridge of his nose. "And it's usually my duty to put the vampires back into the ground where they belong. This- this is different. How do you think he's going to feel when he figures out what you've done to him?"

The look she gave him was affronted. "Unlike Osiris, I don't require anyone to serve me until they die again, I can release them when they want me to."

"He'll still regard it as damnation, Hecate." Anubis glanced away. "A shadow unable to touch or feel anything of the physical world, insubstantial and invisible to most humans. That's not a gift or rescue, that's a curse on top of the one he suffered before death."

She snarled softly and bared her teeth as her red hair darkened to a deep brown, the gray green of her eyes shifted towards a falcon's gold and she spread the wings at her shoulders halfway. "Don't test me, Anubis."

He only sighed, looking away. "If you're looking for intimidation, I don't think showing your natural shape is the right way to go about it. There's very few things that I'm terrified of these days and you aren't one of them, Hecate."

That seemed to cool her temper and she glanced downwards, shame crossing her face. "What does scare you."

Anubis snorted, rueful. "My uncle Aaron, Osiris to a degree or two, Erinyes and Sieh. That's one... spirit I'd just as soon not tangle with, personally. Yes, I could match him for power if I wanted to but his lack of control when he's furious could easily wipe out a good half of the east coast's electrical grid for the next century and a half."

He regarded her tiredly. "But the question is irrelevant to what you're planning tonight, Kate. He won't thank you for this, neither will your parents."

"It's just enough time to give Haydee a chance to say goodbye for real this time," Hecate held a hand out, lighting one of the candles spaced around the circle drawn in chalk on the ugly brown carpet with just a thought. "She deserves that much. It is Daniel we're talking about after all."

He sighed again, giving a soft prayer to the gods for patience. "But she's already gone by now. I haven't been tracking her to any great detail, but I can guess two places she might be. New Orleans or Paris and even with the power you have left, there are rules to things. Daniel won't be able to break them even if you want it. It's like the binding that keeps Sieh from traveling far from the continent. He won't be able to follow her."

"So, we bring her to him," Hecate glanced away, lowering her hands. "Easy,"

"Were it not for my father's curse, Hecate," Anubis said dryly. "No matter how Haydee chases him, he'll always escape her. Your fates only decided it was through death."

He reached out, catching her hand in his. "Or did you miss one of your own stories as a child?"

Hecate quieted, a flicker of blue fire coiling around her free hand before it faded away. "I created some of those stories, Anubis."

"Some of them but not all," He scuffed the salt and chalk line out with a booted foot, extinguishing the candles a moment later. "The Teumessian fox wasn't one of your creations and Thoth turned the pair to stone statues after they passed away. You're a witch but you aren't the psychic I am. I saw Haydee's past. It was enough for me."

Her voice was tired. "I still have to do this, Anubis. Knowing their history or not."

Anubis took her hand in his before releasing it. "Why? He's clearly more than a human boy to you from the sound of things."

She swept a strand of hair from her eyes and sat down on top of the office's small desk. "Because he's kin. Teumessius wasn't, yes. But Daniel is, though the bloodline is distant through my daughter and her human lover. The child they had couldn't shapeshift, but the boy was a witch. It's the child's blood in Daniel's family as much as Teumessius's own gift in Daniel."

Her gaze when she met his was weary. "How else do you end up with the strongest witch in a generation for the LaLaurie family?"

"You don't," Anubis looked away, shoulders dropping at the question. "I don't like this, but I won't stand in your way if it matters to you."

ALSO BY MARK RUNTE

Silver and Salt

<u>UPCOMING WORKS:</u>

Bound in Blood

Eve

Love, Death and Little Shadows